REVIEWERS' PRAISE FOR *STORYTELLER*:

"Smooth, well crafted, and entertaining … It's like a rich chocolate dessert, savor it and enjoy." — *Pub-ioneer Book Review, March 27, 2007*

"Excellence personified! G. R. Grove spins a Welsh tale out of a surprisingly accurate grasp of life in the Middle Ages … Over the course of the novel, the details accrete, and the world we are led through—a picturesque, colorful, delightfully Celtic, and refreshingly whimsical place—unfolds like a blossoming rose in time-lapse. The dialogue too is insightful and precise, and it is written with a subtle edge that affords us a view into the minds of a set of well-drawn characters … Grove is a consummate storyteller … one of the best." — *POD Critic Review, April 9, 2007*

"A unique blend of history, myth and fantasy, circa 6th Century Britain, that's as magical as the old Wales lore… a well written story of Gwernin, a wandering storyteller in 6th century Britain, and his search of fame and glory as a bard. As he journeys in search of the fulfillment of his hopes and dreams, he meets magicians and mythic characters, who may or may not be part of his imagination, and the story weaves elements of reality, myth, and Gwernin's imagination into a gem-like polished whole… unexpectedly moving." — *PODler Book Review, May 4, 2007*

"I was brought up in Wales from the age of seven until I was twenty and hence lived side by side with a culture that attempts to hold onto the very traditions described in this volume… the experience of Welshness comes through with crystal clarity… Whoever picks up this book should be

confident that it is as accurate as it can be and always entertaining ... a truly involving, gently dramatic, introduction to a
saga that has the potential to be as well regarded as the myths
and legends Gwernin turned his attention to relating." —
LeoStableford.com review, May 14, 2007

"The reader will get a sense of both Gwernin the young man
experiencing these wonders and dangers for the first time,
and also of Gwernin the old man, looking back on his life,
telling us of his triumphs, and of his youthful stubbornness
and folly. One delights in Gwernin's successes, but also can
enjoy cringing with his embarrassment. With true understanding of human nature, Ms. Grove has created a character
anyone who has been through adolescence can relate to, yet
firmly rooted in his own time... I eagerly await the next
installment."—*J. Mizrahi, Amazon reviewer, August 5, 2007*

"A pleasure to read ... an extremely friendly read, with a
well-researched foundation, and a light-hearted tone ... You
are introduced to an evolving, colourful cast of characters that
Gwernin meets along the way, as well as those who accom-
pany him on various adventures. As they travel, the reader
hears stories of legendary England, including tales of King
Arthur. You follow Gwernin through various life-
experiences, and even as he falls in love... The first paragraph will snag you and you will be engaged throughout.
Then you will be dropped off at the last paragraph wanting
more ... it has me looking forward to the next installment. I
recommend this book to anyone who just loves a good story;
for there are plenty of those to be had in *Storyteller*." —
Odyssey Reviews, December 31, 2007

Storyteller

OTHER TITLES BY G R GROVE:

Available from all booksellers:

Flight of the Hawk

Available from Lulu.com:

Guernen Sang It: King Arthur's Raid On Hell And Other Poems

Guernen Sang Again: Pryderi's Pigs And Other Poems

* * * * *

*For more information about the **Storyteller** series, visit*

http://tregwernin.blogspot.com
or
http://aldertreebooks.com

STORYTELLER

Being the Wanderings
of Gwernin Kyuarwyd

G R Grove

Lulu.com

Published by Lulu.com
Lulu Press, Inc.
Morrisville, NC, USA

First Printing: January 2007
Second Printing: January 2008

ISBN-13: 978-1-4303-0524-8

Set in 12.5 and 18 point Garamond and 10 point Arial by Aldertree Books,
Denver, Colorado, USA.

Cover image by permission of www.urweg.com

For further information about the Storyteller series, see
http://tregwernin.blogspot.com or **http://aldertreebooks.com**

Dedicated to the Society for Creative Anachronism, and
especially to the people of the Barony of Earngyld,
who saw the beginning and liked it.

CONTENTS

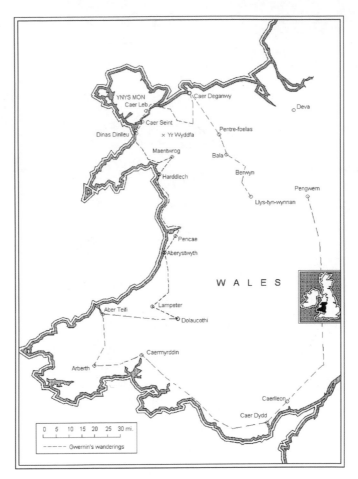

Gwernin's Wanderings

A CIRCUIT ROUND WALES

"ynteu Wydyon goreu kyuarwyd yn y byt oed"

"And he, Gwydion, was the best teller of tales in the world…"

– Pedair Kainc y Mabinogi

I. Ghosts

Blood and fire, gold and steel and poetry, a river's voice in the silence of the night, and the shining strings of a harp—all these and more I have known in my time. Steep mountains, dark forests, and the endless song of the rain; music and laughter and feasting in the fire-bright halls of kings; a dusty road, and a fast horse, and a good friend beside me; and the sweet taste of the mead of Dun Eidyn, with its bitter aftermath: a dragon's hoard of memories I have gathered, bright-colored as a long summer's day. Now they are all gone, the men and women I knew when I was young, gone like words on the wind, and I am left here in the twilight to tell you their tale. Sit, then, and listen if you will to the words of Gwernin Kyuarwyd, called Storyteller.

The place which men name Caerllion, the City of the Legions, lies on the low banks of the river Wysg not far from the sea in south Wales. Even when I first came there it was ruinous, and that was a long lifetime ago. But many men's lifetimes had already passed since the Eagles who built it flew south from Britain and left us on our own, to sink or swim as we could against the Saxon tide. Arthur held them for a while, checked their advance and forced them back into their beachheads of the south and east, and gave us time to breathe. But Arthur died at Camlann three years before I was born, and how long now we can hold the crumbling sea wall he built is anyone's guess. Many a kingdom has gone under already; many a fair fortress lies now beneath that wave. I wonder if I shall not, before I die, see my fair Pengwern herself laid waste, and Cynan's halls home to the wolf and the raven...

But I was speaking of Caerllion, and the wonder that lies there. I saw it first on a mild evening in late spring, when my friend Ieuan and I came humping our packs over the last hill-crest to the east, and saw the hearth-smoke rising from amongst the gray stone ruins at either end of the bridge. Time had not treated Caerllion kindly; the villagers' huts for the most part were reed-thatched shells of houses that had once been crowned in red tile, with wattle and daub filling gaps here and there in their crumbling walls. Only a few buildings near the river gate were still in use; the rest of that stone-walled enclosure was full of broken rubble half grown up in alder and oak scrub, a tangled wilderness where once were only the straight lines that the Romans so loved. In the midst of it all crouched a great brown block like a small hill, its top green with grasses and willow-herb, a silent presence brooding over all the rest. Tumble-down walls and fortresses I had seen before—indeed, I was born in one, though I remember little enough of it, before the Black Year came to sweep away that life and send me to my aunt's house in Pengwern—but this was something new, beyond my previous experience, and as always I hungered to know more.

First, however, there was the question of lodgings for the night. The inn at the east end of the bridge was still open and doing business, and there Ieuan and I made our way. It seemed strange to me, new to the road as I was, to be paying for the food and lodging which my people would have given freely to any passing traveler, but as Ieuan had explained to me, such a small place, home to no great lord, and yet located on one of the main trackways used by the merchant-kind, could not be affording unpaid hospitality to all comers. Besides, the excellence of the landlord's ale was legendary, and well worth the small coins we exchanged for it and our

4

supper, with the promise of more to come if my tales pleased an audience that night.

After we had struck our bargain, and eaten our supper of stew and barley bread, washed down by some of that famous ale, I left my friend chatting amiably in the tap-room and wandered out again, heading for the great ruinous hulk that had earlier caught my eye. *Baths*, the landlord had called them, built like everything else here by the Romans. Palaces, I thought, as I stood staring up at them from the edge of a patch of waste ground, might have been a better term. Fully two-score paces in length and perhaps half as wide, and tall as the lordliest ash tree that graces the slopes of Powys, the Baths dwarfed any king's house that I had yet seen. Their towering walls gazed back at me out of the twilight, pieced with dark window-openings that gaped like empty eyes. I returned their stare thoughtfully, but curiosity still won out.

Crossing the waste ground where the soldiers had raced and wrestled, I picked my way forward over broken stone, clogged with blown dirt and white with bird droppings, until I stood within the gloomy vault itself. Around me the red-brick walls rose up, towering into owl-haunted cliffs and caverns, while beneath them the scummy pools of the baths themselves lay gleaming here and there like tarnished mirrors. There was a strong smell of must and decay, and a sense of ghosts watching from behind one's shoulder. Almost it might have been the mouth of a fairy mound, a gateway to Annwn itself, and the wonders that lay there—or so I thought at the time.

The silence was eerie, with a faint echo in it as of the wind, or the sea in a shell, or distant music, so that when a bit of stone dislodged by who-knows-what dropped from somewhere above and plopped into one of the pools near me, I jumped, and stumbling on the uneven footing, found myself almost over the edge before I knew it. As I teetered on the brink, I dimly saw a leering face with snakes for hair peering out at me from among the broken tiles at my feet, and in the roof above me I heard a rustle of wings.

Then the owl came gliding down, silent as a ghost. Like a pale shadow she came, and passed so close I could feel the chill breath of her wings as they stroked the air, and see her golden eyes, bright in the white mask of her face. She sailed through one of the empty window-vaults and was gone, and the huge cold room seemed the darker and more threatening for her leaving. Yet I stood my ground for a moment more, waiting for I knew not what. And at last it came, one white feather floating slowly down to land at my feet. I bent and picked it up. It lay light in my hand, soft and weightless as a scrap of silk, real as a memory. I put it in my belt-pouch for safety, and came away; I had seen enough to slake my curiosity for that night. Behind me in the darkness I could feel the ghosts of the soldiers still watching as I went, but they were silent.

Outside the twilight seemed bright as day by comparison, the air incredibly fresh and sweet—heavy though it was with the evening scents of wood-smoke and cow byres. I looked back once from the bridge at the towering ruin, looming against the last of the sunset like a young hill. Already those who should know better are beginning to say that the Baths are really the ruins of Arthur's Palace, built for him in the space of a night by magic. Built, so they say, by the King's Bard himself, using nothing but harp-song and moonlight, and a strong spider's-web of spells to bind it all in place. Traveler's tales, or stories for children, but still... On that quiet evening it almost seemed possible. And who should know better than I what feats music may encompass? That night I earned my ale in the tap-room with the tale of Gwydion the Magician and Blodeuwedd, the woman—if she was a woman—who became an owl. And later, in my sleep, I could swear I heard the beat of ghostly wings.

All of this seems a small story to relate, a small thing to remember after so many years. And yet it sticks in my mind for many reasons, not least because of what came after, when I came to know in truth, in bone and blood and spirit, the real cost and meaning of the Gates of Annwn.

But that, O my children, is a story for another day.

II. The Cloak-Clasp

Nowadays I often find, looking back, that the years and journeys blend together, so I can no longer be sure as to which time or place many of my memories belong. One day on the road is much like many another, within the usual gamut of heat and cold, dust and mud, sun and rain and snow; one rough lodging much like the next. Even the faces blend together over the years, various and individual though they all are: bright with interest in my performance, or dull with boredom; young or old, sober or drunken, ill or well. But at the time of which I speak, I was still new to the road and to my trade, and every day was an adventure, every night a fresh excitement as I stretched my growing abilities. So it was with Caer Dydd, my first big festival. Every detail of it is still clear in my mind, bright as a fresh-opened flower, not only for its own sake, but also for what came after.

We arrived there on a fine spring day, not long after our stop at Caerllion. Indeed, it was for Caer Dydd we had been making all the while, and the great Beltane fair that was held there every spring, when the roads and the seas first opened to travelers and traders. Many of them came, as we did, to set up their booths by the strand, and there I first stared open-mouthed at two things I had never seen before: the sea, and the ships that lived and traveled on her back.

It was the sea that caught me first: the sea of which I had heard so often in the tales. On the sea the Romans had come to Britain, and over it they had sailed away. On the sea Maxen Wledig had come to us, and over it he had gone when he left, taking many of our warriors with him to settle Less Britain. Yes, and older still: Brân the Blesséd had crossed the sea to rescue his sister from Ireland, and into the sea had gone Dylan ail Ton after his birth, to bide there with his great seal father, and rule over it in his turn. And over the sea, more prosaically, had come the foreign traders with their bright wares to the Beltane fair at Caer Dydd.

That afternoon the sea near the mouth of the Severn stretched broad and blue away from me, wind-ruffled into short sharp waves, hiding infinite possibilities. The tide was out, and the smell of mud and fish and seaweed, and who knows what besides, was strong on the warm spring air, and the sky above loud with the crying of gulls. Three or four small boats were lying beached on the mud, while other larger ships swung at anchor some way out. Above the tide-line fishermen and traders alike had set up booths and tents, and a busy market was already in progress.

I followed Ieuan as he worked his way through the crowd—a thin crowd as yet, for it was early in the fair—looking for a place to set out his wares. This early in the year his stock consisted mostly of small, light items of bone and horn and wood—double-sided combs, elaborately carved and decorated; pins for the cloak or the hair, painted or wound with wire; cases for bronze needles; and small trinket boxes for a lady's treasures. Rings, too, he had, and a few bracelets, fashioned of twisted copper or silver wire. Ieuan himself had made most of them during the winter, working steadily through the short days and long nights by the fire. Now he would trade them, if he could, for other small, light things of greater value, brought by the traders from overseas, to carry with us on our travels and sell or trade again along the way. Not until autumn would we go home to Pengwern.

In the meantime, here at Caer Dydd, there was the Beltane fair to enjoy, and the competitions to look forward to. Christian though these lands were then, at least in name, yet most of us held also by the old festivals, which are the rhythm of the land and the seasons. And Beltane has always been one of the Great Festivals, the spring festival that follows the first plowing. There would be days and days of celebration, and meat and drink in plenty; plenty of employment, too, for storytellers and minstrels such as we.

Whether because of its position on the coast of south Wales, a popular landfall for traders on their way to Ireland, or because there had already been a settlement there when the Romans came, Caer Dydd had fared better than her sister Caerllion, having been taken over by the local chief as a strongpoint rather than being left to fall to ruin. Some of the buildings in the fort had been maintained, and it was in one of these, on the last night before Beltane, that a storytelling competition took place: for as you know, many tales— Winter-tales—should only to be told in the dark half of the year, between Samhain and Beltane. There it was that I first stood up to speak in contest, to be judged against my peers.

Well I remember the flickering firelight on the roughly plastered walls and blackened roof-beams of that hall, and on the watching faces of my audience, glinting on here a fine shoulder-brooch, and there a gilded bracelet, as the owners moved. I remember the patter of rain on the roof-tiles, and the barking of dogs outside the hall, and the smell of the blue wood-smoke from the central hearth-fire that eddied now and then into my face and stung my eyes. I remember the listening silence of that crowd of men and women and children, broken from time to time by a cough or the scrape of a bench, and the beating excitement in me, half fear and half exaltation, as I first told my tale before so many, weaving with all my skill a net of words to catch and hold their interest.

I wish I could say that I won that contest, but I am sworn to keep to truth in these tales, so far as the truth may be known—for often it seems to me to change with the observer. No, I did not win, but my performance was well received, and toasted afterwards by one of the local lords,

10

who gave me a ring-brooch from his own shoulder in token of his approval. A simple thing it was, but pleasant, made of good bronze, with a red enamel design covering the two terminals of the ring and the base of the pin. It had been fashioned at his own court of Dinas Powys, a short journey to the south and west from Caer Dydd. I wonder now, looking back, if it was not my choice of a tale told often in his home country that commended me to him as much as my expertise. However that may be, it was my first such moment of recognition, and shines the brighter in my memory because of it. Though I have since had many finer jewels, I still keep that brooch as a talisman. Worth is not always measured in weight of gold.

It was the same Lord Dafydd of Dinas Powys who that night issued a general invitation to all the bards and storytellers there to join him at his court for a few days after the fair ended. "For," he said, "it is seldom I have the enjoyment of such an array of riches as you have spread before me here, and I would fain keep it for a little longer. Moreover, I currently have no bard in my hall, and must needs chose one soon," and he grinned, "least my word-fame be lost, and my name vanish with me."

So it happened that on the day after the fair Ieuan and I and several others were making our way up the steep track which led to Dinas Powys, a track deep-rutted from the wagon-loads of wine-barrels and oil-jars that had come up from the harbor earlier in the week to gladden the hearts of the merchant-kind. Ieuan was in a good mood for a change, for his trading had gone well, and our packs rode the lighter on our shoulders for it. He was a quiet man as a rule, given to gloomy silences, but that day he spoke more than usual, asking the others with us about their travels, and about the temper of the country that spring.

"Quiet enough so far," said Kyan Goch, a red-headed man from Dumnonia in southwest Britain. "The Saxons will likely be stirring again before long, though. Still, I suppose we should be grateful for such peace as we have."

"Ah, but where is the glory in peace?" asked another. "No warfare, no glory; no glory, no need for bards to sing it; no need for bards, and we are on the road again!" And he laughed.

"Na, there will always be need for bards," said Kyan. "If not to sing the warriors' deeds now, then to remember those who fought before, and teach those who will fight afterwards the way of it. There is always need for songs of Arthur, and Maxen Wledig, and those who went before. One way and another, there must always be bards, as long as the earth stands, and the stars shine above, and the gray sea surrounds us. We are like the pin in the cloak-clasp," and he touched the great brooch on his shoulder, "the smallest, plainest part, and yet without it the brooch falls away and is lost, and the cloak with it, and the man perishes from the cold. So is it with us. If the bards should ever take the druids' road west, it would be a black day for the Cymry, for what is there to hold a people together who do not remember their past?"

No one answered him, for we had reached the top, and the hospitality of Dinas Powys awaited us.

But that, O my children, is a story for another day.

III. The Power of Names

What power lies in a name? Gwernin Kyuarwyd am I, Gwernin Storyteller. So have I said before. And yet I practice all the bardic arts, so far as I am able—poetry and song and harping, as well as storytelling and the recitation of lore. So why do I call myself Gwernin Kyuarwyd, Gwernin Storyteller, and not Gwernin Fardd, Gwernin the Bard?

Modesty, perhaps. Or a stronger regard for the truth than some display. But mostly for another reason, of which I intend to tell you now.

The feasting at Dinas Powys was behind us, and we were on the road again. Fine indeed had it been while it lasted, for though the Lord Dafydd's hall was smaller than some I have since seen, his table was bountiful—roast meat in plenty, both cow's and pig's flesh; made dishes in the old Roman style; flat wheaten loaves from the bake-stones; barrels of red Gallic wine; and great pitchers of the clear honey-sweet mead with its faintly bitter aftertaste, which seems to light all the world like a golden lantern while it lasts.

Half a dozen bards had performed, all eager to fill the empty chair of the household bard at this wealthy court, and all the other performers got a turn as well, and a gift of silver afterwards for their pains, myself included. Mine was a bracelet in the Saxon style, and not the least by any means of the presents given. I got, too, a word of praise and encouragement from Kyan Goch, which I valued above the silver; he it was who won the bards' contention, and stayed on as the new household bard to the Lord Dafydd. I was glad for his good luck, but sorry to lose the chance of his company on the road, for he seemed more friendly and less full of self-pride than some of the bards there—more friendly, at least, to me...

All and all, then, I was thinking very well of myself by the time Ieuan and I set out on our travels again. Westward the two of us were going, toward Dyfed, following the Romans' old paved road which runs straight as a arrow from Caer Dydd to Maridunum, or Caer Myrddin as it is sometimes called nowadays. As one often does, we fell in with a number of other folk who were also following that road on their way home from the festival. What with the bright spring morning, and my recent moments of triumph, I was in high spirits, and kept the company entertained as we went with jokes and riddles and tales. I mind there was one little fair-haired girl in particular who seemed very taken with me, or at least with my stories. She walked close beside me to hear them, and I was not sorry, for her bright eyes made me feel taller and stronger and wiser, maybe, than I was, or was ever like to be. Ah, well, we were young, and it did no one any harm.

As the day went on, most of the folk dropped away from us, turning off to north or south toward their homes, until at last, when afternoon was fading into evening, there was none left but myself, and Ieuan, and one gray old man. I had not talked much with him earlier, being taken up with my own brilliance, but now I turned my attention to him for lack of any other audience (Ieuan being a silent type on the road, and not likely to be impressed with me anyway).

"And where are you bound, sir?" I asked him as we drew near to the village of Y Bont Faen, where the Roman's stone bridge spans the little river Thaw, and where we were hoping to get lodging for the night.

"To Maridunum, near which I live." His speech was that of an educated man, despite his shabby tunic and faded brown cloak, and I looked at him with more interest.

"We also are bound that way," I said, and smiled. "Perhaps we can travel together and keep each other company on the road."

"Perhaps." I thought he looked a little amused. "What is your name, lad?"

"Gwernin Fardd am I," said I, feeling very splendid, "and I come from fair Pengwern in Powys, where Cynan Garwyn has his court on the banks of Severn River."

"Oh," he said, "it is a bard you are, is it? You look full young for such distinction."

"Why—why, perhaps I am." I was rather taken aback by this challenge, which I had not expected. "But I will grow older."

"And wiser?" The glint of amusement in his dark eyes was very marked now. "Discourse to me, then, O bard, of your wisdom. Why is stone hard, and why is a thorn sharp? What is as hard as a stone, and as salty as salt?"

"Why—I do not know," I had to admit, for the riddles were unfamiliar to me. "That is—"

"Yes?" Then, when I made no further reply, "What is as sweet as honey? What rides on the gale? Why is the nose ridged? Why is a wheel round?"

Deeply troubled, I said, "I do not know."

His smile had reached his mouth, and glinted through his gray beard—and yet I think it was of triumph without malice. "Until you know the names of the verse-forms," he said very softly, "the name of *rimiad*, the name of *ramiad*, until you can name the nine elements by the aid of your seven senses, then I think, Gwernin, that you should keep silent, for whatever else you may be, you are not a bard."

"No, master, you are right," I sighed. "I am plain Gwernin Storyteller, and nothing more."

"That is honestly said, at any rate." Then, when I continued down-cast and silent, he added, "Do not be so discouraged, youngster. By admitting what you do not know, you have made a first step toward wisdom."

I smiled despite myself. "A first step on a very long road! Master, if we should travel together, might you be so generous as to share a little, a very little of your knowledge with me?"

"So. A second step already. Yes, Gwernin, I will." I thanked him earnestly, and he nodded. "But I think that must wait until tomorrow, for look, here we are at the bridge, and the sun is setting." And it was so.

Several days we traveled together, and I learned much from the stranger, who called himself Emrys. We parted at last by the bridge outside Maridunum, we going on into the town to seek our fortune, and he off up the valley toward his homestead. I never saw him again, but I heard tales, long afterwards, and guessed who he was. I will not say his name now, for naming calls, and I would not trouble his rest; it was well-earned, and in times and places which have now passed away. But I remembered his lessons, and began, as I walked, to make and polish—with such clumsy labor and pain, but such pride!—my first songs. This is a craft which cannot be learned too young—or rather, cannot be learned at all. No true bard that I have known ever feels he has got to the end of it, however far he has gone—no, not the greatest of us all. And *his* name I will say: for he was called Taliesin, which means Shining Brow; and his rest I cannot disturb, for he is with me still.

But that, O my children, is a story for another day.

IV. A Fall of Mist

Whoever sits down on the mound at Arberth, or so the story runs, may not leave it until he has either suffered blows or wounds, or has seen a wonder. Well, I sat myself down there one spring day like Pwyll, out of pure mischief, and though I presently left—as I thought—untouched by either fate, yet in a manner of speaking I afterwards suffered both, as you shall shortly hear.

The occasion was some days after my parting at Maridunum with the stranger called Emrys. From there, Ieuan and I had wandered on westward, intending to follow the coast more or less closely, thus continuing our sun-wise circuit around Wales. As luck would have it, however, while entertaining at Arberth we heard rumor of a great feast to be held in a few days' time at Aberteifi, to the north of us. Following the coast as we had planned, we would come there far too late, but by cutting across the peninsula through the Preseli Mountains we reckoned to arrive within two days, three at the most. It seemed an opportunity not to be missed.

So there I sat on Pwyll's mound, looking down at the little village of Arberth, basking like me in the warm spring sunshine as it straggled up the hill from its ford. The mound rises on the bluff above the village, overlooking the spot where the story says Pwyll's palace stood, though no sign of that now remains. Wood rots, stone crumbles, and all our works decay: only poetry stands immortal, so long as memory lasts. But the mound itself, Gorsedd Arberth as it is called, seemed solid and permanent enough that day, crowned with green grasses and pale yellow primroses and little blue violets whose scent hung heavy on the cool morn-

17

ing air. It was also still wet with dew, as I had found to my cost, so that when I saw Ieuan humping his pack up the winding track toward me I was pleased, and more than ready to stand up and set off with him, brushing the clinging damp from my clothes as I went. I never gave a second thought to the *geas* imposed by the mound. Why should I? In truth, I thought such a fair spring morning wonder enough!

The way we went that day was no stone-paved Roman road, such as had sped some of our earlier journeying, but a rough country track barely better than a sheep path. Clearly, though, it knew its way across country, being one of the old ridge-ways that men have followed time out of mind. One ford it dropped to, some three miles north of Arberth, and thereafter kept to the high ground, running straight and clear—if sometimes rather muddy!—toward the eastern end of Mynydd Preseli, which lay long and blue and peaceful ahead of us in the morning sun. The day was fair and warm, the warmest we had had yet that spring. Larks rose singing from the grass ahead of us, mounting into a cloudless blue sky, and cuckoos answered them from the green valleys on either side. We soon saw we would have no trouble reaching our first destination by nightfall, a small village on the eastern shoulder of Mynydd Preseli which would give us shelter, and from which the land drops clear to Aberteifi and the sea beyond. So after we had paused for our nooning, eating the food given us by our host of the night before, we lay down in the lee of a clump of gorse bushes to rest for a bit. We had had some hard traveling lately, and I for one was glad of the pause. The sun was warm, and the air drowsy with the buzzing of bees busy pillaging the golden blossoms of the gorse, and sweet with the honey scent of the flowers themselves. I stretched myself out lazily in the soft new grass and closed my eyes, seeing the sunlight blood-red through my eyelids and feeling it warm on my face. I smiled, and slept, and woke to disaster.

Disaster, that is, in the shape of fog, a cold wet clinging mist that cut off vision a pace or two away, so that the very gorse bushes that had sheltered us seemed dissolving at their edges into shapeless masses of darkness. It was impossible to tell how long we had slept, for the sun was invisible, and the light so gray and dim that direction was likewise uncertain. I started up abruptly, stretching out an arm to shake Ieuan awake where he lay peacefully snoring beside me. "Ieuan," I said, "We are in trouble."

He opened his eyes slowly and lay blinking up at the grayness for a moment, then sat up, reaching for his pack. "*Sa*," he said, "I think we are. Best we should be moving; we will have to go slow in this."

And slow indeed we went. What had been a clear track before us, if not an overly well marked one, had become while we slept a maze of sheep-trods and branching side-paths through marsh and heather and gorse. Again and again we stopped, sweating despite the cold, to consult on the way forward. More than once we lost our straight line, and only knew it when the path we were following disappeared in a bog, or dropped suddenly at our feet into a brushy coomb, leaving us to retrace our steps as best we could and start again. At last, with the light fading, we lost our way, as it seemed, finally and forever, when what we had been sure was the main track led us to a sheep-trampled ford instead of a village.

Ieuan stood for a moment staring at the latest ruin of our hopes, then scratched his head. "What now?"

"I do not know," I said wearily, feeling muddy water seeping yet again into my boots. As I spoke my breath steamed into more mist before my face. Somewhere in the distance I could hear sheep bleating. "Find the shepherd?"

Ieuan nodded, easing his bulky pack on his shoulders, and splashed wordlessly into the stream.

We stumbled about in the heather until it was almost too dark to see which bog we were falling into next. We could hear the sheep, and once or twice we saw them, pale patches in the gloom which trotted briskly away at our lumbering approach. The loom of some larger mass ahead of us gave us hope for a moment, especially when it resolved itself into the sort of dry-stone hut that the shepherds often build for shelter on the moors, but we knew before we reached it that it was cold and empty. And so, by that time, were we.

I dropped my pack by the door-post of the hut. "Let us stop here. At least it is shelter, and a dry place to lie down. I am done."

Ieuan pursed his lips and spat deliberately, then nodded. Wordlessly he doffed his own pack and bent under the low lintel. The hut was dirty and cramped, and dark enough inside to make the fog without look bright, but it was shelter of a sort, and the dried piles of last year's bracken that my groping hands discovered by the wall would make for better sleeping than the bare ground. With flint and steel Ieuan kindled a stub of candle and by its light dug through his pack, emerging at last with a couple of strips of dried meat and a crumbling oat-cake that had lived there the gods knew how long. Pinching out the candle to save it for later, we split the food between us and settled back on the bracken to eat. The meat smelled odd and tasted worse, but I was young and hungry, and choked it down regardless, then wrapped my cloak around me and curled up to sleep.

It was some time in the night when I became aware that my supper was not agreeing with me. I fought the urge for as long as I could, but at last staggered up and out into the fog, leaving my friend snoring peacefully behind me. Stumbling clumsily over the rough ground in the dark, I went some way apart for privacy, and then gave way to nature.

I will draw a veil over the next hour or so. No doubt you can supply the details from your own experience. I will only say that it was a long time before I could face smoked meat again, and longer still before I trusted any food out of Ieuan's pack.

By the time I could once again take an interest in my surroundings, the fog above me was growing perceptibly lighter. Not, as I first thought, with dawn, but with the rising of the moon, a waning crescent faintly visible through the murk, whose appearance meant that day could not be far behind. I lay for a while watching her as she climbed above the shoulder of the hill; then, feeling the cold begin to bite deep, hauled myself wearily to my feet and turned toward the hut. It was not there.

I think now that in my quest for privacy, I had merely gone a little farther afield than I intended, but at the time it seemed a supernatural vanishing. Still, shivering and lightheaded as I was, I pushed off in the direction where I thought the hut should be. A few minutes' stumble through the fog proved me wrong, but as I paused again, wondering what to do next, I saw a tall figure standing silent in the moon-silvered mist ahead of me. A few more steps, and I knew it for a standing stone, a massive dark-gray block like many another we had seen the afternoon before. In my confused state, it was a familiar friend, and I staggered forward to greet it, flinging an arm around it for support and gradually sliding down its moonward side to end sitting on the turf with my back against the stone. Wrapping my arms around myself for warmth, I sighed and closed my eyes, hoping that day would come soon.

Somewhere a hunting horn was blowing, and dogs were chasing a stag. I could hear them coming closer though the darkness, hear the horn and the hoof beats and the baying of the hounds, shining white hounds with red ears, chasing a pure white deer. I knew what the huntsman would look like following such a pack, knew his dapple-gray horse and his gray hunting garb, gray as the mist around him; and I knew, too, his name. His name was Arawn.

Not many miles from where I sat was Glyn Cuch, the Frowning Glen where Pwyll Prince of Dyfed (of Gorsedd Arberth fame) had once while hunting seen another pack of dogs, chasing and killing a stag on his lands. He had driven off that pack, unearthly though they were, their bodies all shining white and their ears all shining red, and fed his own dogs on their kill, only to be interrupted by the hunter himself, who proved to be none other than Arawn, King of Annwn—the Celtic Other-world. Arawn threatened to punish Pwyll for his discourtesy by satirizing him to the value of a hundred stags, unless Pwyll first won his friendship by performing a task for him—and that was a fearful threat, for satire is the weapon of the bards, and in the hands of a master it can kill. And if a human bard's words can have such effect, how much more power might a verse composed by Arawn have over a mortal man?

Such, then, was the Hunter in the night, and such were my thoughts as I crouched at the base of the standing stone, and strained my eyes into the swirling mist around me. Distantly I saw the hunt come and pass, the wraith-like deer and the white hounds gleaming in the darkness. Dimly I saw the rider, gray-cloaked and gray-mounted, pass by, with his followers streaming behind him and the moon striking sparks of silver from their fittings and their horns. They came, and passed like thunder, and dwindled into silence, and I was alone with the moon, and the mist, and the coming dawn.

Or not quite alone. Out of the mist before me came the sound of footsteps, moving steadily over the turf toward me. Through the brightening mist a gray-cloaked figure was approaching, with the white shape of a hound trotting at his side. I stood up slowly, my back to the stone, to meet what was coming to me, my throat dry with more than the rigors of the night. My movement caught the dog's attention, and he started in my direction. I could almost see the Huntsman's face…

Then I was sitting at the foot of the standing stone, blinking up through the first light of morning at a puzzled shepherd who stood staring down at me while his dog licked my nose. "Man," he said, "do you not know you can catch your death, sittin' out like this o'night, in the fog and all?"

I grinned, and forced myself stiffly to my feet, feeling as if I had been beaten. Blows or wounds, or a wonder, was it? I had had full measure. "Never mind," I said, "it was a good dawn, and I seem to have survived it. Do you help me find my friend, who I think is still sleeping soundly in your hut, and set us on our road, and I will bless you thrice over."

With the mist thinning fast before the rising sun, it took little enough time for him to do so, and before long Ieuan and I were dropping down over the shoulder of a hill to the village where we should have spent the night. We got a warm welcome there, and warmer sympathy from the shepherd's wife, who took us in and fed us. And of all the wonders I had seen that morning, the hot oat-cakes she baked for us on the hearth-stone were the most wonderful of all!

Afterwards as we walked I looked back often and often over my left shoulder at the slopes of Mynydd Preseli, as smooth and blue and serene as they had been the day before. They do say that stones from that peak were dragged by the men of old to Salisbury Plain, to build the Giant's Dance. Dragged, or it might be, floated there by magic…

But that, O my children, is a story for another day.

V. Gold

GOLD. It is a word that catches everyone's attention, is it not? Certainly it caught mine that morning at Aberteifi, near the end of the feast which Ieuan and I had hastened so hard to attend, and which had proved so unprofitable to us after all.

Not because the lord of Aberteifi had been niggardly in his rewards, mind you, but because of Ieuan's weakness for gaming. I woke on the last morning of the feast to find myself a beggar, who had been feeling rich enough the night before. And all because Ieuan—who had been holding my purse while I performed, and kept it while I slept—was unable to resist the lure of a game of dice. It was no comfort that he had beggared himself along with me. All I had left was the clothes I stood up in, and my red-enameled brooch from Caer Dydd. It was little enough profit for two months' wandering.

So there I was, rather disconsolately eating bread and cheese in the lord's hall, while Ieuan babbled on beside me, trying to excuse himself, when the word *gold* caught my attention. "What is that you say?" I asked. "Gold? We could certainly use some!"

"Have not I been telling you, then?" Ieuan sounded sullen, for which, in my opinion, there was no excuse. "It is a place where the old Romans used to mine, up in the hills to the east of here somewhere. Caradog knows where, he told me about it last night. He will let us go in with him for shares."

"Was that before or after he won all our money at dice?" I asked sourly.

24

Ieuan brushed it off. "Never mind that, that was nothing. This is our big chance. It will make our fortunes for sure."

"Something had better." I crammed the last of the bread in my mouth and stood up, wiping my hands on my tunic. "Right then, let us go and talk to Caradog."

Caradog turned out to be a foxy-looking fellow with a thin beard and a lot of pointed yellow teeth, which he exposed frequently in what was supposed to be a smile. I took an instant dislike to him which further acquaintance did nothing to amend, but beggars, as they say, cannot be choosers, and it was beggared that we were now. After a certain amount of secretive behavior, casting suspicious glances at all about us in a manner calculated, I would have thought, to arouse curiosity where none existed, he was persuaded to part with the details of his plan—or should I say, his generous offer?

We would all contribute equally, he said, to the venture. His contribution would be the specialized knowledge necessary to find the gold and recover it, using techniques he had learnt while mining tin in Dumnonia. Ours would be enough money or other valuables to feed us all for a month. We would all do equal amounts of the work, and share out the proceeds equally among us.

At this point I interrupted him to point out the obvious. "We have not got any money or other valuables. You won them all from Ieuan here last night." With that I cast a look at Ieuan that should have withered him where he sat, but he remained defiantly unwithered. His mind was on gold.

"Ah!" said Caradog, scratching his scraggly beard. "Well, and it is because of that, see you, that I am for giving you this chance. Do you not worry about your stake, I will loan it to you, and you can pay me back out of your share of the gold."

"Thereby wiping out all of our profits. I do not see the point."

"Gwernin!" said Ieuan in distress, and at the same time Caradog said, "Na, na! Nowhere near that. I tell you, as rich as this thing is, you will get back ten times your stake, and that easy."

"If it is a good as that," I said, kicking Ieuan under the table before he could interrupt again, "why should you want to share it with us?"

"Ah!" said Caradog again, and paused, looking around suspiciously. No one, so far as I could see, was paying us any attention; they were all going about their morning business in the hall. Nevertheless, Caradog bent forward and continued in a hoarse whisper. "It is that I need someone I can trust, see you, and I like the look of you two. But if you do not fancy it, youngster, why, just you say so, and no hard feelings. There are plenty more would jump at the chance."

"Gwernin!" said Ieuan in smothered anguish. I sighed and kicked him again. "All right," I said. "We will join you. Why not?"

"Ah!" said Caradog. "You will not regret this, lad." Reaching for a pitcher of left-over breakfast ale, he filled our cups and raised his in a toast. "To success!" Ieuan drank eagerly, and I reluctantly. I would have been happier if I could have been sure to whose success I was drinking.

Shortly after that the feasting party broke up, and we shouldered our severely lightened packs and started off with Caradog. The Romans, as he explained while we walked, when they first came into Britain, had cast about for the source of British gold, in order to take it over and mine it themselves for their own treasury. Some of it they had found in the North, and some in Gwynedd and Meirionydd, but the best gold mine in all of Britain, it seemed, had proved to be right here in the mountains of Ceredigion, at Dolaucothi.

The Romans, said Caradog, had conquered the Silures of south Wales just to get Dolaucothi, and once they got it, had set themselves up in business there with all their slaves and

overseers and so forth, with a little fort stuffed full of soldiers as well, just to protect the mine. They had kept on
mining for years and years, and then for some reason the
soldiers had to leave—it might have been when Macsen
Wledig marched on Rome. And then all the overseers and
slaves and such had felt uneasy, and left as well, and never
came back, leaving a great heap of ore behind them, rich as
rich, and all ready to process, which nobody but himself
knew anything about... That, at any rate, was Caradog's
story, or at least the gist of it. I found myself talking like him
sometimes, after a while. It was catching.

So off we went, as I said, to Dolaucothi, and gods! If I
thought I had seen hard marching before, I knew nothing
about it! Two days up the Afon Teifi, falling in and out of
swamps and fords and thickets, until even I was sick of the
sight of alder, which is saying a lot! (For Gwernin, O my
children, means Alder-Tree, as you should know.) Then east,
on stretches of road that were sometimes straight enough to
suggest the Romans' handiwork, but naked of any suggestion
of paving. These led us for three more days over what
seemed the backbone of the world, seeing few people, living
on cheese and stale oat cakes and cold spring water, and
sleeping rough. I wondered more than once why Caradog
had not recruited his workforce closer to the mine, but
something held me back from asking. By the time we came
dropping down into the valley of the little Afon Cothi on the
evening of the fifth day, I was ready for a rest. I did not get
it.

Under Caradog's direction, we took up residence in the
ruins of one of the Romans' old buildings—a stable, I think
it may have been—and started to work. Our first task was
cleaning out the remains of one of the old aqueducts in order
to get a trickle of water down to the mine. Then there were
the water tanks to clean out and repair, and a sort of bedrock
trench to muck out as well, with only the three of us to shift

two hundred years' accumulation of sand and silt and mud. I say three, but I noticed after a while that when the hardest work was being done, Caradog was nowhere around. He was always off organizing more materials, or down buying our food at the inn which had sprouted up like a gray stone mushroom in the ruins of the old fortress buildings, or up the hill checking the ditch for leaks or blockages—anywhere but on the end of a shovel.

Ieuan and I stuck it out, though, with hardly a grumble. We had the gold fever bad by then. Our clothes went to rags, and our hands to blisters and broken nails and calluses, until we looked like a couple of wild hairy savages from the back of the north wind, rather than two civilized strolling entertainers, but we made nothing of it. We were going to be rich.

The big day arrived when we were ready to run the sluice—that was the bedrock trench, you understand. After mucking it out, we had refilled it with load after weary load of broken ore from the Romans' stockpile. Then we opened the gate to the tanks, and let all our hoarded water out in a rush. It plunged down the sluice in fine style, washing away all the lighter rock and leaving behind—we hoped!—the gold. At least, that was the theory.

It was not quite so neat in practice, partly because we did not have as much water as we would have liked. Still, it reduced the material in the bottom of the trench considerably. The next step, said Caradog enthusiastically, was hand-cobbing. This, I found, meant hand-sorting all the bigger rocks and pebbles out of the trench into buckets, and carting them away, leaving us finally with a few dozen bucket-loads of sandy mud in the bottom of the trench, which Caradog assured us contained the gold. This precious material we carried to the nearest water tank, where it had to be washed—by hand!—in flat wooden platters until only the gold was left, a back-breaking task in the hot afternoon sun. Of course, we had only two platters, but it did not matter, because Caradog disappeared again before we were through—I suspect to the inn.

That afternoon, though, I finally saw some gold. Only a couple of tiny flakes at the bottom of my first pan, but I told myself there would be more in the next one, or the next one after that. Sometimes there was, a whole clump of little gold spangles, or maybe a angular little golden blob. Sometimes there was nothing at all. Still, by the time the shadows of the mountains to the west came creeping over us and made it too dark to work, we each had a palm-full of gold dust for our trouble, with maybe three quarters of our clean-up still to go. Caradog, strolling back from the inn in the twilight, seemed discretely pleased. Tomorrow, he said, carefully scooping our gold into a little deerskin bag, would be even better.

And it was. We worked from when the sun first peeked over the ridge in the east, until the western mountains swallowed it up again. And what work it was! I could see why the Romans had used slaves. It was hard to imagine anyone in his right mind working that hard for a few flakes of metal. But then, we were mad—gold-mad!—not to mention beggared. We really had no choice. Or so I told myself, as the gold slowly—how slowly!—piled up.

One more day, said Caradog, scooping up our harvest that evening, and that would be the best day yet. Then we could go our separate ways, with a fat poke for each of us as reward for our month's work. New clothes, horses to make our traveling easier—and for me, I thought secretly, a harp, and a chance of finally becoming a real bard. Though looking at my laborer's hands, I knew it would be a while before I could start learning to play it.

The last day's clean-up, scraped from the very bottom of the trench, surpassed all expectations. As the weary hours passed and the gold mounted up, I began to believe it was all true. Caradog was the best of good fellows, a worthy bearer of his noble name, and Ieuan's passion for gambling became in retrospect a virtue. When Caradog poured all our gold together that evening into one of the wooden trays, and divided it into three carefully equal piles before transferring it to more of his deerskin bags, I felt an excitement that I had previously found only in performance. Tired as I was, I doubted I would be able to sleep that night.

"Well, lads," said Caradog, hefting our spoils, "we have done ourselves proud! Let us drink now to our good fortune!" And with that he bent and hauled out from under his bench an actual skin of wine, real wine such as princes and nobles drank. "Brought up here special for us," he said, breaking the wax on the end with his knife and twisting out the leather-wrapped stopper. "Nothing is too good for us now, lads. Drink up!" And he filled our wooden cups to the brim with the pungent blood-red stuff.

I choked on the first swallow, but the rest went down easier, and the next cup easier still. A sovereign remedy, I thought—my eyes crossing slightly—against all discomfort. Under its influence all my aches and pains melted away, until I had never felt so good in my life. Or, suddenly, so sleepy. I felt I could sleep for a week. But overnight, as it turned out, was long enough.

When we woke up, of course, Caradog was gone, and all the gold with him. Bleary-eyed as we were, it took a little while for the awful truth to sink in, but there was really no room for doubt.

"Leave it," I said after a while, breaking in on Ieuan's colorful description of what he would do to Caradog when he found him. "We will not catch him. He has had all night to be gone in, and the wherewithal to buy the best horse in the valley to go on. If we find him somewhere else, it is our word against his. Come on, let us see if the inn-folk will let us work for our breakfast—and hope it does not involve a shovel!"

Later that morning, while I was mucking out the stable at the inn, I heard the sound of trotting horses. Into the yard rode half a dozen mounted men, light-armed with swords and daggers, and in their midst, with his hands tied before him and his horse on a leading rein, was our old friend Caradog.

"Good day to you, Lord," called the inn-keeper from his doorway. "I see you got him."

"We did indeed, just as you said, with the gold from my land in his saddlebags." Sitting at ease on his big bay horse, the red-cloaked leader of the troop was smiling. "We are looking now for his two companions, who he says are still here."

"Ah, and there is one of them now, Lord," cried Caradog, gesturing at me with his bound hands. "It was them as led me into it, they did, almost forced me to join them!"

"So much so that you were escaping from them in the dawn?" But the leader was looking at me with interest nevertheless. "And who might you be, young fellow?"

"Only a wandering storyteller, Lord," I said. "Down on my luck, and forced to work for my breakfast."

"Indeed, Lord, and I think that is true," said the inn-keeper, with a wink at me. "Certainly, I never saw this lad nor his friend up at the mine"—and that was true enough, for he'd never come up there!—"and they do seem to be poor, harmless folk. I doubt they would be mucking out my stable if they had gold in their purses."

"Gold, is it, that you are seeking?" I said. "And stolen? Lord, if you can find aught of gold in my gear or my friend's, then by Pryderi's pigs! May I drop down dead before you from pure astonishment!"

"I believe you," said the young lord, casting a smiling glance at Caradog, who sat fuming in red-faced silence—for to accuse us further was to brand himself doubly a thief! "And your words convince me you are a reciter as well.

31

Come, then, to my court at Lampeter, and tell your stories for our Midsummer feast there in three days time, and perhaps I can amend your poverty." Then, gathering his reins and speaking to his followers, "Ride on, lads. It seems we still have two thieves to catch, who"—and he glanced again in amusement at Caradog—"would certainly not be earning their breakfasts by useful labor, being far too well provided with their share of stolen gold!"

Later that morning I walked away from Dolaucothi without a backward glance, through a fine summer's day bright with bird-song and more beautiful than any gold. And the next time I went looking for treasure in the earth, it was in a different form, and did not involve a shovel.

But that, O my children, is a story for another day.

VI. The Tale of Arthur the Soldier

Our golden weather had gone at last, squandered at Dolaucothi in our search for lesser gold. It had seen us as far as Lampeter and the Midsummer Festival there, and two days farther, up the straight white Roman road that led north through Tregaron and the green hills of Ceredigion. Then, when we were nearing Aberystwyth, the heavens opened and the rain poured down in torrents. Five days latter, it was still pouring.

Leaning on the door-post of the hut where we were staying, I watched the gray veils of rain marching eastward up the Aber Dyfi, blotting out the hills beyond as they went. In our common tongue the word *glas* can mean green, or blue, or gray; that afternoon, it described the whole landscape. The sound of the rain was everywhere, drumming softly on the thatched roof, dripping from the eves, and splashing in the puddles that covered most of the farmyard. The dust of the summer roads had turned to rivers of mud, and I knew without being told that the Afon Dyfi would be roaring over her ford at Machynlleth, too deep by far for our crossing. We might yet wear out our welcome in this friendly countryside.

With a sigh, I turned away from the rain, back to the room within, and the company assembled there. It was time for another story.

Morag, the farmer's comely wife, looked up smiling from her loom as my shadow crossed her web. "Would you be for telling us another tale, then, Gwernin, dear, to pass the afternoon?"

"I would." Mentally I tallied up my resources. The two nights and days Ieuan and I had already spent at Tre Pencae since arriving soaked and weary on the doorstep at twilight had used up most of my regular stock of tales. Still, I had one or two left…

I looked around the room assessingly as I thought. The place was all one big thatched roundhouse in the old British style, not like the squared-off Roman villas I had seen here and there on my travels. In the middle of the room was a central hearth on which the fire never went out from one Beltane to the next, and over it hung a big bronze cauldron with our supper stew cooking in it. All the other activities of the household were arranged around the room as space permitted, with Morag's loom nearest the door to catch the available light. A bed-place in the back, separated off by wicker-work and hanging rugs, gave her and her husband some privacy at night; everyone else, children and farm-hands and guests alike, slept wherever they could find space, on the benches around the walls, or on the hard-packed earth near the fire, or in the smoky gloom of the half-loft above. The farmer and his men were out somewhere about the steading now, rain or no rain, but the rest of the house-hold—four women, seven children, and a dog or two—were all watching me expectantly. Even my friend Ieuan, mending a boot in the far corner, who had by now heard most of my stories more often than he liked, looked faintly interested at the prospect of entertainment. It was better than watching the rain.

The sight of Ieuan reminded me of our recent attempt at gold mining, brought on by the loss of most of our goods and gear. And that in turn reminded me of a story… I took a deep breath and smiled at my audience. "Did you ever hear the Tale of Arthur the Soldier and the Three Truths?"

"No, never," said Morag happily. "So sit you down and tell it to us, do. It is time aplenty we have to fill before the supper is done." There was a chorus of agreement from the household, and as usual seven-year-old Gwion, the oldest boy of the brood, sat himself solemnly down at my feet, fixing his dark eyes on my face as if prepared to memorize my every word. Behind him his grandmother added wool to her distaff, and Morag's sister Heledd, who had been turning the last of the oatcakes baking beside the fire, took up her spindle again and settled down to listen.

"Everyone knows the adventures of Arthur the High King," I began, "Arthur of the Twelve Battles who freed us from the Saxon threat for a generation. But this is a story of Arthur before he became king, when he was still only Arthur the Soldier, War Leader of Britain." I looked around the room. Except for three-year-old Dafydd, busy trying to pull the ears off a big black hound lying by the hearthstone, everyone was listening intently, so I went on.

"Now the trouble with being a War Leader is that soldiers expect to be rewarded for their efforts. And even when someone else pays them—when all the different kings and princes and chieftains raise their own war-bands and bring them on campaign—there is still the question of supplies, of food and drink for the army and all their camp-followers and servants, and pack-horses, and wagons, and tents, and so forth. So the one thing a War Leader can never get enough of is treasure, and Arthur was no exception. At the time of my story, he and some of his friends—just Bedwyr and Cai and a few others—had come into western Britain to try and talk the local kings and princes out of more gold for the next year's campaigning. And he was having hard going at it.

"They had gathered at Dinas Emrys, one of Cadwallon Lawhir's seats close up under the shoulder of Yr Wyddfa, and after a few days of this, Arthur was ready for a break. So when someone reported that a white stag had been seen on the mountain, and suggested a day's hunting, he was all for it.

"Early the next morning, then, they mounted their horses and started for the slopes of Yr Wyddfa. It was a cold, quiet morning, with the scent lying high, such as comes sometimes in late October. Presently the huntsmen found traces of the stag, and the hounds were off baying on its tracks, with all the hunters following close behind them. Higher and higher up the mountain they went, until the ground was too steep for riding, and they had to leave their horses behind them. But they kept on regardless.

"It had been fair enough weather when they started, but before long the clouds came drifting in from the west and gathered around the peaks, dropping lower as the hunters climbed. So it came to pass that sometime in the late afternoon, Arthur and his party, still intent on their hunt, suddenly found themselves overtaken by a drifting bank of mist, that came creeping around a crag and engulfed them before they knew what they were about.

"It was a good thick mountain mist, cold and gray and damp. Strung out across the hillside as they were, Arthur and his men lost sight of each other between one stride and the next. They called out, of course, trying to regroup, but it was no use. The more they yelled and searched for each other, the more they drifted apart. Arthur called and searched as hard as any, but after a while he realized that he could no longer hear any voice but his own. He was alone in the mist, high up on the slopes of Yr Wyddfa, and the light was fading. Soon it would be dark.

"Now if ever there was anyone good at grasping a situation, it was Arthur. So he set himself to work to find some sort of shelter, where he could pass the night in reasonable comfort. Picking his way carefully along the hillside in the drifting mist, he found a sort of overhanging cliff, with a hollow bit at the back, like a cave. As he made his way into it, he found that it *was* a cave, and a good-sized one at that. He was just blessing his good fortune, when somewhere towards the back of the cave, he saw a blink of light in the gloom, and at the same time, he smelled wood-smoke.

36

"Now this gave him pause, for Arthur knew as well as you do what sort of unchancy things can live in mountain caves." My audience nodded back, big-eyed. They'd heard the stories, too. "Still, what with the wet and gloomy weather outside—did I mention that the mist was changing into rain?—he decided to chance it. There was no point in lingering in the front porch, so to speak, waiting for whatever was in there to come out and surprise him. So Arthur summoned up his courage and started deeper into the cave.

"As he picked his way down the passage, the lighter got stronger and stronger, until at last he could see it was a fire burning on a hearth in the middle of the cavern ahead of him. Over the fire there was a tripod, and beside it stood an immense black cauldron. And on the far side of the cauldron was a pile of treasure, gold and gems, cups and arm-rings and brooches, and every kind of precious thing you ever saw or heard of, all sparkling in the light of the fire.

"Now Arthur, as I have told you, had just been spending his days trying of squeeze the smallest amount of gold out of the lords of Gwynedd. So this heap of treasure drew him as a feast would a starving man. There were other strange and wonderful things in the cavern, but he had eyes for none of them. He looked at the treasure, and he looked back down the passage, and he stood still and listened. There was no sound but the crackling of the fire on the hearth and his own hasty breathing. He was alone.

"Surely, he thought, the possessor of so great a mound of treasure would never miss one or two small bits of it. And after all, it was for the best of causes, the defense of Britain against her enemies. So he picked up a couple of gold coins, and put them in his pouch. And then a brooch. And an arm-ring. And a few more coins. Before he knew it, his pouch was full, and he was dropping valuables down the front of his tunic above his belt, and taking off his cloak to make a bag of it. There was still plenty of treasure remaining. Indeed, it seemed that the more he took, the more there was left.

"At last, when he had as much as he could stagger with—and that was a lot, for Arthur was a strong warrior—he turned to leave, for it seemed to him now that a night spent on the hillside in the rain might well be a better choice than waiting in the cave for its owner to come home. And as he turned, what do you suppose he heard?"

"Footsteps," breathed ten-year-old Gwen from beside the fire, where she had been separating her youngest brother from the impatient hound.

"That is right. He heard the sound of footsteps, coming down the passage toward him." I paused and looked around the room at my audience. Everyone was waiting in varying degrees of suspense. Even Ieuan sat frozen, boot in one hand and leather thong in the other, his task forgotten. I smiled and went on.

"Down the passage toward Arthur was coming a very large man. He was so big that he walked stooped over, with his hairy shoulders brushing the roof above him and his huge hands hanging down by his knees. As he came into the light of the fire, Arthur thought that he had never seen such an ill-favored person in his life. Then he caught a glimpse of the old woman who was following the giant, and changed his mind.

" 'And what might you be doing here, man?' asked the giant in a deep voice.

" 'Ah—I was just sheltering from the rain,' replied Arthur. 'But I do not want to disturb you. I will be going now.' And he took a step toward the passage.

" 'Not so fast,' said the giant, and with a huge hand he grabbed Arthur by the shoulder. 'I think you have something there of mine.'

"Now the grip of the giant's hand was stronger than the grip of ten men, so that sweat sprang to Arthur's forehead for the very pain of it. But he stood quietly and smiled. 'Why, what do you mean?' he asked.

" 'Just this,' said the giant, and lifting Arthur suddenly off the ground, he shook him as a dog shakes a rat.

"Gold went flying everywhere. Jewels and coins bounced ringing off the cauldron, and drew sparks from the fire. Bracelets and torques and arm-rings rolled across the floor, and one gold-mounted, ruby-studded drinking horn sailed clear across the room and struck a great harp standing there with a clang and a clatter and a ringing of strings. When at last the shower of gold ended, the giant set Arthur back on his feet, but kept a grip on his shoulder. 'Well, Mum,' he said to the hag grimly, 'what shall I do with this thief?'

"The hag looked Arthur over from his head down to his heels and back again. 'Ah,' she said at last, 'do you tie a bit of string around him and throw him in the corner there. Happen we will be glad of him come breakfast time, for it is empty the pot is now.' And she nodded at the great cauldron standing waiting beside the fire.

" 'I will,' said the giant, and he whipped out a hairy length of rope, and before Arthur could so much as lift a finger, he was tied up tighter than a bundle of twigs, and cast into the far corner of the room, with a verminous old sheep-skin thrown over him 'to keep him warm', as his hosts put it.

"Well, of all the uncomfortable nights that poor Arthur ever spent, this one was one of the worst. The rope around him was rough and strong and very tightly tied, so that after a while he could hardly feel his hands and feet. The ground under him was jagged stone, and however much he squirmed around, some bits of it were always sticking into him—and it was cold as ice as well! And the sheepskin, which was sup-posed to keep him warm, was so well populated that he would most certainly have been very much happier without it. But worse than any of these discomforts was the thought of the cauldron, and what might happen to him in the morning. That fear alone would have kept him sleepless though the night.

"As he lay there, squirming and itching and aching, he was aware of music, the most beautiful music he had ever heard. Craning his head out from under the sheepskin, Arthur saw that the source of the music was the giant, playing his harp beside the fire. Now Arthur thought he had heard great harping before in his life. Only a few days since, he had listened to Talhaearn Tad Awen, greatest of all the bards, playing at Cadwallon's court, and the spell of that music had been such as to call the birds down from the trees, and the stags out of the forest, and the salmon up from the depths of the sea. But the harping of the giant was to all other music as the flowing ocean is to a little brook. The beauty and majesty and wonder of it wrapped Arthur so around, that he forgot all his troubles and wept for pure joy. And at last, worn out, he fell asleep.

"The next thing he knew, it was morning. The sheepskin was lifted off him abruptly, and while he was blinking, the giant plucked him out of his corner and set him, still bound, on his feet. Arthur saw that the fire had been built up and the great cauldron set in place above it, with a little steam rising from its maw. The giant drew a knife from his belt and set to sharpening it, *wheet, wheet, wheet*, on a whetstone. 'Well, Mum,' he said to the hag, 'what do you think?'

"The hag looked Arthur over from his head down to his heels and back again, her eyes very bright and knowing under the rook's-nest of her gray hair. 'Ah,' she said after a bit, 'it is a bonny lad he is, and right enough, though there is not over-much honesty in him. It seems a pity to waste him, when a sheep would serve as well.' And she gave a cackle of mirth. 'I will tell you, my lad,' she said, addressing herself to Arthur, 'if you can speak me three undoubted truths before the kettle boils, I will let you go.'

"Arthur looked at the cauldron, and saw the steam was thickening above it. After the night he had spent, his head felt solid as a block of wood, and his tongue like a strip of old boot-leather in his mouth. Gazing around desperately for inspiration, he saw the harp sitting silent to one side, and remembered last night's wonderful music. Looking at the giant, Arthur said without thinking, 'You are the best harper I have ever heard!'

" 'Aye,' said the hag, holding up a bony finger. 'That is one!' And looking around at her, Arthur realized he had spoken his first truth.

"From the corner of his eye, he could see the steam over the kettle was thickening fast. Nevertheless, he could not help staring at the hag. To say that she was unattractive is like saying that the weather outside today is a trifle damp." There were grins from the household at this; the rain was currently roaring on the roof like a waterfall. "The longer Arthur looked at her, the more she amazed him, and without thinking, he said, 'You are the ugliest woman I have ever seen!' "

There was a collective gasp from my audience, mixed with nervous giggles, but I ignored them and went on.

" 'Aye,' said the hag," I said, " 'and that is two!' And she held up another finger." And I held up a second finger as well.

"Arthur cudgeled his brains in search of inspiration, but his wits seemed to have gone right out of him. He looked around the room again, but nothing came to him. The cauldron was starting to make the sort of muttering noise that comes just before it boils, and the giant had begun sharpening his knife again, *wheet, wheet, wheet,* in a sort of counterpoint to the sound. Arthur looked at the knife, and he looked at the heap of golden treasure which had seemed so valuable to him the night before, and he looked along the passage to where the first sweet gray light of morning was just beginning to bloom. And without thinking, he said, 'If I once get out of here, I will never come back again!'

" 'Aye,' said the hag, 'and that is three!' And the cauldron boiled.

"Quick as a wink, the giant grabbed Arthur by the hair, and with his knife cut the ropes that bound him. 'Go on, then,' he said, turning him loose, 'and keep your word while you can!'

"Arthur took to his heels without a backward glance, and what he had said, he made good. As long as he lived, he remembered that some things are more valuable than gold, and he never came near that part of Yr Wyddfa again. And neither, I can tell you, have I!" And I leaned back on my bench with a sigh, as if I were the one released.

"Ah!" said Morag, when the murmurs of appreciation had died away. "That was a good story, my dear, almost as good as one of our master's. And now, unless I am wrong, it is time we all had a bite and a sup. Cynan, Rhys, Bleiddig, get you out of those wet clothes and into something dry first, it is soaked to the skin you all are!" And I saw that the men had come in quietly from the farmyard while I talked, and were standing grinning inside the doorway behind me, having listened to the end of the story. So in the ensuing bustle, I never found out the meaning of Morag's remark.

Sometime in the night the weather changed, and we woke the next morning to a new world, still damp from its birth and steaming in the early sunlight. Our hosts saw us on our way after breakfast with many kind wishes, and a packet of oat-cakes and cheese for our nooning, and the children waved after us from the gateway for as long as we could see them.

Three days later, looking back south to the green hills across the Aber Dyfi—we had had to wait at the ford as I had expected—I thought again of Tre Pencae, and the strange feeling of belonging I had felt now and again during my stay there. And just for a moment, walking in bright sunlight, I felt cold rain on my face, and tears blurred my vision so that I stumbled on a smooth path.

"What is it?" asked Ieuan from behind me. "Walking in your sleep again, are you?"

"Something like that," I said frowning. It was long and long before I found out the meaning of my moment's vision. I know it now, of course, know it all too well...

But that, O my children, is truly a story for another day.

VII. The Birds of Rhiannon

When Brân looked out from Harddlech, he had quite a view. So I was thinking one fine summer evening as I stood leaning against the turf ramparts of that place and looking out west over the sea. The Beautiful Rock has been inhabited time out of mind, though seldom by very many folk at once. The fort itself is nothing much for most of its circumference—a low wall designed as much to keep sheep and babies from falling into the sea as to keep out raiders—but it does not need to be. The Rock herself drops almost sheer for two-score paces to the water, which laps around her feet at high tide. And the view is stupendous.

To the north you can see right across Morfa Harddlech and the Afon Dwyryd to where the mountains of Eryri climb toward the sky—to Yr Wyddfa herself on a clear day. To the north-west and west and south-west, the whole great length of the Lleyn Peninsula runs out toward Ireland, as if Gwynedd was stretching out an arm toward her in friendship. Though in Brân's day, of course, it was the other way round—or so it started.

You've heard the story, I expect—how Brân the Blesséd, King of Britain, looked out from Harddlech and saw the fleet of Matholwch, King of Ireland, coming toward him over the sea, coming to ask for the hand of Brân's sister Branwen in marriage. How Brân gave her to him, and the heartbreak that followed. How Efnisien her half-brother took offense at the match and gave great insult to the Irishmen, so that even though Brân patched things up and made reparations, the memory lingered with them and turned to hatred of Branwen, and abuse of her. How this led to war in its turn, Brân

44

coming with an army to lay waste to Ireland; and the further ill-doing of Efnisien, when he killed Branwen's little son Gwern, to whom Matholwch would have resigned his kingship, by thrusting him into the fire; and the great slaughter that followed on both sides. How Efnisien in remorse sacrificed himself to overcome the Irish by bursting apart their cauldron of regeneration, and burst his own heart in the process; and how Brân got his death-wound from a poisoned spear, and commanded his followers to strike off his head, and bear it back to Britain with them. How Branwen herself died at last of grief that those two great countries had been laid waste because of her, and was buried on the banks of Afon Alaw by the pitiful remnant of Brân's forces who returned...

"Yes, when we went with Brân, sad journey, save seven, none came back from Iwerddon."

The words were so much in tune with my own thoughts that it was a moment before I realized someone else has spoken. Then I turned to look at the person beside me.

Not a large man, he was, and yet not small. Not young, somehow, and yet certainly not old. His shoulder-length dark hair and his neatly-trimmed beard were untouched by gray, but his face was mature, and not that of a youth. An ordinary-looking man, and yet not ordinary; hard to describe, but also hard to forget. He was dressed as for a journey, in good but well-worn clothes with the dust of the summer roads on them, but the brooch that clasped his cloak was kingly gold, and rich with many-colored enamels. Even so, I thought, might Brân's brother, Manawydan mab Llyr himself, have looked after the Irish expedition. So quietly had he come that I had heard nothing until he spoke. But certainly he was here now, leaning on the rampart beside me as if he had grown there and gazing out over the sea.

I nodded slowly. "Such words were also in my mind."

"Back with us bore we Brân's head, as he himself had bade us." My companion spoke softly and musingly, as if talking to himself alone. "Eight years were we at Harddlech, and four-score more at Gwales, and in all that time his head was to us as pleasant a companion as ever when he was alive. And always there were with us the birds of Rhiannon, whose singing gives forgetfulness and peace. So feasting and forgetting stayed we there, till at last one amongst us opened the door that looks toward Dumnonia, and with that opening memory rushed in, and we knew our loss, and felt the heavy burden of our grief fall upon us. On the White Mount, then, we buried Brân's head, as he himself had bade us, and it kept the coasts of Britain clear, until Arthur dug it up. And that was an evil day."

I stared at him, feeling the short hairs creep on the back of my neck, and a shiver go up my spine. It was not just the resonant storyteller's voice, or the finely-phrased delivery. He spoke as one who had himself truly been there, and seen all that he described. "Lord..."

The stranger gave himself a little shake, as one coming out of a dream, and smiled. "Forgive me, I am a bard, and we speak ever in riddles." He looked at me intently, his eyes very blue and piercing, so that I felt suddenly naked to his gaze. "And you, I think, are also a bard."

I shook my head. "No, I fear I am not—or at any rate, not yet. Only a wandering storyteller am I."

"No very bad thing to be." He was still smiling slightly. "From your speech I think you come from eastern Powys."

"I do indeed. From Pengwern the beautiful come I, where Cynan Garwyn has his court on the banks of Severn River."

"I know it well." His gaze softened; he turned back toward the sea. "Be patient, Gwernin. All things will come in their time."

Something about him stirred a chord in my memory. And he knew my name. Abruptly I asked, "Lord… Forgive me, but have we met before?"

"Met? Not—exactly." He shook his head slowly. "No, not exactly. But I think that we will meet again." He was still looking away, and my gaze followed his, far, far out over the water toward the west, where the sun was now sinking, dropping slowly through the clouds toward the edge of the world, bright sun-dazzle dancing on blue water, blazing, blinding, and in it the singing of the birds…

I blinked and shook myself, my eyes watering from the light into which I had been staring. I turned to my companion to make some comment, but he was gone, disappeared as quietly as he had come, leaving only the empty air behind him. Nor did I see him that evening in the headman's house, where I and my friend Ieuan alone provided the entertainment. He seemed to have vanished away with the wind, as if he had never been there and I had imagined the whole.

I did meet him again, of course—he was right about that, as he was about most such things.

But that, O my children, is a story for another day.

VIII. The Black Stone

Pigs are not my favorite animals. Valuable and useful they are indeed, their flesh making good eating and their skins good leather. Powerful and magical they are as well, for did not Arawn King of Annwn himself give the first pigs to Pryderi, Prince of Dyfed, in token of the friendship that was between Arawn and Pryderi's father Pwyll? And did not Gwydion the Magician steal those selfsame pigs from Pryderi by a trick, and bring them home to Gwynedd, thereby causing bloody war between Gwynedd and Deheubarth, in which many a man lost his life—not least of them Pryderi himself, slain by Gwydion in single combat before both their armies? Slain, so the tale says, "by dint of strength and craft, and through magic and enchantment..." No, I like a nice dish of pig-meat as well as the next man, but I hold with the Irish that the pig-run should be kept out of sight and scent and sound of the owner's house, and not only because of the smell of it.

Pigs, however, were very far from my mind on a certain sunny morning in Gwynedd. High summer it was, some weeks now past Solstice and drawing near to Lughnasadh, with the grain standing tall in the fields and ripening fast, and the willow-herb blooming rose-purple along all the roads. No one, however, was at work in the fields that day, for it was a Sunday, and there was a traveling Christian priest in the village who was going to preach.

So it came about that midway through that fine morning, I found myself—most uncharacteristically!—standing at the back of a crowd of people and listening to someone else talk. The priest, a thin, wiry man with a graying beard and the Celtic tonsure which goes from ear to ear, stood before us on the top of a low green mound at the edge of the village. He spoke well enough, though his voice, I thought, could have used a little more projection, and his phrasing could sometimes have been bettered. I admit I did not give overmuch heed to his words, having come along that morning more out of deference to my hosts than from any religious interest of my own. Instead, I was thinking back to some of my recent adventures, and ahead to Caer Seint, where we would be going in a few days' time, and wondering what stories to tell at the Lughnasadh festival there.

I am not in any case a Christian, though in today's troubled times it is becoming less and less wise to stand up and say so. With the Saxons pressing in ever more savagely at our borders, the Christian faith, along with the Latin language and the ideals of learning and Roman citizenship that go with it, has become one of the things we British cling to, as a bright lantern in our hand here on the edge of savage darkness. Anyone abjuring that faith publicly may be suspected by some, if not of giving help to the barbarians, at least of not totally resisting them to the utmost.

Still, on that sunny summer morning near the banks of Afon Cynfael, I was guilty of nothing worse than daydreaming, while the voice of the priest wore on and on, going over my head without apparent effect. So it was that the stone caught my eye. It stood at one end of the mound from which the priest was speaking, a round black pillar perhaps half the height of a man. Maen Twrog they call it now—Twrog's Stone—in honor of a saint who is supposed to have lived beside it for a while, but in those days it had another name which many still remember, though I did not then know it. I only thought vaguely that the stone and the mound were some sort of tomb or monument from the very-long-ago, and went back to contemplating the story I intended to tell at Lughnasadh. The priest finished his prayers, and the crowd broke up and began to drift back toward their houses by

Cynfael ford. And that would have been all, had it not been for my curiosity, which made me linger and take a closer look at the stone.

It was not, as I had thought at first, a rounded column, but a flattened one, a little too regular to be natural. It stood with the mound in a patch of bright-green sheep-cropped grass at the edge of the village fields. The mound itself had two or three other stones around it, standing or lying in the turf, big rough-coated gray stones, unshaped and shaggy with lichen. The black stone had nothing growing on it at all. It stood smooth and cold and silent under my hand when I touched it, with nothing to say for itself. I wondered what its story was, and if anyone in the village would know.

Straightening up again, I saw in the distance beside the track which leads west from the village another standing stone. And because it was a pleasant day, and I was sure of lodging here for the night, and tired of religious discussions for the moment, I started off to look at it.

It stood almost on the edge of a belt of woodland. Another gray stone, I found it was, but smaller, and of a different kind from the ones by the mound, roughly squared and with the remains of carving on one side. I had seen the like once or twice before in my travels, and knew it for a Roman milestone. With difficulty I spelled out the moss-grown letters carved on its near side: SEG, for Segontium—Caer Seint as we call it now—and something below it that I could not read, which might have once been a number. I was standing on one of the Romans' old roads, the one perhaps that had led from Tomen-y-Mur to the coast. It explained the smooth levelness of the path I had followed, and the half-lost traces of stone paving in the ford by the village. But the black stone by the mound was none of the Romans' work.

I was turning to go back to the village when I heard the music. Snatches of a light, catchy tune, played as it might be on some sort of flute or pipe, came drifting on the breeze from somewhere within the oak-wood behind me. It was not a tune I knew, but one, I thought, that I would like to learn. I turned again and followed the music into the oak grove.

Under the trees the light was green, a pale green like spring. The piping was somewhere ahead of me, and I followed the thread of sound. Between the oaks there were other trees, birch and hazel, and clumps of thick brush. The path thinned to almost nothing where it pierced the thicker clumps, and the bushes pressed in against me from either side with urgent hands. But the music drew me on, now louder, now softer, now fading away almost to nothing. And mixed with it I could faintly hear the sound of running water from the river ahead.

As I paused to listen, I heard a noise behind me, as of something large and heavy moving though the undergrowth. Frowning, I looked back, but could see nothing. Then the music started again, and I went on.

Ahead of me the wood opened up into a clearing. I caught a glimpse of river bank, and beside it a lime-washed hut, pied with sun and shadow from the huge oak that leaned over it. There was a wattled enclosure beside the hut. A scrap of a breeze blew my way, and I wrinkled my nose at the odor that came with it.

Behind me there was a crashing noise, and I whirled to look over my shoulder. Out of the bushes came something big and black, solid as one of the standing stones. Massive and mud-crusted, the black sow glared at me malevolently out of little red eyes, and started toward me at an accelerating trot. I backed a step, and another step, then turned and ran incontinently, heading for the shelter of the wattled enclose. Behind me I heard the thunder of the sow's feet and her grunting breath as she gained on me.

Did you ever know, even as you acted, that you were making a mistake? So indeed that time did I, but events pressed, and my choices were not many. Reaching the fence,

I leaped for the top of the gate and swung myself over it anyhow, rolling and landing heavily on my back on the other side. At least it got me away from the dark one, and what was within was soft to land in.

Behind me the sow hit the gate with a crash that shook the whole enclosure, but somehow it held. Then a voice spoke nearby, biding her quieten and draw off, and strangely enough she did so. Dripping and filthy and shaken as I was, I got slowly to my knees in the pool of muck where I had landed, and looked up to confront the swineherd.

Perhaps a finger's breadth shorter than I am, he was, and I am not tall. He was thin and brown and gnarled as an old alder root twisted by the river, but strong, too, as an alder root, and that is very strong. His dark hair was gray-striped as a badger's pelt, but his teeth showed white in the tangle of his beard when he smiled, and his eyes were bright and merry, green and brown together like a sun-speckled river, and just now very amused as my condition. In the warm summer he wore nothing but a short, sleeveless tunic of gray homespun, and dangled the bone flute he had been playing in one lean brown hand at his side. "Welcome," he said, his voice cool and smooth as river water, and as musical. "We are always glad of company here, though sorry I am if the Lady pressed you. She does get over-eager at times, but there is no harm in it today."

"It is pleased I am to hear it," I said stiffly, getting to my feet. "It did not show in her manner. Does she bring you many visitors?"

"A few." Smiling, he looked me over a minute, as I stood dripping muck and trying to keep my dignity, and then he laughed. "Ah, man, never stand there so stiffly! It is a fine day for washing, and the river is close at hand—and did you not come out today with the intention of getting clean?"

Sometime later that afternoon, I sat on a boulder, dabbling my feet in Cynfael stream, while my clothes steamed slowly in the sunlight on the bushes behind me. I had washed them in the river as best I could, and washed myself as well, and though a sensitive nose might still have detected some hint of pig-reek on the both of us, at least the water had carried away most of the mud and sweat and dust of the summer roads.

I was happy enough at that moment. The silken flow of the water around my bare feet, and the cool, stream-polished smoothness of the dark gray stone beneath me, and the warmth of the sun on my skin and hair—all these were all pure pleasure, as was the thin bright piping of my companion, which mixed and mingled gently with the singing of the small birds in the oak above us. I hardly noticed when the piping stopped, and changed to song instead:

"Oak there grows 'twixt earth and sky–
Rain may wet it, sun may dry.
In its branches broad and high,
One I seek may safely lie.

"And so may we for the moment," said the piper, "though I fear the afternoon is drawing on. What brought you out here this afternoon, Gwernin, my friend, and what do *you* seek?"

What, indeed? "Chance brought me out, or so I thought," I said slowly. "And as to what I seek…" The piper was waiting, watching me with his head tilted to one side like an expectant bird. His raised eyebrows prompted me to go on, but he said no word. "I seek a way forward through the wood of this world, a way to knowledge, and music—yes, and to esteem. Will I find any of those here?"

The piper laughed. "You found some knowledge here today, did you not? Will that not help you to your calling?"

I smiled. "I fear that the perfumes you distill here would not improve my bardic standing—unless, indeed, the tale I was telling was that of Culhwch, he who was born in a pig-run!"

"Ah, but Cynfael river will leave you in good odor with your hosts—or at least, no worse than when you came out! Do you go on tomorrow, then, to Caer Seint?"

"And how would you know," I asked, "that it is to Caer Seint I would be going next? For I have not said so."

"Where else, this soon before Lughnasadh, with the grand festival that is to be held there, and the King himself like to be present?" And saying so, he plucked a pebble from the stream and tossed it in the air. For a moment, spinning in the sunlight, it shone like jewel or coin. Then he caught it— and it was a pebble again, a polished brown stone shiny with river water and nothing else. The piper pressed it briefly to his lips before handing it to me. "When you come to Dinas Dinlleu, look southwest across the sea to where a reef breaks the surface at low tide. Throw this pebble toward that rock for me, as a payment for old debts." He smiled wryly. "I would go myself, but I cannot leave this service, or my pigs."

"But I am going next to Caer Seint," I protested, "not to Dinas Dinlleu, wherever that may be."

"Are you not? Still, take it none the less, and if you come there, remember my request. And as you go back, touch the black stone again for me when you pass, and spare a thought for him who lies beneath it."

"And who would that be?" I asked, stowing the pebble away in my pouch. But I think I knew already.

"You are a reciter, and do not know?" His bright smile flashed white again in his tanned face, but the green eyes were haunted. "Who else, but he who was slain on the Great Sands, and buried above Y Felinrhyd? Heavy indeed is the weight of that stone, Gwernin, for Care himself lies buried beneath it."

"I will remember," I said seriously, and he smiled again. "Do so," he said, and putting his pipe to his lips, spoke no more that while.

So the afternoon passed, and my clothes dried, and at last I went back the way I had come, if not quite the same. The swineherd had charmed the Dark One out of my path, and glad I was of it; pigs will never be my favorite animals. But I touched the black stone again as I passed, and felt the chill in it, and remembered what I had heard.

"Well, Gwernin, and where have you been all day?" asked my friend Ieuan as I came late to my dinner. "Meditating under a tree while we were listening to the good Father?" And I saw that the priest was one of the gathering indeed, and judging by the state of his platter was eating with quite unpriestly zeal.

"Washing away my sins on the river bank," I said lightly, and saw the holy man frown. "Or at least, the dust of the roads."

"You were better on your knees, my son," he said piously. "The state of your soul is more important that that of your body."

"Well, on my knees or on the bank," I said, "if I am not holier than when I went out, at least I am cleaner!" And even Ieuan had to smile at that.

The next day, as we left Maen Twrog, I looked back from across the river at Pryderi's stone, standing quietly in its green field. As I walked, I made a song for him, and thus it runs:

> Deep beneath this stone, now sleeping lies Pryderi;
> Dark beneath this stone, the Prince of Dyfed dear—
> Slain by Gwydion's magic and enchantment,
> But victor over time, deception, age and fear.
>
> His is still the fame, the fame that lasts forever—
> One of only seven who came back o'er the seas.
> Now he lies beside this little river,
> Dreaming of his Arberth 'neath her flowering trees.

STORYTELLER

Bright he burned, the flame, the flame that lights forever–
One of only seven who came back o'er the Irish seas.
Now he sleeps beside the Cynfael River,
Dreaming of his Arberth midst her southern trees.

Rough enough stuff, but better it sounds with the music of the harp—or sung by the shining stings alone, as often I have played it…

But that, O my children, is a story for another day.

IX. Choices

Choices. They are the milestones of our lives—yes, and the branching of the roads by which we travel. Some say there are no choices, that our lives are foretold before our births, set in the stars, and perhaps that may be so. But I think that if I had made a different choice at Dinas Dinlleu that day, my life would have been far different thereafter.

It is not an appealing place, Dinas Dinlleu. A squat, brushy hill it is, set on the coast of Gwynedd and half gnawed away by the sea, with a broken ring of a fortress wall still crowning the remaining top of it. Flat and marshy the coast is otherwise there, but with a view of Ynys Môn across the Menai Strait to the north, and behind you to the east the great rising bulk of Yr Wyddfa, with all his lesser chieftains grouped about him, towering into the clouds. And clouds there were in plenty that day, and rain to go with them, so that standing on the hilltop and looking out to sea as I was, I hugged my billowing cloak tighter around me and shivered, even though it was still summer.

I had come there by a series of chances, not all of them good. Indeed, as I told the swineherd at Maen Twrog a few days before, I had no intention of going to that place at all, but was bound instead for Caer Seint—or Caer-n'ar-fôn, the Fortress beside Môn, as they are calling it now—for the great festival of Lughnasadh that celebrates the first of the harvest. And a bountiful harvest it would be this year, after a summer pleasant and mild, with rain and sun both plentiful in their seasons, so that the corn stood heavy and ripe in the fields, ready for the scythe, and the herds and flocks alike were abundant in their increase. And not ungenerous, in consequence, would be the King of Gwynedd to all those who came to entertain at Caer Seint.

So I was thinking as Ieuan and I took the road that led west from Maen Twrog. A fine, clear morning it was, as I remember, the birds singing in the trees and the willow-herb blooming rose-purple along all the verges, and the roads all powdery-gray with dust after the last several day's sunshine. And powdery-gray we would be, too, before night, from that dust—but it was better than rain. Or so I thought at the time.

Our road took us along the north bank of Afon Dwyryd for a while—a lazy-flowing stream there in late summer, winding back and forth in its flat valley between the hills— and then climbed slowly away, crossing the peninsula of Penrhyn-Deudraeth into the wide, marshy estuary of Afon Glaslyn. We crossed the Great Sands there at low tide on the remains of the Romans' causeway, and headed on west across the marshes, where the swarms of midges and biting flies soon had me wishing for wind and rain instead of placid sunshine. Glad I was when we gradually climbed away from them, up the wide low pass between Moel-y-Gest and the south-facing steeps of the White Cliff.

By the time we reached Dolbenmaen, on the Afon Dwy-for, Ieuan was ready to stop for the day, but I was for pushing on a little farther, impatient as I was to reach Caer Seint. So on we trudged for another hour, over a boggy shoulder of land and into the valley called Nant Coll, where we found a night's lodging beneath the frowning red bulk of Mynydd Graig Goch.

All that day I had been thinking on the names of the places we passed, and the story that lay behind those names—for our journey had taken us back along the very track of Pryderi's beaten army, as he retreated before the forces of Math son of Mathonwy and Gwydion son of Dôn. In this green little valley Pryderi had rallied his men after their first retreat, and here, so says the tale, "there was made an exceedingly great slaughter." Leaning against the house-place door of Cynan's hut that evening and watching the slow summer twilight creep in between the hills, I tried to imagine that resounding battle, and failed. It seemed too ordinary a place; as ordinary as the little cluster of huts at Dolbenmaen which we had passed earlier that day, where Pryderi, after another retreat, had halted and sought to bring about a truce, and given hostages to Math to secure one. It had not lasted long, that truce. Before many miles had passed, the men of the two armies had begun shooting arrows at each other again. And so at last at Y Traeth Mawr, the Great Sands we had crossed that day on the Romans' causeway, Pryderi had challenged Gwydion to meet him in single combat, to settle with their own bodies and blood that bloody quarrel—for it was Gwydion's trickery in stealing Pryderi's pigs that had begun the war in the first place. "And by means of strength and craft," says the tale, "and by magic and enchantment, Gwydion conquered, and Pryderi was slain…"

Gazing up at the twilight hills, I shook my head slowly, and went in to my dinner, and the entertainment I would owe the household afterwards.

The next morning we were up betimes, to find the weather had changed. Instead of bright sunlight, we were met with a gloomy grayness, a wet twisting fog that hid the mountains above, and made uncertain even the road beneath our feet. Ieuan was for waiting till it lifted a bit, but I was still on fire to reach Caer Seint, and no little bit of mist was going to quench my enthusiasm. So after a brief bite of breakfast, off we went up the valley, Ieuan muttering under his breath at the weather and me whistling. Ah, but we were a well-matched pair!

A broad, gentle pass it is, there above Nant Coll, despite the steepness of the hills on either side. And so, when we came to a fork in the path, there in the drifting gray mist, and took the right-hand branch as we had been told to do by our overnight host, how were we to know that this was not the branching he had meant?—the left-hand path being, as every local knew, merely the lane to Bwlch Derwen farm, and not a proper road at all! And so a little while latter, faced with another and equally unmarked choice, how were we to know that the more heavily trodden left-hand way led westward to the coast at Clynnog-fawr, and not to Caer Seint as we thought? Though we found that out for ourselves before many hours had passed, when we broke suddenly out of the fog at the end of a steeply dropping stretch of the track, to see the wide gray expanse of the Western Ocean no very great distance ahead of us. By then there was nothing for it but to turn right-handed along the coast, following the coast-wise track that would eventually bring us back to the road we had left, some miles to the south of Caer Seint.

Our next check was at the Afon Llyfni. A small stream it would have been, had we crossed it higher up its course as we were meant to, but here at the coast it was broad and brown and tidal, and of course the tide was in. By the time it had withdrawn enough to let us pass the ford, afternoon was well advanced, and a rising west wind was breaking up the lingering shreds of fog—and incidentally bringing with it rank upon rank of thick dark clouds which threatened rain before night. By the time we had walked for another hour or so, and crossed two creeks and the Afon Llifon, even I was beginning to think there was much to be said for a short day—all the more so as a misstep at the last ford had left me soaked to the waist and above, with a corresponding damp-ening of my spirits. But by then we were into a wide, flat expanse of coast, increasingly marshy and open, and sparsely populated in consequence.

So when at last, through a hurrying spatter of rain, we saw and smelt the ragged blue feather of peat smoke from a low thatched hut some little way ahead, we were more than ready to take the offered hospitality of its owners and stop for the night. Nor was I surprised to learn from the folk in the hut that we had somehow missed our way again, and were heading, not for the road leading to Caer Seint, but out along a marshy thumb of land that thrust itself into the southern waters of the Aber Menai. "Naught out there," they said, shaking their heads at our foolishness, "naught but marsh grass, and sand, and the old fort on the hill."

"What fort is that?" I asked, suddenly seeing a pattern.

"Dinas Dinlleu," they said. And putting my hand on my pouch, I felt the hard, round shape of the pebble in it, and remembered my promise to the swineherd of Maen Twrog, and knew why I was here.

And so the next morning found me standing on the top of Dinas Dinlleu, my cloak billowing out around me like wings in the wind and Ieuan beside me gloomy as another rain cloud. *When you come to Dinas Dinlleu*, the swineherd had said, *look southwest across the sea to where a reef breaks the surface at low tide. Throw this pebble toward that rock for me, as a payment for old debts. I would go myself, but I cannot leave this service, or my pigs.* In the spell of that summer's afternoon, it had seemed a natural enough request. Now suddenly I had my doubts. With a frown to match Ieuan's, I reached into my pouch and brought out the round, heavy object I found there. Opening my hand to look at it, I saw—no pebble, but the glint of gold!

Ieuan saw it, too. "Gwernin! Where did you get that?"

"I am—not sure." I was regarding the object warily, uncertain as to what form it might take next. What I saw—and continued to see, squint at it though I would—was a gold coin, two fingers' breadth in width and correspondingly thick. There was a portrait of a man's head on it, seen from the side, with Roman lettering around him, and on the back, two draped figures sharing one chair. The letters were too blurred to read, but the head was clear enough, with a wreath of leaves and flowers encircling the brows like a crown, and a fine eye on him staring straight ahead. I stood gazing at it entranced, struck as much by the beauty of the thing as by the value it represented.

Not so with Ieuan. "You are not sure? What sort of answer is that? How could you be having such a thing as that with you and not know it? Let me see it!" And he made a grab for the coin.

"No!" I jerked it away, suddenly angry.

"I was only wanting to look at it," Ieuan muttered sullenly. "It is gold! Where in God's name did you get it?"

"I tell you, I do not know. But I think—" I paused, licking dry lips, knowing how this was going to sound.

"Well?"

"I think—it was a pebble when I got it," I said slowly. The coin on my palm gleamed brightly, making a nonsense of my words. Surely even gold had no right to shine so brightly on such a dull day?

Ieuan looked from my face to the thing in my hand and back again. He shook his head. "It is slow indeed I must be today, I do not see the joke. Never mind. What are you planning to do with it?"

When you come to Dinas Dinlleu, the voice in my memory repeated, *throw this pebble toward that rock for me...* I remembered the pebble shining in the sunlight as the swineherd tossed it in the air, shining like jewel or coin—and then, in his hand, a pebble again. Which was truth, and which was seeming? And did it matter? I stared at the beautiful thing in my hand, and knew that I desired it. And I had made no promise, or at least none in words...

"Gwernin?" prompted Ieuan, reaching out again.

"No!" I closed my hand reflexively, feeling the weight of the coin in my palm as I did so. The tide was in; I could see no reef, but some way out there was a spot where every now and then a wave broke. A submerged rock? It might well be.

But still... *Throw this pebble toward that rock for me, as a payment for old debts.* What sort of debts, and whose? And why did I seem to know the name, Dinas Dinlleu...?

"Gwernin!" said Ieuan impatiently. "What is the matter with you? I am not trying to steal your gold, I am only wanting to look at it. If you keep on dancing around like that you will fall over the cliff!" And it was true that we were close to the edge.

"It is not mine," I heard myself say, in a voice not quite my own. "I cannot keep it, and I cannot spend it. It is owed to someone else." And before I could think any more about it, I drew my arm back and threw the coin far out over the sea. It sparkled as it fell and vanished without a trace into the wind-torn waves.

Ieuan gave a howl of pain and grabbed for me, too late. "Gwernin! What—why—are you mad? You *must* be mad!"

"No," I said sadly, "merely honest, I am afraid. It is a serious handicap for someone in my line of work." And then I noticed that Ieuan was saying nothing and doing nothing, but only staring fixedly out over the sea. Even as I turned to look that way myself, I felt a disturbance of the air beside me, a lessening of the wind as if something had come between me and it. A man was standing there next to me, close enough to touch. Reflexively I gave back a few paces from him, to leave him more room between myself and the cliff edge, while I stared at him in surprise and dawning recognition.

Perhaps a finger's breath taller than I am, he was, and I am not tall. His long hair was black as a raven's wing, and his teeth showed white in his tanned face as he smiled. His eyes were green as the wind-torn waves behind him, and glinted with amusement as he surveyed me. "Well, Gwernin," he said, his voice cool and smooth as silver, "well met again! It seems that I owe you a reward." And he held out toward me a small, heavy bag that clinked as it moved. "This gold you will not have to throw away. Take it! You deserve it."

63

I looked at the bag of gold, but made no move to touch it. "And will it turn to dulse and seaweed in my hands if I do so, Gwydion, my friend?"

At that he threw back his head and laughed. "Ah, Gwernin, I see you do know me now! Yes, it might—that is the risk you run! Are you saying you would prefer another sort of reward?"

"I am not claiming any reward at all from you," I said frankly. "What I did for you was little enough, and freely given."

"But that is to leave me in your debt," complained Gwydion, "and to that I will in no wise consent!"

"Then the problem is yours, is it not?" I asked, smiling.

"You are right." He snapped his fingers, and the gold disappeared. I was a little sorry to see it go, but only a little. Gwydion spread his arms wide, his dark cloak billowing about him with the wind from the sea. "Until we meet again!" he cried. And suddenly there was no man before me, but an eagle, its wings beating strongly as it sprang into the stormy sky above. I blinked, and he was gone, only the harsh cry of the bird trailing back down the wind behind him. Beside me Ieuan stirred into life again, while I still stood open-mouthed, staring into the sky.

After a moment I realized that Ieuan was speaking to me. "What did you say?"

"I said you are a fool, Gwernin, and I do not know why I put up with you."

"Neither do I," I said absently. "Come on, it is time and past we were setting off for Caer Seint."

"There at least you have said a true word," grumbled Ieuan, shrugging his way into the pack he had dropped earlier. "Though it is little enough use of our going, with you in the mood to throw a fortune to the winds for a scruple."

Gazing into the distance, I paid him no heed. Far off to the north, I thought I could still see the flicker of great wings, as the eagle flew on toward Caer Seint.

But that, O my children, is a story for another day.

X. A Debt Repaid

Lughnasadh, as you may know, falls in late summer, halfway between *Alban Hefin* and *Alban Elfed*, and is a festival of the sun, of the harvest, and of the god Lugh. *Calan Awst*, the First of August, some are calling it now in the common tongue, and so it is, though it lasts considerably longer than the one day. People come together at that time all across the land to meet and make merry and celebrate the first fruits of the harvest. And in this particular year that I tell of, the greatest festival in Gwynedd was to be held at Caer Seint. Warriors and weavers, poets and potters, harpers and horse-breeders, traders and tellers of tales—all the world, it seemed, was going there for the festival, and Ieuan and I went with them.

Now Caer Seint, or so the stories tell us, was once the Roman Segontium, and it was Maxen Wledig's capital when he was Emperor in Britain, before he set out to conquer Rome as well, and there lost all his fortunes and his life, and many a British man with him. Nowadays it has dwindled to a collection of huts alongside the Afon Seint where it comes down from the foot of Yr Wyddfa to the sea, with the ruins of the stone-built Roman fort on the hill above them. When I first saw it, though, with Ieuan, it did not look like a ruin, but was bright with tents and banners, and busy with people, buzzing like bees around a happy hive.

We had arrived early in the festival, despite our detour to Dinas Dinlleu, and were able to get accommodation in a run-down bit of a shed at the upper edge of the village, where the path goes up to the old fortress above. Later arrivals slept under canvas—when they slept at all!—or rolled up in their cloaks in the open air, and took no ill from it, for the weather was warm and dry, as often comes this time of year. Indeed, some of the days were almost too hot for comfort, so that more than once I wished that I had a greater choice of clothing, other than the one good woolen tunic given me by the Lord of Lampeter, and the rags remaining from my gold-mining adventure at Dolaucothi—for having a performer's dignity to defend, I could not strip to my trews and be comfortable, like the half-naked horse-boys leading their charges to the stream, and wading beside them in the water while they drank.

And horses there were in plenty around the camp, some of them fine-bred animals indeed, for horseracing is always part of Lughnasadh, and this year the King of Gwynedd was offering a fine prize to the winner—a great cauldron, so rumor said, full of three hundred pieces of gold. For this, men had come from near and far, even from as far as Ireland across the sea, bringing their swift horses with them. Ieuan's eyes brightened at this news when he heard it, for there was nothing he liked better than a horse race—unless it was the betting that went with it. He was in and out of the horse lines almost before we were well settled in our hut, and little enough did I see of him for some days to come.

Not that I spent much time looking for him, you under-stand. For there were contests a-plenty there for men as well as horses—contests in wresting and in running, in poetry and in singing, in harping and in storytelling, and in every sort of music and dance that you can imagine. And there was meat and drink in plenty while you watched, all given in his generosity by the King of Gwynedd—cauldrons full of boiled pig-flesh, and whole roast sheep and oxen, and mountains of wheat- and barley-bread, and great open vats of beer and of mead!

I ate and drank with the rest, and watched the wrestling and the running, and wandered through the place of the merchants, gawking at the fine cloths and the splendid weapons and jewels they had brought for sale, while I waited my turn in the contests—for the storytelling would come midway through the festival, followed by the singing and the harping, and culminating in the Contest of the Bards. *That* was the thing I was waiting and wanting to see. I had heard great names—Taliesin Ben Beirdd, so they said, was there, he that was used to be Bard to King Arthur himself, and Ugnach mab Mydno, and Kynan Delynor, and others too many to mention. Now and again I had seen them at a distance among the *uchelwyr*, the nobles, with their many-colored cloaks around them like bright feathers, and sometimes a narrow band of silver holding back their hair, and there was a longing on me such that I cannot describe it, to become one of them: and not only for the glory of it.

So the bright hours passed, and the day of the horse race dawned hot and clear. All of us went streaming down from the village toward the sea in the early morning. The tide was well out, and the pale sands lay smooth and firm and level, as fine a racecourse as you could want. The early sun shone on the glossy flanks of the horses as they lined up, and on the many-colored clothes of the people crowding the start, and glittered here and there on a bright jewel or a fine sword hilt. The air was thick with the mingled odors of horse droppings and seaweed, of smoke and beer and many excited bodies. I saw Ieuan standing near me in close conference with a group of Irishmen—the cut of their tunics marked them out from the rest of us even before you heard them speak—and wondered uneasily how many bets he had made already on this race, and with whom.

Another minute, and the riders were jostling for the start, the horses snorting and sidling and sweating, and then at the sound of a horn they were off, plunging headlong down the beach with clots of sand flying around them in a cloud. Along in the distance, fully a mile away, I could see the pole where they were to turn—half a tree it was, but looking a mere twig at this distance. The crowd was yelling already, cheering on their favorites, and I found to my surprise that I was yelling as loudly as any of them.

Almost before I knew it, they had reached the turn, the flying skein of horsemen wrapping itself briefly around the distant pole before starting back toward us again. Looking straight down the beach toward them as we were, it was hard at first to pick out single riders from the pack, but as they came closer I could see that the red stallion belonging to one of the Irishmen was in the lead. From hardly seeming to move, suddenly they all came down on us like lightening, and the drumming of their hooves on the beach was thunder itself. The screaming of the crowd rose to a peak and died away with their passing, the red horse leading still by two clear lengths. Then the riders were pulling up, and turning back towards us, toward where the King of Gwynedd stood waiting for the winner.

For some reason, at this moment of triumph when all eyes were fixed on the grinning Irishman and his horse, I happened to look sideways at Ieuan, and what I saw hit me like a blow under the heart. His face was white as milk, his mouth half open and his eyes staring as though he looked on a ghost—or on his own death. I even saw him sway a little, like one about to fall. The next moment he had himself in hand, and made a joking remark to the Irishman beside him, and dragged a sleeve across his brow, wiping away a sheen of sweat that was certainly not all from the heat. Then everyone was surging forward to see the winner, and I lost sight of him in the crowd. Only the unease of what I had seen remained with me.

It was late in the afternoon before I saw Ieuan again. I had come up to the hut for some reason—I think to add some trifle to my pack—and there he was, crouching in the darkest corner and rising up cautiously as he recognized me. "Gwernin," he said urgently, "can you loan me some silver?"

"Ieuan, you know how little I have," I said. "A couple of rings and a copper pin is the extent of it. Why, have you run yourself into the ground already?"

"I was thinking—that coin you had, at Dinas Dinlleu." His voice was trembling, I thought with eagerness. "You have no more of them, have you?"

"I have not," I said firmly. "That was a thing to itself, and glad I am that it is gone."

"I thought—I hoped—if only you had kept it!" Ieuan burst out. "Gwernin, I am in trouble. I bet with the Irishmen against their horse, and—you saw the race!"

"Why, then," I said reasonably, "you have lost your stake. It is sorry I am to hear it, but..."

"No, no, you do not understand!" Ieuan's face twisted with fear. "I was *holding* the stake, and I used the Irishmen's money to bet with other people. I can not pay the half of my wagers, they will take me as bondsman for my debts, unless you can help me!"

Fear, it seemed, was catching. I took a deep breath to steady my voice. "Lie hidden here until after the contest tonight. If I win, I will pay your debts. If not... we will think of something else. But whatever happens, do not show yourself at all until then." And I turned and left the hut, whistling cheerfully on the path as though I had not a care in the world, and taking with me the image of Ieuan's gray face and staring eyes.

Luck was not with me that night. Mindful of all that was riding on my venture, I was nervous as I had never been before, and I am afraid it showed. I spoke not too well in that contest—to lie would be bad!—but through the generosity of the King, I still carried away a silver armlet for my efforts. I was weighing it in my hand as I came up the path toward our hut, wondering if it would be enough to compound with the Irishmen, and knowing it would not be. Perhaps tomorrow I could think of something else; the fair still had two more days to run, and there were other contests... though the thought of presenting myself in some field in which I was not competent—singing, perhaps, or even poetry!—in order to win a pittance made me shrink as from thorns.

So was I thinking as I strode into the hut. "Ieuan," I called softly, "it is I." But there was no answer. The boothy was dark and silent, and when I struck a light, the signs of struggle were everywhere. Ieuan was gone, and not by his own desire.

"Aye, I saw them," said the old woman in the third hut down the row. "Just after sunset they came, five hulking sailors and a little bit of a man leading them. They went into your hut, and I heard yells and the sound of blows, and after a while they came out with your friend, hands tied behind his back and a rope around his neck, and hobbles to keep him from running. They will be taking him away with them, I hear, to sell as a slave for the money he owes them... Is it true, then, boy?"

"It is," I said gruffly, and left her with a word of thanks. How I was going to do it, I did not know, but I had to get Ieuan free, and everything I had was not enough to buy him. That left only theft, which is better by night.

Down through the camp I made my way, to the beach. Most of the boats there were small, and lay drawn up on the sand safely above high water, but the Irishmen's was a bigger ship, and had not been beached with the rest. Later they would have to strand her to load the horses, I thought, but just now she rode safe to her mooring in the river's mouth, a dark bird brooding on a silver sea. Not too far, maybe, for me to swim—those born by Severn River, as I was, mostly learn to swim before they walk—but too far for Ieuan, who was a poor swimmer. If, of course, he was aboard her at all, and not secured somewhere else about the camp.

He was. It took me a while to find out for sure, asking an idle question here, overhearing a remark there, but there was no doubt of it. What I could not determine was whether any of the Irishmen were aboard as well. I had not paid so much attention to them as to know them individually, and moreover there was more than one party of them in the camp. I would simply have to trust to luck.

By then it was full dark, or as dark as ever it gets at that time of year. This time when I went down to the beach I took my cloak with me, with Ieuan's few belongings and my own hidden under it. Once I got him away, there would be no time to spare for collecting our gear. It seemed I was going to miss the Contest of the Bards after all.

As I came softly down the sand past the stranded boats, a man rose up beside me from behind one of them. "Good evening, friend," he said quietly. "Can I do aught to help you?"

My heart thumping loudly in my chest—for he had taken me by surprise—I looked him over as well as I could in the darkness. About my height he was, or a little taller, and strongly built. His voice sounded young, and he spoke with the intonation of Gwynedd. If he was not a friend, I was already in trouble. And if he was...

"I need the use of a boat," I said deliberately, "to save my friend from slavery. He is in debt to the Irishmen, and they have him aboard their ship. What do you say to that?"

"Not hard," said the other, and on the words he bent and lifted his own boat from where it lay beside him. It was a coracle, a lightweight basket of wood covered with a stretched bull's hide. One man could lift and carry it at need, and it could—I hoped!—take three. "Put your gear in here," said the boatman, "and take you the other side. If it is ready you are now?"

"I am," I said, and complied.

The young moon had already set, but the faint glow from the summer stars let us see what we did, and there was light still in the northern sky. We pushed the little boat out through the gentle surf and climbed aboard, her owner easily and I with a little more difficulty. He took the oars, and sculled us out lightly toward the Irish ship. "Is your friend alone?" he asked in a voice just above a whisper.

"I do not know," I replied at the same pitch.

He chuckled softly. "Then we will find out."

Before I expected it we were beside the ship. The boatman brought us softly up to her stern, and caught hold of her without a sound. For a while we hung there listening, and heard nothing but the lapping of the waves against the hull. Then I stood up cautiously and peered over the side. There was no sound of movement, but somewhere forward someone was snoring. As silently as I could, I hauled myself into the ship. "Gwernin?" breathed a familiar voice from the deck close beside my feet.

"Ieuan?"—"Here." As I groped my way toward him, I hoped they had only used ropes on him, and not chains. I had no file.

They had not. I had my knife out and was dealing as best I could with the ropes in the dark when a sound behind me made me look up. Just in time I twisted aside from under the Irishman's blow. Then we were locked in a confused hand-to-hand struggle, with poor Ieuan underfoot and trodden on equally by us both. Not that I had time to think of him, for the Irishman was bigger and stronger than I, and was winning. It would have gone hard with me, but suddenly an iron hand took my enemy by the throat from behind and yanked him away from me, and before he could get his feet under him again, its mate had grabbed him by the hair and cracked his head against the side of the ship. After that the strength went out of him, and he was no trouble. Another gentle tap put him to sleep for the rest of the night, and I could turn my attention back to Ieuan, while my friend the boatman bound and gagged his prisoner.

We were climbing down into the coracle—and that most carefully, for the three of us filled her rather full—when the question arose of our destination. "We could put in on the other side of the river," said Ieuan, "and go back south the way we came. At least we know the road."

"Na," I said, "that is what they will expect. They can ask questions as well as anyone, and do not forget they have horses. Better that we head north, toward Yr Wyddfa. They will not think of that."

"We will have to lie up until day in that case," protested Ieuan. "We do not know the road."

"I could run you across to Môn," the boatman offered. "They will by no means be looking for you over there, and you can wander up the coast, and find someone else to put you back across beyond Pwll Ceris, where the strait narrows."

It sounded a good enough plan to both of us, and we took him up on it gladly. And so some while later, as the sea mist was thickening and the summer twilight was brightening toward dawn, our rescuer ran his boat aground in the mouth of a little creek on Ynys Môn and let us ashore. His thanks already said, Ieuan started up the beach with our gear, but I paused in the act of running the coracle out again. "Friend," I said to the boatman, as I stood thigh-deep in the summer sea, "we owe you a very great debt, and have no means to repay it."

"Na, na," said the other, and leaned on his oars, so that the boat drifted away from me as he spoke, vanishing as it went into the gathering mist. "You owe me nothing." Something about his voice was suddenly familiar. I wondered, could I see them in daylight, if his eyes would be green.

"Farewell, Gwernin," came the voice from the mist, distant and receding. "All debts between us now are paid. In the future, keep your friend from horse races and salt water, if you can!"

"I will remember," I called. "And good going to you, friend, wherever you may travel, and my thanks!"

There was no answer, only the sound of the waves. I waited a moment, then followed Ieuan up the beach. And in speculating on the identity of the boatman, I forgot his parting warning; and this was an ill forgetting, and brought about much sorrow.

But that, O my children, is a story for another day.

XI. Ynys Môn

What do you think of, when you think of Ynys Môn? Some would say, of the shining fields of that island, wide and green and fertile, that make her the granary of Gwynedd. Others, of the great wooden palace at Aberffraw, the court of the Kings; or of the saints in their monastic, bell-tongued seclusion; or even of that quiet green mound beside the Afon Alaw, where Branwen died and was buried on her return from Ireland. All of these and more are found on Ynys Môn, but they are not what comes first to my mind. When I think of Ynys Môn, I think of Druids.

The Romans, or so it is told, only suppressed two religions in the course of their conquests. One of these was Christianity (in which case, as all the world knows, they were not successful), and the other was the teachings of the Druids. The reason given, in both cases, was the horrible bloody sacrifices—human sacrifices—offered by the priests to their gods (this from a people whose highest entertainment was the slaughter of thousands in their Circuses!), together with the refusal of the initiates to acknowledge the supremacy of Roman law over the commands of their own religion. The Christians adapted and changed, and eventually conquered their conquerors. The Druids—ah, that is another tale entirely, and one too long for the telling here, even if I had the whole of it under my tongue, which I have not. But Ynys Môn, or so the stories tell us, was the last and greatest Sanctuary of the Druids in Britain. And here the Romans came with steel and fire, in the year when Boudicca rebelled, and left behind them blood and ashes only, and silence.

None of this was in my mind, however, as Ieuan and I came trudging up the dusty path to Caer Lêb farmstead in the afternoon following our escape from Caer Seint. I was thinking only of my empty stomach, and where we might find a bed for the night, and whether the story of our misfortunes would have yet reached this isolated place. Ieuan beside me was silent, sunk in gloom as he had been most of the day. Since leaving the boat which had brought us across the Aber Menai, he had said hardly more than "yes" and "thank you." Not that he was talkative at most times, except when some scheme struck him—and that usually ended in trouble!

A black man, Ieuan was, black-headed and black-eyed, and came originally from somewhere in the hills east of Powys, in lands now lost to us and held by the Saxon invaders. A man some years older than I, but known to me from my childhood (for he wintered always in Pengwern), he had agreed to take me with him this year on his circuit, to company with him and learn the ways of the road. He was not a reciter, as I was, but a news-bringer, a deft juggler, and a surprisingly sweet singer with many an old ballad and new in his store, which I was slowly learning. A trader, too, he was, of small light items such as are easily carried, and an inveterate and unlucky gambler, which had more than once gotten the both of us in trouble, as in this present instance. For it was Ieuan's unwise and dishonest betting with the Irishmen at Caer Seint which had led to our nocturnal flight from that festival, and brought us here to Ynys Môn, where we had not meant to come.

The farmstead at Caer Lêb sat within a fortified compound, surrounded by two walls with a ditch between, and a gate on the eastern side. The walls themselves were five-sided and ancient, and built perhaps as much for show as for defense, being overlooked by higher ground to the east. The buildings within were newer, though old enough in their own right, having mostly the right-angled shapes beloved of the

Romans. The whole looked impressive enough as we came trudging up the dusty path toward it, through the pale fields already bare from the harvest and holding now only a few gray sheep grazing on the stubble. Westering sunlight danced on the water in the ditch and on the thatched roofs within, but left the eastern walls in shadow. The warm wind in my face brought me the smell of peat smoke and baking bread, and other things less desirable, and reminded me again of how empty I was, having eaten nothing since the night before.

As we came closer, a yellow dog lying chained in the gateway stood up and began to bark, and was joined immediately by two more from within. Then a skinny child in a gray tunic came out and hushed the dog, and shrilled the news of our arrival to the household. The yellow dog sniffed at us suspiciously as we passed, but made no further complaint. The stone shadow of the gateway washed over us like cool water, and then we were in the courtyard, being greeted and inspected by a swarm of children and dogs, while behind them the women stood back smiling.

The main house-place was raised a little above the level of the rest of the court, and built man-high of dark gray stone, with a tall thatched roof above. As we approached it, a woman appeared in the doorway, a tall woman in a red gown, with hair the color of ripe corn and a face that was neither young nor old. In her hands she held a guest cup of dark polished wood, the rim bound in silver, and this she offered us, saying, "Drink, strangers, and be welcome."

"Gladly will I drink," I said, and took the cup. The wine within was cool and strong and sweet, and tasted of herbs and of honey. The woman's eyes were a pale, smoky gray with dark rims to the iris, and coolly appraising. They weighed me thoughtfully, and moved on to Ieuan, and lingered as he drank in his turn. Then we were following her into the house, and the moment was over.

Presently, sitting by the hearth and eating barley cakes and broth, we heard that most of the men of the steading were gone to Caer Seint for the Lughnasadh Festival, but would be back in a few days. We for our part admitted to having been there ourselves until the previous day. I left it to Ieuan to explain our early departure, which he did readily enough, saying that after the horse race there had been ill feeling between himself and some he had bet with, so that he had felt it safer to come early away. Our hosts took this at face value, but I felt a touch of shame to be so misleading them, and changed the subject as soon as I well could. Traveling with Ieuan was at best a mixed blessing.

It was along towards sunset, and we were out in the courtyard getting a breath of fresh air before bed—for the evening was still and close within the house—when I heard the bell. A small, bright sound it was, clear and sweet as the sky above us. "What is that?" I asked someone beside me.

"It is the monks' bell," she said—it was one of the older girls, a fine slender lass with curling dark hair that I had noticed before.

"Monks?" asked Ieuan, looking up from where he sat on the doorstep, regarding his two hands as if he had never seen them before. "What monks?"

"The Christians at Llangaffo," said the girl readily enough. "They ring the bell every morning and evening for services. It is a few of them only are there. Saint Caffo founded the *clas* long ago, so they say, before I was born."

"Monks," said Ieuan again, but softly, more to himself than to us. "Yes. Perhaps that is it." The girl gave me a wondering look, and I shrugged and shook my head, and she smiled. Then her eyes went back to Ieuan, where he sat staring at nothing and frowning, and her gaze grew thoughtful. But she said nothing more, and presently we went in.

In the morning, when we would have left, our hostess bade us stay. "For," she said smiling, "we have not heard the half of your stories; and moreover, it is good to have two more men here with us while our own are gone. Stay one more night, at least—unless you are in haste to be off?"

We denied it, and accepted her invitation. And as we were doing so, we heard again the Christians' bell on the still morning air. At that, Ieuan began to question our hostess about the monks—how many they were, and how long they had been there, and what they did. "Man," she said smiling at last, "is it of joining them yourself you are thinking, that you ask so many questions?"

"It is indeed," said Ieuan seriously. "For I think perhaps God may have brought me here for this reason. My life has not been good, and I have had warning to amend it."

At that there were exclamations all round, and an argument broke out, some of the women seeming to think it a goodly idea, and others holding that Ieuan was as yet far too young and comely a man so to retire from the world. At last our hostess brought the discussion to an end, saying, "Enough! Are you truly resolved, friend, to take this step?"

"I am," said Ieuan, but with less determination than he might; I think the feminine debate all around him had shaken him.

"It is a grave decision," said the lady seriously. "Bide here yet a day and a night and think on it, lest you do what you may regret." And Ieuan accepted her invitation.

As for me, I was startled by this sudden announcement, and thinking mostly of myself. Traveling with Ieuan had sometimes been less than a joy, but I was used to him, and would miss him sore if he left me here. Even silent company on the road is company still. And yet I felt that I had not the right to beg him come, if his heart bade him stay. There was another worry on my mind as well, and that was the homecoming of the men of Caer Lêb. Ieuan, I suspected, had bet with quite a number of people at Caer Seint, and I had no idea who the most of them were. I wished I could be quite certain that none of them lived in this part of Ynys Môn.

So the day passed, and Ieuan and I entertained the household as best we might, and twilight came again. And in the courtyard the chime of bells sounded faint and sweetly on the evening air.

"Do you think he will really go to the monks?" asked a voice beside me, as I stood in the court that evening, gazing at Ieuan where he sat again by the door. I looked and saw the little dark girl of the night before—Anwen, I think her name was.

"I do not know," I said, and sighed. "I was wondering the same thing."

"It would be a waste," said Anwen softly, more to herself than to me.

At that moment Ieuan stood up and came toward us. "Gwernin, I am going out to walk and think. Do not wait for me, I may be very late."

"Where are you going, then?" I asked.

"I do not know. Where the Spirit leads me."

"Go, then," I said. "I will see you in the morning." As Ieuan passed out through the gateway, my eyes met Anwen's, and she smiled.

"I think I am also going for a walk," she said.

"Go, then," I said, smiling back, "where *your* spirit leads you." And I turned and went into the hall to my bed. Ieuan came back very late indeed that night, and when he came he did not sleep alone.

"So," the Lady Braint asked us the next morning, "will you stay with us yet one more day and night, and entertain my man when he comes back from Caer Seint? Or are you, today, the one for the road, and the other for the monk's cell?"

"For my part, Lady, I will stay gladly," I said, and looked at Ieuan. He had the grace to blush a little.

"I also will stay, Lady," he said. "I think perhaps I am not meant to be a monk after all."

"That is well, then," said the lady, and smiled, and went about her business. So the day passed, and Ieuan and I entertained the household as best we might, and evening came again. And with it came the men of Caer Lêb.

I was in the hall when they came, telling the story of Arthur the Soldier and the Three Truths, and had just reached the part where the giant comes striding down the tunnel and catches Arthur with his hand in the pot of gold. When the sound of dogs and horses and men in the courtyard broke into the listening quiet of the hall, I brought the story to a momentary close and turned to face the door, feeling not a little like the hero of my tale. I was still not easy in my mind about what else Ieuan might have done at Caer Seint, and I could see from his face where he sat by the wall with Anwen beside him that he was worried also.

Into the hall came a tall, red-headed man whose face was familiar to me, though I had seen it before only at a distance. One of the *uchelwyr*, the nobles, he was, who had thronged round the King of Gwynedd in his splendid pavilion. My heart sank within me, for if the Irishmen had complained of us to the King, this man would certainly know of it. It only remained to see if he recognized us.

He did. His eyes fell on me first, where I stood by the fire, and then searched the room until they found Ieuan, who was trying to disappear into the shadows. "Why, Wife," he said, "what is this you have for me here?"

"Entertainers," said the Lady Braint, "and good enough ones, too. They have been with us some days now. Why do you ask, Husband?"

"Because I have seen them before, and that recently. Of this one I know no ill"—and he indicated me—"save that he is a not-too-competent storyteller, but the other is wanted badly by a number of people in Caer Seint, most especially"—and he grinned—"by a bunch of horse-trading Irishmen who are just now seeking his blood all up and down the coast of Gwynedd. Well it is for him that he is on Ynys Môn instead, and better still that he is in my house and not in some others, for I do not love the Irish. I have seen"—and his voice was dry—"far too much of them over the years, from behind a war-spear!"

"Indeed you have," said his lady, but she was frowning. "Yet it seems that these two told me only half a tale. What, then, is the rest of it?"

"Why, only that the dark one"—and he indicated Ieuan, who was trying not to cringe and only half succeeding—"bet rather more with the Irishmen than he had, and lost their stake as well; and when they took him as bondsman for his debt, he escaped in the night, helped, so they said"—and he looked at me dubiously—"by any number of fierce, bloodthirsty warriors. Is that the truth, Storyteller?"

"It is, the most of it," I said frankly, "though I cannot swear to the bloodthirsty warriors."

At this the red-headed man laughed hugely. "By all the gods I swear by, an answer after my own heart! Will you stay on here for a few days, then, Storyteller, and show whether you speak better alone than in contest?"

"I will," I said, "and that gladly!"

"And as for you," said the red-headed lord to Ieuan, "you are welcome for as long as he, so long as you bet me here no bets! Can I trust you for that?"

"You can, Lord," said Ieuan, rather faintly. "You can indeed!"

We stayed five more days with the lord of Caer Lêb, and then journeyed on up the coast of Ynys Môn, visiting other houses at his recommendation, so that the moon which had been new when we were at Caer Seint was full before we left that island. I in particular went from Caer Lêb richer than I had come, new-clothed and new-shod and with a silver-gilt brooch to my cloak, the red-headed lord having agreed that I did indeed speak better alone than in contest. As for Ieuan, it was hard to say whether he gained or lost from that visit. He took away with him some presents, but he parted hard from Anwen, who had held by him still despite her lord's revelations.

I mind it well, that misty summer morning when we were rowed back to the mainland, and Ieuan's profile beside me, still turned to the west, to the island, with a sort of longing on him. For the bell, or the girl, or the both of them? At the time I did not know, and nor, I think, did he.

For myself, I have other memories of Ynys Môn, darker memories and wilder, from a later visit.

But that, O my children, is a story for another day.

XII. The Reciter's Tale

Bright and hot and clear that morning was, hot even for late summer, when Ieuan and I started up the valley of Nant Ffrancon. It was not the way we should have been taking, but Ieuan went still in fear of the Irishmen whom he had cheated at Caer Seint. So rather than following our normal route through Bwlch y Ddeufaen, the old pass that the Romans had used as part of their high road from Deva to Ynys Môn, we plunged instead south-eastward into the mountains, up the steep course of Nant Ffrancon, which drives straight and sharp as a sword-edge into the heart of Eryri. And straight, as it happened, into the path of a late-summer storm.

Storms in those mountains can come on almost as fast as the lightening they carry. One moment, it seemed, we were walking peacefully along the stony path, watching the white cloud-masses soaring over Yr Wyddfa to the south (though we could no longer see the Snow-Peak herself by then, the intervening mountains being too close and steep); the next, the afternoon sunlight dimmed and changed color, as the great bluish-purple bulk of the storm came sailing over the gray-brown ramparts of rock that almost closed the valley's narrow head. Then the rain came, rain like silver spears that fell on us and blinded us, roaring like an army. We broke into a run, heading for the hut we had seen some way ahead, now almost invisible in the rain and sudden darkness. By the time we reached it we were soaked and breathless—bruised, too, from the hailstones that were mixing now with the rain!— and glad beyond telling of the shelter, rough though it was. The woman who kept it for the shepherds welcomed us in and turned to building up the fire, while we huddled around it trying to wring rainwater out of our clothes and hair, and no doubt looking half-drowned the while.

I was rubbing my hands over the flames, and wondering why the running had not warmed me better, when between the peals of thunder I heard a splashing of feet on the pathway outside, and the leather curtain over the door was thrust aside by an urgent hand. The short, wiry fellow who followed it in looked even wetter than we were. By the pack he carried, he was no shepherd, but another traveler like ourselves, though his good clothes were soaked and plastered against him by the rain—muddy, too, where he seemed to have had a fall in his haste!—and his tawny hair hung limp and dark with streaming wet. It was only by his voice I knew him, as he thanked the goodwife who was taking his dripping tunic, and offering him a rough blanket to wrap around himself while his clothes dried. He was one of the storytellers against whom I had competed at Caer Seint, almost a moon ago. Competed unsuccessfully, I might add, for though he had not won the prize in that contest, he had done a great deal better than I myself.

"Holy Jesus!" he was exclaiming. "Did you ever see such a storm? I swear the Devil himself was in it, for I never did!"

"Aye, they come on quick here amongst the mountains," said the shepherd's wife placidly. "Is it food you'd be wanting then, lads? I have oat cakes fresh from this morning's baking, and good ewe-milk cheese in the crock by the door."

Presently, as we were sitting around the fire and steaming gently in its warmth, the newcomer, who had been frowning at me over his oatcake, said, "Surely your face is familiar to me, friend, but I cannot say from where."

"Caer Seint, belike," I said, "for yours is familiar to me as well, from the storytelling contest there."

"Of course! How could I forget it? And your name is…"

"Gwernin. I come from Pengwern, in Powys. Yourself?"

"Edern mab Rhys am I, from Aberdaron, in Penrhyn Llyn." He looked at Ieuan, frowned, and looked away. Ieuan was staring into the fire, and did not notice. "Yours was the story of Arthur the Soldier, as I remember. It was well done."

"Not so well as it might have been," I said wryly. "Yours was much better. The Dream of Macsen Wledig, was it not? I never heard it told so before."

Edern grimaced. "Each knows his own faults best," he said. "Now, if I were a poet... You were there, surely, for the Contest of the Bards, and heard Taliesin speak?"

"Alas, I was not—circumstances prevented," I said. "Did he take the prize, then? Tell me of it, I beg you! Of what like is he, and how did he speak? How many others contended, and who were they? Tell me everything!"

"Easy, easy," said Edern, laughing. "One question at a time, as I have only one mouth to answer! Yes, he took the prize, and deserved it. Ten or twelve stood against him— some, I think, merely to say that they had done so! He spoke last, after all the rest were done, and so subtle were his rhymes, and so great the force of his *awen*, that all the rest were shown to be mere prologues to his story, like sand-hills at the foot of Yr Wyddfa. Not for nothing is he called Taliesin Ben Beirdd, Taliesin Chief of Bards!"

I sighed in mingled happiness and frustration. "I wish I could have been there! Do you remember any of his verse?"

Edern shook his head. "Fragments only. I meant to listen and remember, and thought myself well able to do so—I am a reciter, after all!—but it went over me like a dream, or like a great wave that falls upon the land with its mighty power, and drains away, leaving no trace of itself behind on the beach. The small puddles caught in the rocks are no measure of what went before."

I sighed again. "Who else contended? I heard some names..."

"Ugnach mab Mydno, of Caer Sëon, was first among the others. Before the contest started he and Taliesin exchanged some *englynion*." Edern smiled. "It seems they had met once before some years back, and exchanged sallies, Ugnach inviting Taliesin to stay with him and Taliesin declining—and all in verse, of course!"

"I have heard something of that," I nodded. "I do not suppose…?"

"Possibly, possibly," said Edern. "Let me think a little. Since it was at the beginning, my memory may be clearer." He sat frowning into the fire for a while, while I waited with what patience I could muster. The thunder and lightening had died away to occasional distant grumbles, but the rain was still drumming on the thatch of the *hafod*, though more softly now. I doubted we would go on that night. The woman sat in one corner, listening to us with interest—poetry appeals to all of our blood!—and Ieuan had drawn back a little from the fire and seemed to be dozing. The fresh scent of the rain came in around the leather curtain in little puffs of air, and mingled with the peat-smoke and the smell of wet wool. I shifted my position slightly for comfort on the earthen floor and waited.

"Yes," said Edern after a while. "I think I have the most of it. Like a bright ball that encounter was, tossed from hand to hand…" He sat up straighter and pushed the tawny hair back out of his eyes. "Taliesin spoke first—but you will see that. Here it is, then, as best I can give it." He took a deep breath and began:

> "To Ugnach mab Mydno, my greeting–
> long years is it since our last meeting–
> an encounter which proved much too fleeting!"

Edern's voice had changed and grown deeper as he spoke. His eyes were a little unfocused, staring into memory. I held my breath.

"Taliesin Chief Bard, my pleasure
to see you—in memory I treasure
our meeting—recall you its measure?"

This voice was different, lighter and with more of the accent of Gwynedd, but still pleasant. Edern, I thought fleetingly, was good at his work.

"Ugnach, I recall it most clearly—
wine, feasting and gold won most dearly
you offered, not fire and bed merely."

I smiled with pleasure at the intricacy of the rhyme. Then it was Ugnach's voice again:

"Yet none of those offers could lure you
to my household, wherein, I assure you,
whatever your ills, I could cure you!"

I frowned a little at that one. A bit presumptuous, surely—or perhaps not? Bards were not only poets—some were seers and magicians as well. Some were druids. Edern's voice went on, speaking as Taliesin:

"Ugnach, I had cause to deny you—
yet longer I will not defy you—
invite me again, and I'll try you!"

I smiled again. There was light-heartedness in that reply, and humor.

"Taliesin, you fill me with gladness!
Not to ask you again would be madness—
your refusal before caused much sadness!"

A good answer, that—and a good use of rhymes. Would that I could do so well after much thought, never mind on the fly! Edern was frowning, his eyes almost crossed with concentration. I held my breath.

"Ugnach, if I may be excused,
you will not thus again be abused—
I, Taliesin, say
to you fairly I'll pay
the visit that once I refused!"

I laughed aloud at that middle couplet. It was a pun, of course—the bard punning on his own name. "Taliesin" is usually translated "Shining Brow"—*tâl iesin*—but it can also be understood to mean "Fair Payment". I thought I was right about the light-heartedness.

Edern looked up, smiling, at my laugher. "I hope that sounded well enough—you seem to have enjoyed it, anyway. Though it was a candle to the sun compared to what came later."

The woman was laughing, too, and even Ieuan was smiling. I realized that several other people had come in while I was listening—two men and a boy, all shepherds by their dress. The little hut was suddenly rather full.

"Thank you, Edern," I said. "That was wonderful. I hope I can remember some part of it."

"My pleasure," said Edern. "And now, if the rain has stopped, perhaps I should be going."

The shepherds would not hear of it. Not only was the weather still uncertain, they said, but they had missed the first part of Edern's recital, and begged him to stay and do it again. The upshot of it was that we all stayed the night.

Late in that evening, when I stepped outside for a moment before retiring, Edern came with me. The rain had ended and the sky was slowly clearing, the great stars of late summer coming out as we watched. We stood for a few minutes talking of this and that before going back into the peat fug inside to lie down, and so I returned at last to one of my earlier questions, still unanswered. "Of what like is Taliesin, then?"

"Not easy to answer, that," said Edern musingly. "I judge that if you met him in passing, he might seem a slight, dark man of no more than middling height, though maybe looking taller. But when he speaks with *awen*, you would swear he was a giant like Ysbaddaden Bencawr himself! He must be of middle years at least, even if he was only a boy when he served Arthur, and yet he moves like a young man, and his hair is as dark as your friend's."

"I think I saw him once, when I was a small child," I said. "He sang then at Pengwern, at the court of Brochwel Ysgithrog, our present lord's father. I remember him as a man immensely tall and lean, dark-haired but beardless, and with a beautiful voice, rich and dark and flexible, the sort of voice that Gwydion mab Dôn might have, if he wished, to conjure or persuade... But that is only a child's memory, and dim with time. I doubt I would know him again if I met him on the road."

"It would also depend, I think," said Edern seriously, "on whether he wished you to know him. By the Risen Christ, they say the man is a magician, and I believe that it may be so! I would go far and far to hear him speak again, but further to avoid him, were he to take against me." He gave himself a little shake, and yawned. "Well, I am for my bed. Which way do you go tomorrow, Gwernin, up-valley or down?"

"Up," I said.

"Then our roads lie apart."

"Pity that is," I said, "for I have enjoyed your company, and would have had more of it."

"And I yours." Edern yawned again, and laughed. "Ah, well, we may yet meet at Caer Deganwy. Do you go there for the fair?"

"I do not know," I said. "I had not heard of it before. When is it?"

"It is at full moon," said Edern. "I am going, I think. Perhaps I will see you there in contest."

"Perhaps you shall," I said and smiled. And with that, we turned and went inside, and spoke no more that night.

The next day dawned fine and clear, with a hint of mist in the hollows, and a high, pale sky the color of a robin's egg. The stony tops of the mountains wore touches of gold that had not been there the morning before. Almost imperceptibly, the wheel of the year was turning towards winter. Time soon for birds to be flying southward, and for wanderers to be thinking of home.

I said as much to Ieuan, when we stopped that day for our nooning in a sunny hollow on the far side of the pass, near the headwaters of Afon Llugwy. "How long, do you reckon, is the traveling from here to Pengwern? For I think autumn will be upon us before we know it."

Ieuan scratched his head thoughtfully, and I noticed that evenly dark though his hair was, there were a few threads of silver starting in his beard which had certainly not been there last spring. In the clear light of midday he looked a tired man, and that was odd, for we had been traveling by easy stages since Caer Seint. "Twenty days, perhaps," he said after a while. "It might be a little less. That is if we held by the old track through the hills south of Berwyn, rather than taking the Romans' road towards Deva. Why, are you so eager to get home?"

"Na, na," I said, "I only wondered. Edern was telling me of a fine Fair to be held at Caer Deganwy not many days hence. Is it too far out of our way?"

"Two or three days, at least," said Ieuan, frowning, "to Aber Conwy, where the river meets the sea. Afterwards we could drop back south to the Romans' road easily enough, and go on east towards Deva. Do you want to go, then?"

"Why not?" I said. "Edern implied there will be contests, so who knows who we might see? Perhaps even Taliesin himself, if the King has a *llys* there! Yes, I would like to go to Caer Deganwy, by all means."

"Then we will," said Ieuan smiling, and thereby sealed his fate.

But that, O my children, is a story for another day.

XIII. Green Shadows

Under the trees the light was green, green and dim as evening. The air was heavy with the scent of leaf and root and branch, of growth and decay; and always there was the sound of running water, from the roar of waterfalls descending into the gorge, to the small music of single drops falling from the trees into the pools below. Ageless and nameless, the Old Forest ruled the lower course of the Afon Llugwy that day as ever it had before. Behind your back there was a feeling of eyes among the branches, watching, watching...

"I think we have missed our way, Gwernin," said Ieuan, turning a pale face to me in the gloom. "We should have found that track to Llyn Geirionydd by now."

"You may be right," I said. "Still, if we carry on, we should come sooner or later to the Afon Conwy, should we not? And a broader valley?"

"We *should*," said Ieuan somewhat doubtfully, "if we are not benighted in this alder swamp first, and end up spending the night in a tree, for fear of wild pigs or worse." And that was true enough, for we had been seeing pig sign ever since we came into the forest.

"Go on, then," I said briefly; pigs, as I have remarked before, are not my favorite animals. It did seem to me that the light was fading already, though it should not have been dusk for some hours yet. Clouds moving in, perhaps—and that could mean more rain. Not a pleasant prospect, I thought, squelching after Ieuan, in a place already as boggy as this one. The path we were following seemed made of equal parts of roots, rocks, and mud, and twisted around the boles of the big trees in a leisurely manner, as if in no hurry to arrive at its destination.

By the time we saw the light ahead of us, we were both mired to the thighs and growing weary, and Ieuan was limping from a fall and a bruised knee. At first it seemed merely a thinner spot in the trees, but as we came closer I could see it was a clearing, a small patch of cleared land perched on a narrow shelf where the gorge widened slightly. The last of the day's sunlight found its way down into this hole in the forest from a sky which was filling now with tumbled clouds, and touched for a moment the pale thatch of the small hut which stood at the back of the shelf, tucked tight against the mountain. There were a few rows of beans and cabbages in front of the hut, and a little brown hen with a yellow beak and a bright eye scratching in its doorway, and best of all, a thin finger of blue wood-smoke filtering out through the smoke-hole at one end of that pale, new-thatched roof, promising fire and food and hospitality for the night. It was altogether better than we could have hoped for, and I felt my spirits lighten as I looked.

As we came closer a woman appeared in the doorway and stood waiting for us. A tall woman, she was, of an age neither young nor old, with long pale hair the color of wild honey bound into two heavy plaits on either side of her face. She wore an old green gown of fine-spun wool, much faded, and deerskin shoes on her narrow feet, and a single amber bead on a thong around her neck. Her eyes were bright and questioning, and alive with some secret amusement, but her manner as she bade us come in and seated us by the fire was friendly enough, and the cheese and barley bannocks she offered were fresh and very welcome.

"You will stay the night, of course," she was saying as she handed round the food. "Dark it will be soon enough, and a storm maybe coming on, and you needing rest." This last was to Ieuan, who had stretched out his bruised knee with wincing care, and was beginning to unwind the leather straps which bound his coarse linen trews in order to come at the damage. He readily agreed that he had walked far enough for one day, and thanked her.

"*Sa*," she said, watching him, "you will be better for the rest. A fall, was it, in the forest? I will make you a warm poultice presently, which will help take the swelling down. Do you sit, the both of you, at your ease while I go out to gather the herbs."

We thanked her and did so. Though the day had not been long, we were tired, and it was pleasant to sit still in the house and watch the small flickerings of the fire on the hearth, when we had not long ago been contemplating the prospect of a night spent in the fork of a tree in the forest.

It was some time before the woman came back, and when she came she carried a bundle of green things caught up in the full of her skirts. Dumping them down beside the hearth, she took up her copper cooking pot and filled it with water from a jar by the wall, and hung it from the hook on the chain which came down over the fire. Then carefully she picked up her herbs and dropped them bunch by bunch into the pot, muttering words that I could not catch under her breath the while. Some of the green things she used I knew—thousand-leaved yarrow was there; and *llysiau'r miltwr*, the soldier's herb; and chickweed in its great green masses— but others were strange to me. An aromatic steam began to rise from the pot and fill the house, and the woman sat back at last, brushing her hands on her skirts, and smiled at us.

"It will be needing to boil for a while and a while first," she said to Ieuan. "How is your knee?"

"None so bad," said Ieuan, from where he sat massaging the joint in question. "It is only that I struck it on a rock when I fell, that caused the trouble."

"Let me see it, then," said the woman, and rose and went to him. I saw that her hands as she felt the broken bruise were careful and knowing. "*Sa*," she said after a moment, "it should be well enough. Do you stretch out now and rest, so, and it will soon be better still." And she went back to her task, which our arrival had interrupted, of grinding meal in a quern by the door.

"Would you hear a story while you work, Lady?" I asked her—our hostess seemed as silent by nature as Ieuan, and I was growing restless. "I am a reciter, and my friend here a singer."

"Certainly, if it please you tell one," said the woman, but I thought she seemed amused. "What story would you be telling?"

"The story of Arthur the Soldier, and the Three Truths," I said, and started into my recitation.

Now, you will have heard me mention this tale before— it was one of my favorites then, and I told it many a time that summer, all up and down the coast of Wales—told it to audiences of one or two, and to whole families, and in the halls of chieftains; and told it also in contest at Caer Seint (though not so well there as I would have liked). And I was familiar with every reaction that an audience could have to that tale, and knew how to anticipate and shape that reaction. So now I told the tale in the hut by the Afon Llugwy, and told it well indeed. And yet throughout that telling, our hostess kept still her look of slight amusement, glancing now up at my face, now down at her work, as I spoke; and though I managed not to let it put me off, still I was disconcerted.

"Well done," she said at the end. "Well should you know the power of words, you who deal in them. What is your name?"

"Gwernin Kyuarwyd am I," I said, "from Cynan Garwyn's court of Pengwern, in Powys. What is your name, Lady?"

Her amusement seemed to deepen. "Gwen, you may call me," she said after a pause. It is a name that means "white" or "holy." "And your friend?" She looked down at Ieuan, who answered for himself.

"Ieuan mab Meurig mab Pedr, and I come originally from the Eastern Hills, near Venonae, where my father had a farm."

"Ah," said the woman, "the lost country. I thought you looked to have a touch of the Roman in you." And with that she brushed the last of her flour into a bowl and covered her quern with a cloth. "Lie you still, then, Ieuan mab Meurig mab Pedr, and I will see what I can do for that knee." And taking the pot, which she had removed from the fire some little time before, she lifted out her green stuff bit by bit, and spread it onto Ieuan's swollen knee, and bound it there with strips of clean linen.

"That feels better," he said when she was done. "My thanks to you, Lady."

"Lie you still, then, so long as you can," she said. "That is the best way to thank me, and help yourself. Gwernin, I need more water to start the supper. Would you come with me, and carry back the jar?"

"Gladly, Lady," I said, standing up and taking the heavy jar from her hands. "Is there a spring here?"

"Sa, but the best water is from one across the river. Come you with me and I will show you the way."

I followed her out into the early evening. The clouds which had been broken and tumbled when we arrived now covered the sky, and the light was fading fast. Gwen led me across the little clearing and into the trees, where a steep path switch-backed its way down to the river. The green gloom under the leaves was intense, deepening as we went down until we seemed to swim through it as through dark water. The voice of the river, flowing here in a narrow channel amidst great stones, was loud in the dimness.

At the bottom Gwen halted beside a fallen log which bridged the stream. "The spring is over there," she said.

"Wait you until I have crossed, then follow me." And with that she stepped out onto this improvised roadway as if it were a clear path. From the far bank she turned and looked back, her face a pale oval in the gloom. "Come on," she said.

I followed cautiously. Under my feet the log was smooth and slippery from much use. It also swayed perceptively under my weight. Beneath me the river roared and foamed among its boulders, seeming both close and very far away. I was glad to reach the other bank.

Gwen was waiting for me beside the promised spring. Sweet and clear, the water bubbled silently out of the black rocks and gathered briefly in a natural basin before dropping in a thin cascade to the river below. I knelt to cup my palms and drink before filling the jar. "That is good," I said.

"*Sa,*" said Gwen. "It is better than any on the other bank. That is why I come here." She filled the jar and gave it to me, and we started back. The log swayed again under my weight as I crossed; I did not like it. When we reached the clearing, the evening light seemed bright as noonday in comparison with the woods below

Once back in the hut, Gwen set to work on our dinner, putting beans and onions to stew together in the pot while she formed barley bannocks from her meal and set them to bake on the hearthstone. I sat watching the deft movements of her hands, and the firelight dancing on the worn planes of her face, and thought. She puzzled me; I did not know what to make of her. She lived alone, as it seemed, in this hut in the woods, but not in poverty: she had good shoes, and a copper pot, and the hand quern to grind her meal, and grain she had not grown in her own garden. And she had no fear of strangers. It added up to status or power of some sort. Perhaps strangers should fear her instead?

Just then she looked up and caught me watching her, and smiled. There was still that glint of amusement in her eyes, like that of an adult watching a clever child. "Where are you bound for going next, Gwernin?" she asked.

"To Caer Deganwy," I said. "There will be a fair held there at the full moon, so I hear. I go to tell my stories, and to watch others in contest."

"Contest," she repeated thoughtfully. "*Sa*, there will be many contests there, and many prizes won or lost. Will you stand in the Poets' Circle, Gwernin, when the time for contest comes?"

"Not I," I said and sighed. "I am not a bard."

"And yet you work with words. Have you made no verses?"

"A few," I admitted. "But not good enough for contest! I doubt I have the knack."

At that she laughed softly. "Had you the knack of walking, then, when you hung at your mother's breast? But you could learn, and did, through you fell often enough in the trying. Why should this skill be different?"

"Why—perhaps you are right," I said slowly. "But–"

"Na, na," she said, "I know I am right. You will see." And reaching behind her for something, she overturned the water jar. Water ran eagerly everywhere—across the hard-packed floor, into her skirts, even hissing into the edge of the fire, where it spat out ash to flavor the barley cakes.

"No harm done," said Gwen, shaking out her skirts, "only now we need more water. Will you go down to the spring for me, Gwernin, and fill the jar again? There is just light enough left to see your way."

"Gladly," I said, and took the jar, and headed out the door, still turning over her suggestion in my mind. I, to enter the poets' contest at Deganwy? Yes, and stand against Taliesin, belike! No, the thing was impossible; I should not have the courage. And yet everyone starts somewhere...

Behind the clouds the sun had set, and it was growing dark. Under the trees I could barely see the path. The green gloom rose up around me, blinding me as I went down. I had to feel for every step before I took it. Once I slipped and caught myself on a branch before I could tumble headlong. At the bottom the fallen tree was waiting for me, a darker bulk in the darkness. I paused before it, wondering if there was not an acceptable spring on *this* side of the river, after all, but Gwen had shown me none. I could hear the drumming of my heart above the sound of the water. Taking a deep breath, I stepped out onto the log.

Under my feet it swayed gently, like a living thing waiting to throw me off when I least expected it. The river roared, black water among black rocks. I could see nothing, not the log, not my feet, not the water below. I wanted to run, but must shuffle slowly with small, careful steps, feeling my way. Though it was a cool night, I was sweating before I reached the far bank.

I found the spring by touch and memory, and knelt beside it. Setting the jar down—carefully, so I could find it again in the darkness!—I scooped up handfuls of the cool water and splashed them on my face and neck, then drank deeply. What was wrong with me? There was no reason for my fear. Here were no enemies, no wolf or wild pig to threaten me, only the green darkness of the forest—and myself. But my heart went on racing as if I had been running, and the hands that held the water trembled. I could feel eyes all around me in the dark. The Old Ones of the forest were awake.

I filled the jar and stood up, trying to breath more deeply and evenly. Why should I feel so afraid—I, Gwernin, who had talked with Gwydion mab Dôn, and watched the Wild Hunt pass? I who would be a bard one day, if the stranger at Harddlech spoke true? But the Old Ones were unimpressed. From the green mounds they came, from under the trees, from out of the hollow hills themselves, older than any. I could feel them all around me now, coming closer, closing in.

From the corners of my eyes I caught glimpses of movement here and there in the dark, streaks and glimmers of light that disappeared when I looked at them. Little puffs and eddies of cold air brushed my sweating face like groping hands and sent shivers down my spine. I was afraid to move, and afraid to stand still.

At last I tore myself out of my paralysis, and set foot upon the log. More than ever I could feel it was alive, trembling under my feet with expectation. The river roared hungrily from the abyss below, its voice seeming to shake the air about me. A step, a step, another step–

I slipped, my right foot sliding off the log as my weight came on it. Somehow I twisted myself and came down astride the wooden thing, my left arm around it, while with my right I clung desperately to the water jar that was bruising my ribs. I could feel water splashing out of the jar, wetting my belly and thighs. Beneath me the log bucked like a frisky colt, intent on throwing me off. I clung to it, gasping, until it steadied, then sat up carefully and checked the water level in the jar. It was still three-parts full, and I let out a sigh. I would not have to go back and start over.

Cautiously, clutching the jar, I began to inch my way forward, still seated on the log. It was so dark I could no longer tell earth from sky; I could have been in a cave. My legs hung down into darkness; darkness enclosed me like a bag; the river roared beneath me like the sea. Slowly I pulled myself along the log, stopping now and then to ease my legs over limbs or staubs. It seemed to take a very long time; there was no time; time was endless. When my right leg struck against something hard, I started and cried out. Only gradually did I realize that it was a rock: I had reached the bank. Crawling off the log, I found my legs would barely hold me; I was a weak as a newborn child. At last I started up the path on hands and knees, feeling my way, and clinging to the water jar as if it held my life.

The clearing above seemed bright as day when I reached it, and the firelight spilling out of the little hut was the most beautiful thing I had ever seen. Behind me from the woods as I went I could feet the Old Ones watching still, but drawing back, drawing away. And yet no one and nothing had touched me. All the fear, all the threat, came from myself.

When I entered the hut Ieuan was dozing by the fire, and our supper stew was bubbling in the pot that earlier had held herbs. From beyond the fire, Gwen looked up with a warmer smile than any she had given me before. "You were a while and a while at that," she said. "Is it well with you?"

"Oh, yes," I said, handing her the water jar, still three-parts full. "It is very well with me indeed."

We stayed another day and night in that place, while Ieuan's knee healed somewhat. Gwen showed me how to gather the herbs she used for the poultice, and much other useful lore; and Ieuan took his knife and carved for her a new ladle for her pot, and other things besides.

"Remember," she said to me as we were parting, "what you have learned here, Gwernin, when the time of your need arrives."

"I will," I said, and I did so.

But that, O my children, is a story for another day.

XIV. Taliesin

The Conwy is a big river, and broad and tidal at its mouth. We crossed it some way upstream at the old Roman ford near Caer Rhun, avoiding alike the boatmen of Deganwy, who would have charged us for the crossing, and the example of Maelgwn's bards and harpers, who were forced by their King to swim across and then compete with each other. The bards won the ensuing contest handily, for they sang, though wet, as sweetly as ever, while the harpers' strings had suffered from the crossing, leaving them unable to play anything at all. Neither fate, however, befell Ieuan and I, and we arrived dry-shod at the end of a soft, gray, early autumn day, and found a temporary lodging in a bit of tumble-down boatshed near Deganwy strand. It was not, as it turned out, a wise choice, but we were not to know that until later.

The fair, which was being held by the King, Rhun mab Maelgwn Gwynedd, to celebrate the marriage of his youngest daughter Angharad to one of the Princes of Powys, was only just beginning when we arrived, and promised to be a good one. Aside from the usual eating and drinking, wrestling and running, there would be contests for singers and harpers, storytellers and poets—and also, as I soon heard, a horse race. That last news pleased Ieuan, who could never keep from the horses, but it made me uneasy, though I could not say why. I only begged Ieuan to be moderate in his betting this time.

"Of course I will, Gwernin," he said indignantly. "I learned my lesson at Caer Seint!"

"Just so you do not forget it!" I replied. "I have no wish to be hauling you out of an Irish ship again at midnight!"

"Do not you worry," said Ieuan shortly, adjusting the set of his belt and combing his fingers through his curly black hair. "You will not have to. I will not make *that* mistake again!" With which response he went out, leaving me to wonder rather sourly what mistake he *would* make next.

Still, once I had some of the King's good meat and drink in my belly, I felt in a better mood. It was hard to stay sullen with gaiety and celebration all around me. This marriage feast might not be so great an occasion as the Lughnasadh Fair at Caer Seint, but Deganwy was a bigger town than the crumbling remains of Roman Segontium, for Rhun had one of his forts here, built on the rocky crags above the town. Built first, so legend said, by the early British before ever the Romans came, it had been refortified time and time again, most recently by Rhun's great father Maelgwn of famous memory. I determined to have a look within its walls later, for I had heard that many of the Roman customs were still kept there, and fine indeed was the entertainment in the court of Rhun the Tall.

We had been there two days when the trouble started, though I did not know it for such at the time. I had been passing the time most pleasantly before the contests started, having met up with the storyteller Edern, whom I had last seen in Nant Ffrancon. He was a young man not much older than myself, and we found that we had much in common. From Aberdaron he came, in the Lleyn Peninsula, and had been at Caer Seint earlier in the summer for the Festival, where he had bettered me in contest. We were looking forward to a rematch here.

"Have you heard the news, Gwernin?" he asked, coming up to me where I stood gawking at the display of knives in a merchant's stall. "They say Cyndrwyn is coming, and has brought with him quite a train. Bards and harpers and I know not what else, and some of the best horses you ever saw, to run in the race! Llys-tyn-wynnan is near your Pengwern, is it not?"

"None so near," I said, "though—yes, it *is* in Powys. Some days west of us in the hills, I believe—I have never seen it myself. I will be going that way myself ere long, I expect—perhaps Ieuan and I can follow the wedding party back! It is time and past we were thinking of heading home for the winter."

"Yes," said Edern, "the summer passes so quickly! Never mind, you will have some good days here yet. Where is your friend keeping himself? I have not seen much of him lately."

"Down by the horse lines as usual, I expect," I said, and sighed. "I only hope he stays out of trouble this time."

Edern laughed. "Yes," he said, "there was quite a fuss at Caer Seint after you left. He would do well to keep his head down here—there may be those that would know him again."

"As long as none of the Irishmen shows up, we should do well enough," I said, and laughed. "And they ought be safely home by now! Is the wedding party here yet? Shall we go and look? I wonder what bards Cyndrwyn has brought with him, and what meter they will use in contest?" And with that, we fell to technical discussions and walked away, paying no heed to the slight, dark-haired man in the blue tunic who had been standing beside us at the knife stand, and who had certainly overheard every word we said.

With the bridegroom's arrival the festivities redoubled. The horserace would be held at the end of the festival, after the contests and the wedding feast itself. This time, I felt sure, I would be able to see the Contention of the Bards, which I had missed at Caer Seint. Indeed, I had been turning over in my mind the thought of entering it myself—not with any expectation of triumph, given the great ones who would be present, but just for the experience of the thing. I had even polished up one or two verses in my head of which I was not ashamed. But whether I would have the courage to go through with it was another question.

Meanwhile, there was the storytelling contest. The day for this dawned bright and clear, with a high, pale sky that made me think again of the turning year. I was up early—indeed, I had slept little all night—and went out leaving Ieuan still snoring in his corner of the boatshed. I was too nervous to eat, but wanted a drink, and a chance to walk around and prepare myself. The contest would start early, and might run most of the day, and there was no telling who the judges would call on first. The King would not be there all that time, of course—he had better things to do with his day!—but the winner would perform before him at the wedding feast, three nights hence. That recognition, I thought, determining to do my best, might be worth more than the prize itself.

So I walked for a while along the shore, enjoying the fresh morning breeze, and listening to the cries of the gulls. The tide was well out, and the flat brown sands lay smooth and glistening in the morning sun. Not too far offshore was a big ship, which seemed to be making straight for us. Something about the cut of her looked familiar to me, but I could not place her. I wondered if she was bringing more guests to the feast, and who they might be. Already I had seen some I recognized from other places, including Cadwaladr, the red-headed Lord of Caer Lêb in Ynys Môn, who had sheltered us after our flight from Caer Seint. I wondered if little dark-haired Anwen in his court still remembered Ieuan and missed him.

In the open area when the contests were held, the story-tellers and judges were assembling. Even so early, there was a thin scatter of audience as well. I saw Edern in the group and went over to join him. He grinned at me and pushed the tawny hair back from his face in a gesture I was coming to know, but said nothing. Two of the three judges were speaking with a tall, black-browed man who was most splendidly dressed in a robe of red and blue and gold. I had not to my knowledge seen Taliesin Ben Beirdd yet, though I knew he was to be present at the feast. Now I wondered whether this was he, and my heart started to beat fast and hard with excitement. Since I was a boy I had heard stories of Arthur's great bard, and the thought of seeing him now in the flesh—nay, of performing before him!—had me suddenly sweating with nerves.

The judges settled themselves in their chairs, and the black-browed man sat down beside them. The chief judge, an oldish man with a full gray beard, called the first contestant. It was Edern. He walked forward into the center of the circle, and stood for a moment while the crowd rustled in anticipation and then was still. Then he began. The story he told was an Irish one, about a man who waited seven years to catch the great Salmon of Wisdom that dwelt in the pools of the Boyne, and what happened after he caught it.

I was listening like the rest, caught up and borne along by the story, when I became aware of a disturbance in the middle distance. Quickly it came closer and got louder, sounding first like a quarrel, and then like a brawl, and finally like a pitched battle. The judges were frowning, everyone was looking up, and poor Edern seemed uncertain as to whether or not he should continue. Then the running fight reached the outer edges of the crowd, and I saw that Ieuan was in the middle of it.

He was doing his best to escape from a couple of big, blond men who were trying to grab and hold him, and being helped and hindered by any number of others. Even as I leapt up and flung myself into the fray in his defense, I recognized his assailants as two of the Irishmen from Caer Seint, and knew why the incoming ship had seemed familiar. Then I had no time for thinking, only for fighting.

Blows were being swung wildly on both sides, without much concern over who they hit. As I struggled to come at Ieuan, he tore himself out of the Irishmen's grasp, leaving a handful of tunic behind, and turned to run—and stumbled. Before he could recover, one of the Irishmen had borne him to the ground with a sort of flying tackle, and they disappeared under the feet of the swaying crowd. Then a great voice was uplifted over the clamor, biding us hold, and a man on horseback came forcing his way into the crowd, laying about him with the flat of his sheathed sword.

The combatants broke apart, flinching aside from his blows and the horse's feet, and the horseman brought his mount to a halt beside the place where the Irishmen were still determinedly pinning Ieuan to the ground. A tall man he was, big every way, with thick curly hair and a beard that still showed more red than gray despite his years. The sheath of his sword glittered with gilding and precious stones as he restored it to his belt, and there was more gold on his horse trappings, and massive bracelets of it on his sinewy arms. With fierce blue eyes he glared around him at the silent crowd, and demanded, "Who dares to break the peace of Rhun mab Maelgwn Gwynedd? Stand forth now and explain yourselves!"

One of the Irishmen stood up, the other keeping Ieuan pinned the while. "Lord," he said, "asking your pardon I am for this disturbance, but my brother and I were for taking this man, who is an escaped bond-servant of ours. He cheated us at Caer Seint, taking our stake for a wager and then not paying his debts, and when we seized him for it, he fled in the night. All around Caer Seint we sought him to no avail, and then this morning, as soon as we landed, what should we see but him, bold as brass, walking out of some boatshed upon the strand! Aye, and if we had not seized him, he would have been off again! Lord, we ask only justice, and trust you to give us our due!"

"So you may trust," said Rhun, "when I have determined it. You, on the ground—what do you say to these charges? Let him up, man, so that he can speak."

Ieuan, released, came slowly to his knees, spitting out dirt and grass, and trying to staunch the blood which was flowing copiously from his nose. "Lord," he said somewhat thickly, "I ask your mercy and protection! It is not true, what they said, I did not do it, I was not there! In God's name, I beg you, save me from these murdering Irish barbarians who would slay me!"

"He lies, Lord!" cried the Irishman. "I can bring witnesses, there are those who saw him there!"

"Enough!" said Rhun. "I cannot sort this in the open field. *Penteulu*"—and he spoke here to the captain of his bodyguard—"bring these, and all who speak for or against them, to my hall, and I will hear them there, and give justice where it is due."

The Court of Rhun the Tall was all that rumor had said. Within the stone-built Roman walls of the fort were stone-built Roman buildings, not ruinous, like those I had seen elsewhere, but in good repair, from their square gray walls to their tiled and thatched roofs. From Commandant's house to barracks blocks, stable to bathhouse to latrines, all was as it should be, if not precisely as the Romans had left it. Walking behind the men of the bodyguard who were escorting Ieuan and the Irishmen, I could not help gazing around me in wonder. It was like walking back into the past.

But within the stone-built past, I found, lived the present. The long forecourt and central atrium of the Commandant's house had been thrown together and roofed over to form the hall of a Romano-British chieftain, complete with wooden benches around the wall and a low fire burning on the central hearth, and a blue smother of wood-smoke finding its way out through the unglazed windows in the upper walls. At the far end of the room a low wooden dais supported three massive chairs, and was flanked on either side by several benches, on which various brightly-clad men were seated. I recognized some of them as being bards who had accompanied Cyndrwyn. The rest, I supposed, must belong to Rhun himself.

Slowly the hall filled with people. When the murmurs and shuffling of feet had died away to nothing, Rhun himself came in, accompanied by his prospective son-in-law, and took a seat on the dais. If the King of Gwynedd had appeared large on horseback, inside he was gigantic, a true descendant of Maelgwn the Tall and Cadwallon Long-arm. It did not need the purple and red of his fine-combed wool tunic, or the narrow golden crown on his head, set with polished rubies, to proclaim his status. Beside him Cyndrwyn seemed a squat, brown man of no importance.

"Stand forth, peace-breakers," said Rhun, "and you that they accuse, and state your names."

"Lord," said the Irishman who had spoke before, "Connor son of Ráth am I, and this is my brother Snedgus. We ask only your justice."

"You shall have it," said Rhun, "whatever it may be. And you, what is your name?"

"Ieuan mab Meurig mab Pedr am I," said Ieuan, "and I come originally from the Eastern Hills, near Venonae, though I winter always in Pengwern. Your mercy and protection I ask, Lord, against these who have attacked me without cause."

"That also I will determine," said Rhun. "Connor son of Ráth, speak first, and tell me all your case."

"I will, Lord," said Connor, and launched into his narrative of the events at Caer Seint. Listening critically, I had to admit that he spoke well, and mostly spoke the truth, only a little embellished here and there. Rhun heard him out in patient silence until at last the wells of his eloquence ran dry. Then he looked at Ieuan.

"Ieuan mab Meurig mab Pedr," he said, "now is your chance to tell me your story. What do you say to all this accusation?"

"Lord," said Ieuan boldly, "I say they lie, though whether from malice or mistake, I know not. I was not at Caer Seint when the race they speak of was run, and therefore I cannot be the man who stole their stake. Maybe all the Cymry look alike to them, as the *Gwyddelod* do to us."

"Maybe," said the King dryly. "Connor son of Ráth, what do you say to that? Can you produce witnesses to support your claim?"

"I can, Lord," said the Irishman with emphasis. "Ifor mab Rhys and Cadfan mab Gwyn will speak for me. They are two of your own, and presumably *can* tell one of the Cymry from another."

The witnesses were called forth, and agreed with all that Connor had said. Rhun turned his gaze back to Ieuan. My mouth was dry; I knew what was coming next, and wished I could escape it. I would have to lie.

"Ieuan mab Meurig mab Pedr," said Rhun, "have you witnesses as well?"

"I have, Lord," said Ieuan. "My friend Gwernin Kyuarwyd is here with me, and can swear to the truth of my story."

"Gwernin Kyuarwyd, stand forth," said the King. "Can you support the testimony of this man?"

"I can, Lord," I said. If it must be done at all, it must be done well. "What he says is true."

"Have you other witnesses?" asked the King. "One is hardly enough."

"Lord," said Ieuan, "I saw the Lord Cadwaladr, of Caer Lêb in Ynys Môn, in your assembly. He can testify that when he returned from the Lughnasadh, I was in his court, and had been for some days already."

"That is so, Lord King," said that tall red-headed lord from behind me, and I remembered his avowed dislike of the Irish. And what he said was true, so far as it went.

Rhun mab Maelgwn Gwynedd ran his eyes slowly over us all, accusers and accused and witnesses alike. "Not easy, this," he said, and turned to look over his shoulder toward the assembled bards. "Can you help me sort this tangle, Head of Song?"

From behind that brightly-feathered crew, a slight, dark man stood up, setting aside the small harp with which he had been toying quietly. His long tunic of blue wool was rich and fine, but plainer than most of the others; nor was he bedecked with gilded ornaments, save for the thin band of silver that held back his hair, and the great brooch on his shoulder. As he came forward I realized with a start that I knew him: he was the man I had once met at Harddlech.

Not a large man, he was, and yet not small; not young, somehow, and yet certainly not old. His shoulder-length dark hair and neatly-trimmed beard were untouched with gray, but his face was mature, and not that of a youth. An ordinary-looking man he was, and yet not ordinary; hard to describe, but also hard to forget. He came to a halt beside Rhun and stood looking us over, and a stray beam of sunlight from the high windows sparkled on his circlet and turned his eyes to blue fire. Those eyes moved along the group assembled to testify, and stopped on me. "Gwernin," he said, "come here."

I came. When I stood before him, he seemed taller to me than Rhun the Tall, though our eyes were almost on a level. He looked me over very thoughtfully, as if memorizing my face. At last he asked quietly, "Is what you have said the truth?"

Meeting his eyes, I knew I could not evade, though I felt Ieuan's desperation behind me like a physical thing. "No," I said. "The Irishman spoke truth. I lied."

He nodded, as if he had known it all along, and turned to Rhun. "There is your answer, King of Gwynedd." Behind me I heard a rising wail of despair from Ieuan. As for myself, I stood like one newly dead, or turned to stone. I had destroyed myself to no purpose.

"Connor son of Ráth," said Rhun, "the judgment is yours. Take this man with you where you will, his liberty is forfeit."

"Wait," said the red-headed lord of Caer Lêb. "May I speak, Lord King?"

"Speak."

"Connor son of Ráth, will this buy your prisoner?" And he took from his arm a gold bracelet, and held it up, sparkling, in the sunlight.

"It will, Lord," said Connor, blinking, "him and six more like him!"

"Take it, then, and give him to me." And Cadwaladr tossed the bracelet to the Irishman. "There is one in my court who values him, though I cannot see why, and I grow weary of her tears and sighs. Come you with me, Ieuan mab Meurig mab Pedr, but mind! If ever I catch you betting so much as a pebble on anything again, I will have your head!"

"Lord," said Ieuan, very sober, "you may, with my good will!"

A little while later I was standing in the forecourt of the hall, wondering what to do with myself—Ieuan and I having parted with bitter words—when a boy came up and touched my sleeve, and asked me to follow him. Curious despite my misery, I did so. He led me through the maze of the court, and left me at the door of a small lime-washed room. "Lord," he said, "here is he," and went away. And stepping into the room, I found myself face to face with the man from Harddlech.

"So, Gwernin," he said after a long moment, "you did not do too well today."

I winced at the acid in his voice. "I did what I could for a friend."

"And was he grateful?" My silence answered him. "You did very ill by yourself. What you have lost is not easily found again."

"I know." I shrugged helplessly. "I will have to do without it."

"If you can." I made no answer, and he went on. "Gwernin... does my judgment seem harsh to you?"

"It does," I said bitterly. "It does."

"Listen to me. What I am—what you would wish to be—is not an easy thing. A bard's word is, must be, absolute in truth. Do you understand?"

I looked back at him in silence, and nodded jerkily. My throat was too tight for words, and in any case there was nothing to say against that burning blue gaze. I waited for my dismissal.

It did not come. Instead, "Do you want to learn the harp?" he asked.

Somehow I found a voice. "Yes!"

"Then go out to the forecourt of this hall, and speak to the old man you will find there, and tell him that I sent you. He needs a boy to travel with him and help him. In return he will teach you such of his skills as you can learn." Then, seeing the disappointment in my face, his expression softened and he shook his head gently. "Na, na, I cannot do it, not just now. Will you take the thing offered instead?"

Swallowing down my disappointment—for one blazing moment I had thought he meant to teach me himself—I nodded. "I will."

"Good." Almost he smiled. "He will not be an easy master to you, but he is a good teacher. I know, I studied with him once."

In the doorway I turned back. "Lord..."

"Yes?"

"Who shall I say sent me? For I still do not know your name."

At that he smiled fully; it was like the sun coming up. "Tell him," he said, gleaming, "that Taliesin Ben Beirdd sends you to him."

So I went out, still dazzled with his smile, to do his bidding. And what came after, O my children, is another story.

WINTER IN THE HILLS

"llym awel llum brin. anhaut caffael clid."

"Sharp is the wind, bare is the hill; hard it is to get shelter."

– Canu Llywarch Hen

XV. Talhaearn

In the days and months that followed that moment at Deganwy, when Taliesin had thrust what seemed the sum of my desires into my hands, I sometimes wondered whether he had in fact sent me to study with my new master, Talhaearn, out of kindness, or as a punishment. There were days, indeed, when I was sure it was the latter. But I think now that it may have been both, and neither, for as I came to know later, his motives were seldom simple, and his ends always beyond what most men could foresee.

Nevertheless, my apprenticeship started well enough. I had gone out into the forecourt of Caer Deganwy, still dazzled as I was with Taliesin's smile, to seek the old man to whom he had commended me. *He needs a boy to travel with him and help him,* Taliesin had said. *In return he will teach you such of his skills as you can learn...* And there, sure enough, was the old man himself, dozing on a bench in the afternoon sun, with his small harp cradled securely in his arms. A tall man I thought he was, gaunted with age but still strong, and his iron-gray hair and beard were streaked with silver. The woolen gown he wore was a deep red-purple in hue, and enriched at neck and cuffs and hem with wide bands of many-colored embroidery, which were in their turn partly hidden by the massive necklaces of red amber that bedecked his breast. He looked what he was, a harper-bard to kings and princes, and too fine, perhaps, for the likes of me.

I had stopped before him, and was taking my chance to look him over unobserved, when without opening his eyes, he suddenly addressed me: "Speak up, youngster, and state your business with Talhaearn."

His voice was deep and strong, and made me jump. I cleared my throat nervously. "Lord, I am—I was sent to you by Taliesin Ben Beirdd. He said that you need a boy to travel with you and help you, and that in return you would—you will—teach me the harp?" I stopped, so to speak, on one foot, and stood waiting, feeling more unsure of myself than I had in many a day.

Talhaearn opened his eyes, mere slits of faded blue in his weathered face, and peered up at me. "Hmm," he said after a moment. "What is your name, boy?"

"Gwernin Kyuarwyd am I," I said, and paused uncertainly.

Talhaearn grunted, and closed his eyes again. "Oh, yes," he said, "the storyteller. I heard your performance this morning in hall... And on that showing, Taliesin thinks you would make me a good pupil, does he? I see he does not come to tell me so himself. Or is this another invention of your own, Gwernin-who-is-sparing-with-the-truth?"

My hands clenched themselves into fists at the insult, but then I sighed. I had deserved this reproach, and more like it, when I lied to the King of Gwynedd in open court, though I spoke to save my friend Ieuan from slavery. "No, lord," I said steadily. "It is no invention that Taliesin sent me, nor that I would gladly serve you in return for your teaching. But if you do not want me"—I paused here to steady my voice, which showed an unwelcome tendency to quaver—"I will understand, and trouble you no more."

Talhaearn was silent for so long a time that I thought he might have fallen asleep again. Then, just as I was summoning up my resolution to turn and walk away, he chuckled. "Yes," he said, "you have determination, at any rate. Perhaps it will carry you through the course... Take this." And he held out his harp to me.

I took her with astonishment, and held her carefully, as if she were some infinitely fragile thing that might crumble to dust in my hands. Small she was, but surprisingly heavy, being made of some dense black wood that nevertheless sparkled in the sunlight with the luster of much handling. Her intricate carving was touched up here and there with fine paint and gilding, and the string-shoes that clasped the base of her fifteen horsehair strings were of wrought silver. Sturdy though she was, she had a kind of liveness to her, a singing hollowness even when she was still. I had never touched a harp before. I never wanted to be without one again.

I do not know how long I stood there, rapt in my trance, before the spell was broken by Talhaearn's dry chuckle. "Yes," he said, "I think you will do well enough, Gwernin-the-Storyteller. Hand her back to me now, and sit down here beside me, and I will give you your first lesson." And so he did, his fingers moving surely on the strings as he named them and showed me their notes, and demonstrated the use of the bronze tuning key that hung at his belt, delicately tightening the bone pegs until their strings rang true. Then he played a few notes, a short sparrow's whistle of a tune, and handing the harp back to me again, coached me in the placing and use of my fingers, until—how clumsily and haltingly, but also how proudly!—I also played his tune. It was only at the end, when we both stood up, and he placed his hand on my shoulder and bade me lead him to his room, that I realized his eyes had been closed throughout the lesson. Talhaearn was blind.

The rest of that Wedding Festival at Deganwy passed for me in a happy daze, though I sat in the shadows and watched others perform, and fetched and carried and acted as my master's eyes when he needed me. I found that he was not entirely without sight, as I had thought at first, but his vision was blurred and dimmed with that clouding that comes sometimes with old age. Best he could see in twilight or near-darkness, when the candle of the eye opens its widest, and poorest his sight was in broad sunlight, as when I first met him. But so well did his fingers know the strings of his harp that they seemed to have eyes of their own, or to need none at all, and his voice and mind were alike undimmed by time, as our first meeting had proved.

So I watched and listened, while Talhaearn played and sang for the King during the Wedding Feast, and my friend Edern—who had won the storytelling contest after all, despite the rude interruption he had suffered!—spoke his tales before the hall, and many another performer showed his skills. And last of all, and best, came Taliesin. This was a signal honor to all present, for master bards of his stature seldom performed in open hall like any traveling minstrel. But this last night was special.

I had been lounging on a bench with Edern at the side of the crowded hall, the two of us sharing one drinking horn, and many a comment besides on the various performers. There had come a pause in the entertainment, and the babble of many feasting voices rose within it to fill the hall, so that we could hardly hear ourselves speak, though we shouted each in the other's ear. Then, from the corner of my eye, I was aware of movement at the High Table, and looked around in time to see Taliesin stand up and take his place before the King.

No simple blue tunic for him tonight, to blend unnoticed in a crowd, but the full panoply of his rank—and yet I think he would have commanded our attention had he been dressed in rags. The torchlight gleamed redly as he moved on the silver circlet that bound back his dark hair, and sparkled on the great jeweled brooch he wore on his left shoulder, bright with many-colored enamels, a treasure fit for a king. As he took his position heads turned, first a few, and then more, and the noise in the hall died away to a murmur.

Then, when everyone was waiting, Taliesin began to sing, in the half-speaking, half-chanting style of the bards, and all that crowded hall grew still as listening midnight around his voice, his words falling like drops of crystal into the pool of their silence. His poem was a simple praise song, extolling the beauty and virtue and nobility of the King, and of Angharad his daughter, and of Cyndrwyn of Powys, who was taking her to wife; but so lovely were the linked phrases, and so clever the alliteration, that we all listened entranced, as though we had never before heard praise of man nor woman.

As Taliesin sang, a young man seated at the left end of the dais accompanied him on a small harp, the sweet mellow notes forming an interweaving counterpoint to the words of the song. About my own age he was, with dark red hair, and thin clever harper's hands that walked the strings as if born to them, and the fierce proud amber gaze of a hunting hawk—or a warrior prince. Neirin mab Dwywei, I had heard someone say his name was, and he came from the far North, from the old Votadini lands beyond the Wall, the part which men were nowadays calling Manau Gododdin. He had sung the day before in the poet's contest, and done none too ill. I had watched and envied him then, but now my eyes noticed him only as an accessory to Taliesin's song, while my ears and mind alike were held by that commanding voice. When at last it fell silent, there was a long moment of quiet, out of which we all woke only reluctantly to move and to applaud.

Presently, at his patron's urging, Taliesin sang again, a shorter song extolling the generosity of the King himself, and his might in battle; but after that he only shook his head to further urging, and retired, smiling, to his seat, leaving the way open for any others who dared perform after him. And such was the esteem in which he was held, that not even the King of Gwynedd dared press him further to perform against his will.

It was some while later when, sighing, I took one last pull from the drinking horn I was holding and handed it to Edern. "Finish this for me," I said. "It is time I was going, my master may be wanting me soon."

Edern took the horn, but made no move to drink. Frowning a little, he put a hand on my sleeve when I would have risen. "Wait, Gwernin. Tell me this first: how do you find your new master?"

I stared at him in surprise. "Why, he is all that I could hope for! What makes you ask?"

"Has he been kind to you?" pursued Edern. "Thoughtful? Generous in his instruction?"

I flushed a little, remembering my first encounter with Talhaearn, but put the thought aside. "Why, yes, for the most part. Why?"

Edern was still frowning, with an earnestness that sat oddly on his broad, good-natured face. "Because that is not his reputation," he said slowly. "Folk here call him a proud, cold man, with a tongue that can flay you alive while you stand. You have not seen it?"

"A little, perhaps, at our first meeting," I said, trying to be scrupulously honest. "But that was only a sort of testing. He has been good to me since."

Edern sighed. "Well, I hope you are right. But tell me this, if you can: why did his last boy leave him? And that abruptly, before he could find a replacement?"

I was frowning now in my turn. "I do not know. But surely…"

"But surely what?" asked Edern, when I said no more.

I shook my head. "Never you mind, it was only a passing thought. I must go now, Edern, he will be wanting me soon. If I do not see you again before we leave, the sun and moon be on your pathway, and good traveling to you!"

"And to you," said Edern, raising his drinking horn in a toast to me, "and much music!"

I smiled and left him, but I could not shake the slight unease his words had planted in me, or the thought which I had not voiced aloud. *But surely,* I had been thinking, *Taliesin would not have sent me to Talhaearn if he were a bad master...*

Or would he? What, after all, did I really know about either of them, beyond their great talent? *Enough,* I thought strongly, *enough to judge!* And soon I would know even more...

The next morning my doubts were forgotten, submerged in the excitement of our departure—for Talhaearn had agreed to travel into Powys with Cyndrwyn, and spend some time at his court. I mind me still the fine display we made, riding out though the great stone gates of Caer Deganwy in the early sunlight—or at least, Talhaearn was riding, mounted by the Prince as befitted his age and dignity, while I came on behind, leading his pack pony as part of the baggage train! A fine, mild day it was, late in the Harvest Month, with the fairest of blue skies overhead, and the early-turning willows just starting to put on their autumn foliage, and dropping a few golden leaves here and there down the breeze into our pathway. My heart was high to be on the move again, and heading somewhere near to my own home country. Perhaps, if we wintered with the Prince—as could well happen!—I might even see Pengwern again before the spring, and my cousins. A dear thought, that was, after so long a wandering, and me still new to the road as I was then—though I can tell you truly now, from sore experience, that separation grows no easier with age...

But that, O my children, is a story for another day.

XVI. First Lessons

Traveling with a Prince of Powys might have been an honor, but it was doing nothing for my comfort. That was my conclusion, after only a few days of it. Before, as a wandering storyteller, I might have stayed at many a humble dwelling, but while there, I was the most important guest, and merited whatever rough attention to my comfort my hosts could contrive. Now, although I lodged in the halls of chieftains, my only status was as my master's apprentice, in a place already overflowing with many more important folk; and such hospitality as came my way was rather hit-or-miss, to say the least. I counted myself fortunate to find a dry place to lie down at night, whether on the floor of the hall among a crowd of others, or in the straw of the byres—and the latter was often the more comfortable bed!

My days were as full as my nights were crowded, for though we did not travel at speed—I was by no means the only one afoot in the Prince's train—we still contrived to cover more miles in a day than I might have done if left to myself. Moreover, I had the pack-pony to load and unload and care for; and when that was done, I waited on my master Talhaearn, packing and unpacking his belongings, serving him at table, and generally fetching and carrying and acting as his eyes if needed. In my spare moments—such as they were!—I had to get my own food and drink, keep myself clean and tidy, and snatch a few hours' sleep. Altogether, it was a tiring life, and not at all what I had been used to.

There had been no more harp lessons since we left Deganwy, for my master owed his own Bard's duties to his Patron, often playing and singing in the evenings to honor the lord of the hall where we stayed. So I was pleased when I found we were to linger a few days here at Pentre-foelas, while Cyndrwyn tried the local hunting at the behest of his host, and his servants took a well-earned rest.

It was then two days before Alban Elfed, that halfway point between the poles of the year when nights and days are briefly equal in length, before the dark closes in. Autumn was nearly gone, and Samhain and Winter lay no very great distance ahead. Sometime in the last few days, unnoticed, I had turned sixteen, for September is my birth-month—I who was begotten beside the Midwinter fires, and raised in their ashes. I had almost forgotten the day myself; but now, watching the familiar beginnings of the preparations for the feast, on this mild golden morning that belied the waning year, I remembered and felt a little homesick, as I had not done since I set off last spring with Ieuan, to walk with him on his circuit around Wales, and seek my fortune. Now Ieuan was on his way to Ynys Môn, bound to the Lord of Caer Lêb by bonds stronger than steel, while I headed back to Powys in stranger company than ever I could have expected, and as far as he was from being my own master.

It was an odd thought, and I carried it back with me into Lludd's thatched timber hall, to where Talhaearn sat in the shadows tuning his harp, with the remains of his breakfast stir-about cooling forgotten on the bench beside him. At my step he looked up, so keenly that it was hard to believe he was nearly blind. "So, Gwernin, where have you been all this bright morning?"

"Down to the stables to see to Llwyd." That was the gray pony, named for his color. "Why, have you been wanting me?"

"On the contrary," and Talhaearn's voice was dry, "it is you, I think, who have been wanting *me*. Or my attentions, at least—unless the thought of music lessons on such a fair day has no attraction for you?"

I had been thinking that very thing, and was not unnaturally taken aback. "Why—of course not," I said after a moment. "Only I had begun to think you were too busy to teach me."

"That is impudent of you, and also untrue," said Talhaearn softly. "You should not use words so carelessly, Gwernin. I believe you have been reproved for it before, and not only by me."

"Yes, master," I said, wondering how he knew. Perhaps Taliesin had told him? It seemed unlikely.

"Are you agreeing, then, with my verdict, or merely making polite noises?" Talhaearn placed his harp key carefully on the bench beside him, and tried the strings he had been tuning. A small cascade of notes descended into the silence between us. "You should know better the value of words; you who have worked with them as a storyteller. Used unwisely, they can turn in the hand like an ill-made knife, and wound their wielder. And used with music, their power is all the greater, for each alone is a potent form of magic."

Magic. The word seemed to hang for a moment in the air between us. And yet I knew that it was so. Why else was I here?

"I apologize for my impudence, master," I said carefully, "and for my impatience. It is true I have been wanting more lessons, and you have been too busy to give them to me. And it is true I have been reproved before. But I did not think..."

"Yes?" said Talhaearn after a moment. "It seems likely enough... But *what* did you not think?"

I frowned, trying to get it right. "That you would be teaching me more than the harping. That was why Taliesin sent me to you—or so I thought." I paused, suddenly hearing a voice in my memory: *In return, he will teach you such of his skills as you can learn...* "Perhaps I was not listening."

"Perhaps you have not been listening a great deal of the time," said Talhaearn with sudden fierceness. "There is more to being a bard than music, much more! Do you think this is a peaceful trade I follow, because I carry no sword? Words are the weapons of the bard, Gwernin, words and inspiration. I am as much a warrior in my way as any you may meet. My ash spear and shield are my *awen*, sharper than blue steel and more deadly, and when I sing for princes, I reave as much reward as any raider."

I blinked, thinking back over the nights of entertainment, back to the feast at Deganwy, and the golden gifts there given. "I see... I think I see."

"Do you?" Talhaearn smiled wryly. "Well, that is something to the good, at any rate. Now, if you are ready, sit you down beside me here, and show what you remember from your last lesson. And fear not, you will get your due in practice time today, and something over, while Cyndrwyn hunts his deer."

Talhaearn spoke true, and more than true. By the time that lesson and my subsequent practice were over, morning was passing into midday, and my arms and wrists and hands were aching with strain, and my fingertips burning from the pressure of the strings. Yet such was the lure of the music, I was reluctant to stop. I was beginning to learn my second tune.

At last Talhaearn took his harp from my hands, and bade me go out and enjoy the afternoon. "You will have time enough to play again tomorrow," he said, smiling thinly, "for I think we will be here for two more days at least. And you will not make yourself a bard overnight by wearing your fingers to the bone now. Give it time, boy, give it time! All things will come in their season."

So I went out into that golden afternoon, feeling myself more of a boy than I had in months—but not to idleness. Instead I went to join the reapers who were getting in the last of the corn, as I would have done at home, and spent the rest of the day sweating with them in the fields, coming back

dusty and tired in the gloaming to see the hunters ride in with
their hounds and their slaughtered deer. That night and the
next there was feasting in Lludd's hall—for the next day
followed the same pattern—and I served my master at table,
and watched with new eyes as he played and sang to honor
the Prince and his hosts. The fierceness that was in him
showed ever in his song, controlled and curbed though it
was, and few, I think, would have dared to challenge him at
such times, with the *awen* burning within him like cold fire;
for blind though he was, he was of the warrior build, and
spear-straight still despite his years and his gray hair, which
shone in the torchlight like the iron helm of his name.

Alban Elfed dawned cold and bright and clear, though a
few high feathers of cloud promised a change in the weather
before long. There was to be feasting and celebration all that
day, for the last of the harvest was in, finished the night
before, and the village fields stretched pale-stubbled and bare
along the road and river to the foot of the enclosing hills.

Pentre-foelas lies near the headwaters of the Afon
Conwy, in the last broad stretch of valley before the hills
close in. And big enough hills they are, compared with the
lands of eastern Powys where I was bred; but beside the
mountains of Eryri, though which I had lately come, these
were only hillocks, and gentle ones at that. With the autumn
colors burning brighter upon them every day, red and gold
and amber, they seemed dressed as much for festival as we.
Soon the herders would be bringing the sheep and cattle
down from the high pastures for the culling and slaughter
that precedes Samhain, but for now it was enough to celebrate the fruits of the fields.

Despite the bustle and busyness of that day, Talhaearn
found time for me to practice and to learn. We spent a long
golden afternoon in the orchard, where a few late apples still
hung, russet and crimson amidst the gilded leaves, glowing
like fairy fruit and scenting all the air around them. They

reminded me of a story that I knew and sometimes told, and that in turn led to another thought… "Master," I said somewhat diffidently, when the lesson was over, and Talhaearn was carefully putting his harp into her case before carrying her back to the hall, "do you think they will be needing more entertainment this evening than is already arranged?"

Talhaearn paused, an arrested expression on his face. "I do not know," he said slowly, "yet I think that rare indeed is the feast with too many entertainers. What is in your mind?"

"I am—I have been—a storyteller," I said cautiously. "Such craft as I own has been hard come by, and honed through much practice. I should hate to see it rust for lack of use. But I cannot perform without your leave."

"And you are asking me to give it to you." Talhaearn completed the bestowal of his harp, and slung the bag over his shoulder. "What story would you tell, if I gave you leave?"

"The Tale of Arthur the Soldier, and the Three Truths. It has," I said wryly, "much meaning for me."

"So." Deliberately Talhaearn sat himself down again on the log we had used earlier for a bench. "Tell it to me now, that I may judge the standard of your performance." And he settled himself to listen, with a curious expression on his face which I found impossible to read. At the end he only nodded. "Yes," he said, "I think you will not shame me before the company. I will arrange it." And setting his hand on my shoulder, he bade me lead him back to the hall.

So I stood up that evening in hall for the first time since Deganwy, to speak my tale before the Prince Cyndrwyn. There was nervousness in me, for I was very conscious that the last time I had stood so before this particular lord, it had been as a liar self-confessed in the Court of Gwynedd. The knowledge that my master trusted me, as much as my pride in my own craft, carried me through, and I got at the end my due measure of applause, as well as a silver armlet from the lord of Pentre-foelas for my efforts. But my best reward came much later in the evening, when I was helping Talhae-arn to bed. "Well, Gwernin," he said, as I stood behind him, combing out his long gray hair, "you spoke none too ill this evening, and I think from the heart. I will find you other chances to perform, and teach you more material. Only do not presume to speak so unless I give permission."

I thanked him stumblingly, but he only shook his head. "Na, na, thank yourself, not me, for you have earned it. Now leave me, and get your own rest, for I think that we travel on again tomorrow." And so I did.

That night I dreamed of an eagle, flying over the sea, and knew when I awoke that he was Gwydion mab Dôn. Snug in my cloak within my nest of straw in the quiet stable, I lay and thought about it. A clear dream it had been, with a strange feel to it, more true than daylight waking. I could see in memory each single feather in the eagle's wings, and feel his fierce joy in flight as though it were my own. The blue-green sea, foam-flecked with breaking waves, stretched wide and wide below him, pierced here and there with sand-girt rocks and islands, each with its own small cluster of dark trees. It was very real, that sea, but none that I knew. I wondered if I would ever sail its reaches for myself, and walk upon its islands. And even more I wondered where Gwydion might be going, and why, and whether I would ever meet with him again in this life.

I got my answers to all these questions eventually, though some were a long while in coming.

But that, O my children, is a story for another day..

XVII. The Tale of Tristfardd

As blue as the sky and as fathomless, the great lake stretched away before us in the afternoon sunlight as we came down from the hills toward the little village of Bala. Some call that lake Llyn Bala, after the village, but most name it Llyn Tegid, for a chieftain who once had his court beside it. Beside, or as it may be, *under* it—for legend holds that this valley was not always filled with a lake. Some say that a holy well, carelessly left uncovered, overflowed in the night; others—especially the Christians—attribute the flooding to an act of divine vengeance against Tegid himself. But as to why that vengeance fell upon him, they do not say.

Whatever its origin may have been, the lake was a welcome sight to me that afternoon, promising the end of another long day's journey in Prince Cyndrwyn's train, leading my master's pony and breathing the dust of the roads. I have no quarrel with going afoot—I have done so much of my life—but I prefer to do it at my own pace, and with only a few companions beside me. Still I bore the hardship ungrudgingly that day, for it was part of the duty I owed my master for his teaching. Dust is a small price to pay for music.

We had left Pentre-foelas that morning, as early as might be, and headed south through the hills toward Bala. There we would stop for two nights to rest before the hardest part of our journey, the climb over Berwyn. After that it was mostly downhill, threading our way through the wooded valleys of western Powys until we came to Llys-tyn-wynnan and Cyndrwyn's court, where Talhaearn and I would likely spend the winter. And winter might well be close upon us ere we reached it, for the Harvest Month was running now to its end, and Samhain lay only a moon ahead. Already frost had touched the trees to autumn fire, so that oak and alder, ash and willow and thorn, all burned with bonfire brilliance along the valleys as we came, and the high tops of the hills showed here and there crowned with kingly gold.

Warm was our welcome within the wooden walls of Meigen mab Eidion that night, and warmer still the glances that Meigen himself cast at the lady Angharad ferch Rhun, Cyndrwyn's bride. Indeed she was worthy of appreciation, with her skin white as new snow on Yr Wyddfa, and her sparkling eyes blue as Llyn Tegid itself, and her hair the bright burning gold of the frost-touched ash and alder in the forest outside. If I have said little of her until now, it is because to me in those days, nothing—not women, nor horses, nor wealth unmeasured—came before my pursuit of my craft. But I had noticed Angharad—oh, yes, I had noticed! And even so that evening, with better reason, did Meigen our host.

Seated she was that night at the high table during the feasting, seated at Meigen's left hand as Cyndrwyn was at his right. Often during the feasting he turned to speak to her, or merely to look, assuring himself that she was happy and well-served, but the look in his eyes was not merely that of a host. And she knew it, and began to respond, basking in the glow of his admiration—to put it no higher! Serving my master Talhaearn, who as *pencerdd* sat also by right at that high table, I saw much of the interaction between them—more, perhaps, than did Cyndrwyn her husband. A young man of generous and unsuspicious nature, he was busy discussing the hunting planned for the morrow with the warrior seated on his right, all unaware of the other and more perilous hunt already underway beside him.

The next morning dawned clear and cold, and the hunters gathered early, a brave sight in that torch-lit courtyard, with their bright cloaks wrapped around them, and their breath and that of their horses smoking white on the frosty air. Torchlight gleamed redly from spear-point and knife-hilt, red as the blood that would color them later, and the harness of the horses chimed like small bells as they moved restlessly in the cold. I had come out to watch their departure, though I had no errand here; and some of the excitement of their day transferred itself to me, so that I too felt my heart beat faster with theirs, and almost wished for a moment that I was also a warrior, and going with them. That I was not had been in large part my own choice, and I did not regret it, but I was a man, and young, and my blood was not cold. I watched the other young men ride off into the brightening morning, along the path by the lake shore and into the trees beyond, and then I turned back to the smoky hall behind me, and the music that awaited me within.

The day that had begun in light and fire ended in rain and darkness. Before ever the sun was clear of the eastern trees, thin wisps of gray cloud had begun to drift in from the west and north, growing thicker and heavier as the day wore on. Long before the hunters returned, the first of the autumn rains had begun to fall, turning the afternoon to sodden evening, through which we peered anxiously from the fire-lit hall, feeling as if winter was already upon us.

The hunters came back from their day wet and weary, and some of them bruised and bloody as well from falls in the darkening forest, where the rain was making all tracks treacherous that night. And though they brought with them a slaughtered stag, they had paid a high price for him, for they carried with them also one of their own number in an improvised litter slung between two horses. And that one was the prince Cyndrwyn himself.

Alive he was, but still unconscious, with blood on his forehead and in his brown hair, and his face white as milk under the stain of his summer tan. His horse, so they said, had fallen on a steep bank, and thrown the prince into the rocky stream below, to his undoing. I stood anxiously with the rest in the rain-whipped courtyard, watching in the smoky torchlight as they took him from the litter and carried him away to Meigen's own quarters, his young wife going with him. Rain or no rain, I thought then, we would not be riding onwards in the morning.

Nor did we. For though Cyndrwyn, warmed and tended in his host's own bed, came presently to his senses, he was so bruised and battered from his fall that he would have been hard pressed to rise unaided, much less to mount and go. All the next day he lay drifting in and out of sleep, while the rain roared on the thatch above and the wind shrieked around the shutters, filling the hall with gusts of smoke from the open fire that set us coughing. And in the hall and out, Meigen and Angharad found time to exchange words and glances—if nothing more!

After the evening meal was over, when I was getting my own supper on one of the benches at the side of the hall, I was summoned to the high table, where Meigen and Angharad and a few others still lingered over their mead, with Talhaearn harping softly beside them—so softly, indeed, that the shrieking of the wind outside sometimes drowned his music. Angharad smiled at me as I came up and stopped before her. "Time hangs heavy on our hands this evening, Gwernin," she said. "Can you give us a tale, to help it pass?"

I looked at her lovely face, flushed with the firelight, and it was all that I could do to deny her. "Lady," I said, "I may not. Not without my master's permission."

"And truly does he speak," said Talhaearn's voice from beside us. "But if you wish a tale, Lady, I can give you one."

"I wish it indeed," said Angharad, and others agreed, turning expectantly to face the old bard.

"Then you shall have one," he said. His eyes went from her to Meigen close beside her, and for a moment I would have sworn that he could see. "Have you heard the story of Urien Rheged and the bard Tristfardd?"

"No," she said, frowning a little, and Meigen echoed her "no." "I think not."

"Na, you would not have." A grim little smile tugged at the corners of Talhaearn's mouth for a moment, and then was gone. "It happened in the years around Camlann—before you were born, like enough." He drew his hand across his harp, and in a momentary hush in the storm outside, a scatter of bright notes rose like mournful birds and lingered in the air. "Listen, then, Lady, and believe," said Talhaearn, his voice growing deeper, "for I myself have sung in the court of Urien Rheged, and I know that this tale is true."

He paused for a moment, gazing into the fire as if seeing there the past of which he spoke. "Urien Rheged, King of the North, you will know well by repute," he said at last. "He has not now a Chief Bard in his court, nor has he had one for many years, only lesser bards who come and go with the seasons. But once he had such a man in his service, and that one was called Tristfardd.

"Three sorts of music there are that a harper-bard must command: the music of joy, and the music of sleep, and the music of sorrow. All of these Tristfardd could play, but it was in the last, the *cerdd drist*, that he excelled, and so he got his name.

"In those days Urien was a young king, recently come into his lordship in Rheged. And young also was Urien's wife, Modron ferch Afallach, and she was of surpassing beauty. As he played one night in Urien's *llys*, Tristfardd gazed upon her, and as he looked, he fell in love with her, so that every part of him was filled with desire for Urien's wife. And she looked upon him, and though he was not comely, the enchantment of his music entered into her heart, and she loved him in return. And when Urien was next away from his court, they found opportunity to be together, and to fulfill their love; and they were happy. But then Urien came back, and they were apart, and miserable again. And so they went on for some time.

"At last Tristfardd could no longer bear this having-and-not-having, and he determined to go away. For three years he wandered throughout the land of Britain, without coming near to the court of Rheged. And in all that time he had no peace, and his heart was eaten up with longing for Urien's wife. And he knew that it was the same for her.

"Finally he decided to try and see her again. It was then autumn, as it is now, with the winter closing in, and threatening soon to shut all the ways with snow, and the thought of spending another half-year away from Modron was more than Tristfardd could bear. So he set out toward the court of Rheged. It was cold, wet weather, as bad for traveling as that which we had today, and as he drew near to Urien's *llys* it grew worse, so that by late afternoon he was so chilled and weary that he was forced to stop for a while in the shelter of some woods and build a fire to warm himself. And while he was trying to start the fire, with the wet wood hissing and spitting and refusing to burn, he heard a horseman coming; and peering through the cloud of smoke around him, he saw a tall man on a gray mare. As the man came closer, Tristfardd saw that he was all muffled up in a heavy hooded cloak against the rain, so that nothing could be seen of him but his beard, which was gray-streaked like the pelt of a badger. Tristfardd called out to him, and asked him if he had been recently at Urien's *llys*.

" 'I have that,' said the stranger.

" 'And was Urien then at home?' asked Tristfardd.

" 'He was there when I was there,' replied the stranger.

"Then Tristfardd asked the stranger to carry a message to Urien's wife, and beg her to meet him tomorrow at a place near the court which they had been wont to frequent. The stranger agreed, and rode on his way, and Tristfardd lay down happily to rest beside his fire, certain that he would soon be seeing Modron again. But what he did not know was that the stranger with whom he had been speaking was Urien himself; for in the three years since they had last met, Urien's beard had turned gray.

"When Urien arrived at the *llys*, he confronted his wife with what he had learnt, and ordered her to meet Tristfardd the next day and send him away. She went as he had commanded her, but as soon as she and the bard saw each other, they knew they could not bear to be parted again. Even though she warned Tristfardd that Urien knew of their love, he would not leave her, and she could not bring herself to send him away. And so they lay together as they had done before.

"When Modron returned to the *llys*, Urien asked her if she had sent her lover away, and she admitted that she had not. Then Urien was angry, and he took his sword and went out to slay the bard. But when Tristfardd saw him coming, he knew him, and begged Urien to spare his life, and to let him stay at the court, where he might at least see the queen, for without the sight of her his life was not worth the living. And Urien agreed, on two conditions: that Tristfardd should no longer entice the queen to love him, and that he should never again speak to Urien of his desire for her. And Tristfardd swore that he would keep to these terms, and he returned with Urien to the *llys*. And that night Tristfardd sang again in the hall of Urien Rheged, as he had been wont to do, and he had the sight of the queen in his eyes to comfort him, and she had him in hers.

"So things went along for some time. But at last neither the queen nor the bard could bear to be always seeing each other, and never touching, and so they found a chance when Urien was away to come together in secret, and they once more became lovers. But they were careful to keep this from Urien.

"At last it came to pass that Urien went out hunting one day, and on a whim took Tristfardd with him as one of his party. After they had killed and were on their way back, they shared around a skin of strong wine among them, and Tristfardd, who was very weary, drank more of it than he ought. Presently his horse went lame, and as they were then approaching a river, Urien took the bard up behind him on his own mare to ford it.

"As they were crossing the river, Urien said, 'A fine little mare this is indeed, who bears the both of us on her four slender legs.'

" 'Fine also,' said Tristfardd, the wine speaking through him, 'are the *two* slender legs that bear us both.'

" 'Ha!' cried Urien, 'I see that you taunt me again with your lust for my wife!' And on reaching the bank, he pulled out his sword and slew Tristfardd, so that the river ran red with his blood; and that place has ever after been called *Rhyd Tristfardd*. And from that day to this, there has not been a Chief Bard in the court of Urien Rheged."

There was a moment of silence with only the sound of the moaning wind in it, and then Angharad spoke up. "That is a tale indeed," she said to Talhaearn. "But tell me, did Urien afterwards slay his queen as well?"

"Oh, no, Lady," said Talhaearn gently, and his face was stern. "He did worse than that by far to her. He let her live." And with that he picked up his harp and began to play, and there were no more stories that night.

"Tell me, Gwernin," said Talhaearn later when I was preparing him for bed, "what was Tristfardd's greatest offense?"

I thought about it as I combed his long gray hair, but the answer seemed obvious. "His deception of Urien."

"Not entirely. He swore an oath to Urien, and he broke his word. For a bard, that is unforgivable."

"I understand," I said after a moment.

"I wonder if you do?" Again there was that trace of a smile in his voice. "Promise me, Gwernin, that when you stand in the court of Urien Rheged, you will remember Tristfardd."

"I will," I said soberly. And I did.

But that, O my children, is a story for another day.

XVIII. Encounters on Berwyn

Berwyn stands high. Clouds hang often round her, and rough weather; snow covers her in winter, and summer sees her crowned with lightening. Home has she been in her time to wild men and to wolves, and kings has she defeated. But on the morning when we set out from Bala, she shone fine and fair before us, innocent in sunlight. So easily appearance may deceive, and fortune change swiftly as the weather.

We were climbing that day over Berwyn herself, that long, high ridge which divides the north- and east-flowing headwaters of the Afon Dyfrydwy from those flowing south towards the Severn, on the last leg of our journey to the Prince's home at Llys-tyn-wynnan where Talhaearn and I would winter. Two more days' journey, at most, should see us there; and high time it was, with Samhain close ahead of us now and winter breathing down our necks.

A gay enough party we were on that autumn morning, glad to be out and on our way again after days of being held indoors by rough weather. Even those like myself who went afoot, leading the baggage ponies in the rear of the line, stepped out briskly for pleasure at the change. The ponies themselves were frisky for want of work, while the higher-bred horses ridden by the Prince and his retinue were fretting and light at hand—so much so indeed that I more than once glanced anxiously at my master to see how he did. In deference to his age and lack of sight, the Prince had given Talhaearn a sweet-tempered brown mare, and set one of his men to guide her with a leading-rein. This had served well enough till now; but even calm mares can grow skittish on a frosty morning. However, the old bard seemed to have her well in hand, and I soon gave over worrying about him, concentrating instead on the muddy road, all the worse for the passage of the horses ahead of me.

At first the going was easy enough, along the river-meadows of winding Dyfrdwy where she flows out of the great lake, with here and there a remnant of the old Romans' road to help us. Before many miles, though, our way led south, away from the river and into the hills, and the trees closed in around us. Their gold and russet cloaks were shabby now, and the scent of dead leaves and autumn earth hung heavy on the air. Our track led steadily upward, following a small stream and sometimes crossing it, and here we suffered the effects of the recent rains. So rough was that road at times, that I think we in the mud were less discomforted than the ladies in their horse-litters—for the Prince's new wife, Angharad ferch Rhun mab Maelgwn Gwynedd, was too high-born a lady to jaunter about the country on horseback, prey to the wind and the rain like the rest of us. She and her chief handmaidens rode instead in covered litters—though I doubt if that day they were grateful for the privilege!

Presently our path drew away from the stream bed, and the going was easier, if no less muddy. A steady climb it makes, that old road, and steady its demands on man and beast. At last, though the grade never slackened, we saw the forest begin to open up and fall away from us, and knew we were nearing the barren heights, which until then we had seen but poorly though the woven net of branches that lay above us.

At the crest of the pass we broke out of the trees entirely, and bore to the right up the slope, following the old ridge-way track that cuts across the south face of that shoulder of Berwyn. We should by now have had a hawk's view over a wide expanse of country, had it not been for the sea of fog which covered all the lands to the south, and rose to meet us at the pass, at first in spidery wisps and tendrils, and then in thicker clots and clumps like drifting smoke. Soon we found ourselves in the midst of it, enfolded by its clammy embrace and cut off from the bright sunlight that had pleased us earlier. Had not the old track we followed been so clear, we might have lost our way. As it was, we grumbled at the wet and went on, pulling our cloaks closer around us for warmth in the drifting grayness that chilled hands and feet and faces and left a million tiny dewdrops on our clothes and hair.

After some time the track bent to the right again around a knob of rock, and looking up I saw trees ahead, and realized we had come to a lower spot in the ridge. Perhaps, I thought hopefully, we would stop here for our nooning. Though it was hard to tell in the fog, I felt it must be well past midday, and I at least was hungry.

As I had hoped, we stopped on the edge of the woods. It should have been a pleasant, sheltered place, with wood and hill to temper unkind winds and cup the warming sunlight. Unfortunately there was no sunlight, and the fog found its way everywhere, even into the covered litters, where the ladies shivered in their furs. Riders dismounted and stretched stiff muscles, horses and ponies were picketed, and we all sat down to rest and eat the food our last host had provided. I spread a saddle pad on a rock to make a seat for Talhaearn, and brought him a cup of water from the leather bottle on Llwyd's back, there being no spring or stream to hand. He thanked me absently, frowning with closed eyes as if he listened to some inward voice. It was a look I would later come to know.

All too soon our break was over. Cups and bags and leather bottles were restored to saddlebags or packs, horses were re-saddled and mounted, and the ladies, who had come out of their shelter to stretch and move about, returned reluctantly to the litters. I could not help noticing how the

Lady Angharad, even in this gray light, shone brighter than any other would on a sunny day, her hair burning golden as the absent sun himself. All men noticed her, and showed it in their ways. Prince Cyndrwyn himself helped her back into her litter (not that she needed help, graceful and assured as all her movements were) and tied its leather curtain-strings with his own hands before springing up again onto his tall horse. I gave my master a hand up, and went to take Lloyd's rein from the man who was holding it for me. And that should have been all, were it not for what happened next.

It came as we were starting back onto the track, away from our little patch of shelter. Suddenly a hare, which had lain all this time in concealment, leapt up from under the very hooves of Cyndrwyn's horse, which reared up in alarm, snorting and bucking and frightening the other horses. Panic spread down the line like wildfire, and one of the horses most alarmed was Talhaearn's mare. First she tried to bolt and was forestalled, more by an iron hand on her reins than by the man who was leading her—he, like most of the rest, was taken up with the horse-litters, which were being well-nigh overset by the antics of the horses bearing them. Balked, the mare sat back on her haunches and reared, trying another way of escape. I dropped Llwyd's rope and started toward her, only to see her brought down to a shuddering stand by the leading-rein, as the man holding it finally remembered his duties. Even as I stopped, uncertain, I heard behind me the sound of receding hoof-beats. Our gray pony was decamping with all of my worldly goods, and of most my master's as well.

Talhaearn had mastered his plunging mount without further help, and now sat solidly on her while she stood shivering and sweating. His eyes met mine, and—not for the first time!—I could have sworn he was sighted. "Gwernin," he said, "what have you done?" The mist streamed darkly past us; in the distance I thought I could still hear the pony's receding hoof-beats. No one had caught him; the retinue had been busy with the horse-litters and their own charges.

"I let go of Llwyd," I said, "but do not worry, I will get him back."

He looked at me a moment longer, then nodded, still-faced. "You will."

"Master," said the man holding the leading-rein, "we cannot stay for this, it will take us most of the light to get down from this ridge as it is. Perhaps one of us could ride after him…"

"Na, na," said Talhaearn shortly, shaking his head. "He must mend what he has made."

The man shrugged; it was none of his business. "See, lad," he said, turning to me, "when you have found him, follow the track down, it is clear enough. There are those in the valley below will give you shelter, if you do not come up with us before night."

"That is well," I said. And to Talhaearn, who sat listening and cradling his harp where she sheltered under his cloak—for he never let her ride on Llwyd, and now I could see why!—"I will be with you tonight, if I can. If not, I will come to you at Llys-tyn-wynnan."

"Be sure you will." He nodded grimly. "Off with you, then. You have no time to spare." I sketched a salute he could not see, and turned, and went, following the pony's tracks into the drifting fog.

I am not—I will admit it!—the world's best tracker. The pony's hoof-prints were clear enough at first in the soft ground under the trees, but when I came out into the bracken and low-growing heather on the ridge beyond, it was a different story. In the drifting gray fog I could often see only a few yards ahead. I stopped now and then to listen, but could hear nothing, only once the distant call of an owl from the forest below. I whistled for the pony but got no answer, so I went on, picking my way from hoof-print to hoof-print. They were harder to find now; the ridge was growing stony.

Suddenly the fog opened up before me like a curtain. Without knowing it, I had crossed over again onto the south face of Berwyn. Ahead of me now and to my right a lower ridge branched off, a broad horn of land dropping steeply away from me into the mist. On its crest, just before it disappeared, I saw a mound, one of those round, green hills left by the Old Folk in the very-long-ago, with a standing stone beside it. I paid them little heed, for ahead of me, just above the branching-off place of the horn, stood the gray pony Llwyd, grazing peacefully. A scrap of sunlight broke through the fog and fell on him for a moment, turning his gray coat to silver. Then it passed, and he was as he had always been.

I whistled, and his head came up, but he did not move. I started forward slowly, careful not to startle him, and picking my footing with care. The slope here was not gentle; there were loose rocks in the heather, and the frost-burned bracken snatched at my feet as I walked. The pony stood and watched me come, alert and indecisive. I called his name softly and spoke to him, and his ears flicked back and forth, back and forth, listening. Slowly, carefully, I came on, talking to him as I came. I did not notice the fog closing in again, until suddenly his outline blurred before my eyes. But I was almost up to him by then, and paid it no mind.

At the last minute, with my hand almost touching him, he decided to run. I saw it happen, saw him throw up his head and start to turn, and I flung myself forward, reaching for his headstall. I missed. A stone turned under my foot, and I fell, and down the hill I went, rolling over and over in the bracken until I struck my head on something and fell into darkness—and seemed to fall right into the hill itself.

On bright green grass I stood, greener than any I had ever seen before. Above me the sun shone golden, in a sky more blue than blue, and the air around me was the warm, sweet breath of spring, heavy with the scent of flowers. Arching over me was an apple tree, with pale-pink blossoms and small green fruit and ripe red apples growing all on the same branch. Before me was a woman, sitting in a golden chair and playing on a harp of gold. Her hair was bright as the sunlight, and her skin as white as the snow of one night, and her eyes bluer than the sky above her. Green as the grass beneath my feet was the dress she was wearing, and over it she wore a cloak of nine colors, held at the shoulders with gold enameled brooches that changed their shape as I watched, so that they were now birds of the air, and now beasts of the forest, and now fishes of the sea.

When the woman saw that I was aware of her, she stopped her playing and smiled up at me. "Ah, Gwernin," she said, "well met!" And putting down her harp, she took in her hands a cup from a table beside her, and standing, offered it to me. "Drink of this," she said, "and be welcome."

I took the cup from her hands, and saw that it was made of some dark wood, carved and polished and bound with silver, and within it a clear pale mead, fragrant with the scent of apple-blossom and honey. Delicious indeed was its scent, and there was suddenly on me such a thirst, that I felt as if I had drunk no drink for a year. And yet I hesitated. "Lady," I said, speaking with an effort through the dryness in my mouth, "What will happen to me if I drain this cup?"

"Why, what should happen?" she asked, and her voice was sweeter than all the birdsong in all the springs of the world. "Only that you would be welcome in my land, and your tongue would be loosened and your words freed to sing the songs that are in you, and you would sing them for me."

Still I hesitated with the cup in my hands.

"Well," she said, "if you will not to drink it, then you need not," and the cup was gone. But the thirst that was on me remained.

"Sit down," she said, and there was a couch beside me, and I sat. "You are a bard, are you not, Gwernin?"

I started to speak, and thought, and then thought again. "So I have been told," I said. And that was true.

She held out to me her golden harp. "Play for me, then, O bard, upon this instrument," she said, and smiled.

The harp she held out was the most beautiful one I had ever seen or imagined. The music she had played earlier on it was as clear and as bright as the chiming of stars in the heavens, or the singing of the birds of Rhiannon upon their golden bough. Even the movement of the air through its shining strings brought forth melody, and I knew that if I took it, it would answer as sweetly to my hand. My fingers ached to hold it, and yet I hesitated. "Lady," I said, "What will happen to me, if I take your harp?"

"Why, what should happen?" she asked, and her voice pierced me through like the voice of the harp itself. "Only that you will play the music you have in you, and have always wished to play, and you will play it now for me."

Still I hesitated with the harp before me.

"Well," she said, "if you will not to play it, then you need not," and the harp was gone. But the desire for its music lingered on me as a pain in my heart, and my hands were empty with its loss.

"Be at ease," she said, and I found that I was reclining, and under me a bed all draped with silks and furs, and easy beyond belief. And she sat down beside me and smiled, and her smile promised all the pleasures I had ever dreamt or imagined. Her hair hung down over her white shoulders like cascades of sunlight, and I could feel her warmth and smell the perfume of her skin as she leaned over me, and I trembled with her nearness.

"Well, Gwernin," she said, "you will not to drink, and you will not to play. What do you want? Do you know it?"

"Yourself," I heard myself say huskily, and I reached up to touch her hair, that was light as gossamer under my fingers. "You are what I want, I know it. You are all my desire."

She smiled, and bent forward to kiss me, her long hair brushing my face, her breath warm on my cheek—

—and it was Llwyd's mane, brushing my cheek and waking me, and his warm breath on my face. I lay on the cold hillside at the foot of the standing stone, alone but for my gray pony—and very glad I was to see him. He was not used to people lying down in the heather and not moving, and once I had creased to pursue him, he had come back to see what ailed me, and what new game I would be at now. I tried to sit up and groaned, so stiff and cold and bruised as I was from my fall. Only by holding fast to the pony's neck could I get to my feet at all. My head spun dizzily, and there was a spot behind my left ear too tender to touch, and the wet of the fog-drenched bracken had soaked into my clothes so that I shivered as I moved. Altogether, I was in a wretched state—but I was myself, and alive.

Presently, grasping the headstall, I turned the pony in the way I thought we should go, and keeping a hand in his mane for support, began to lead him back up the slope through the rough heather and bracken. I was uneasily aware that the light was dimmer than it had been, and there was in me now no desire at all to spend the night on this hill. Of what I had seen within it, I would not let myself think. That, no doubt, would come later.

The owl was calling in the twilight woods when at last I came stumbling around another bend in the track, to see before me the tree-filled darkness of the pass I was seeking—and in that darkness, the flickering light of a fire. As I paused, wondering who could be there, all alone on the hill, I heard faint and distant the sound of a harp. For a moment my feet seemed to freeze to the ground, and my blood ran cold. Then I realized that the harp was an ordinary horsehair-strung mortal one, a little out of tune with the wet, and the song was one I had heard at Deganwy not so many days before. My courage came back to me, and I went on.

There were two of them by the fire, and the harper at least I knew, if only by his build, and his red hair, and his thin, clever hands that walked the strings as if born to them. Even in an autumn wood at twilight, Neirin mab Dwywei was not easy to mistake. Then the other man turned to face me, and my heart leapt within me, so that I wondered how I could have failed to know him at once.

"Well met, Gwernin," said Taliesin Ben Beirdd, and smiled.

Presently, while Neirin was rearranging the pack-ponies' loads to get me a mount (one of their three being saddle-broken to serve as a spare at need), Taliesin sat me down on a rock to check me over, seeing no doubt from my white face and unsteady gait that all was not well with me. When he touched the lump behind my left ear, I cried out despite myself.

"Ah," he said with satisfaction. "That is the worst of it?"

"Yes," I got out, as well as I could through clenched teeth. To tell the truth, my head was throbbing like a drum, and I felt sick.

"Lean back against me, so," he said, "and be still," and I obeyed. He touched my head again gently, cupping his left palm over the source of the pain. His hands were warm, and under their touch I began to relax, closing my eyes and drifting, for I was very weary. He smelled of horses, and damp wool, and wood-smoke, and altogether human. Under his breath I could hear him humming something, very softly. Almost I knew the song...

Then, "That is better," he said, and took his hands away. I blinked and sat up, moving my head cautiously. Most of the pain was gone, leaving only a dull ache behind. "Thank you!" I said in surprise. "What did you do?"

He only gave me that glinting smile again for an answer. "Get up, lad," he said, "we have riding to do, and little left of the light." And it was so. I saw that while I sat dreaming Neirin had finished repacking the ponies' loads, and now stood holding the black one ready for me. He met my eyes unsmilingly as he gave me a leg up, then turned to mount his own dappled gray and take the pack-ponies' lead ropes from Taliesin.

Behind us the fire had dwindled to ashes, and the owl called again in the trees. Between my legs the black pony went easily, as well content with the change in his lot as was I. So we rode down from the mist and into the last of the sunset, burning across the sky above us in bars of glowing gold. The light turned the red of Neirin's hair to smoky flame, and lay on our skins like gilding. Around us the shadows were blue and royal purple, and I felt richer than kings. And in my pleasure I forgot my meeting with the woman in the hill, and the fear and desire I had felt there— forgot, or as it might be, ceased for a while to remember...

But that, O my children, is a story for another day.

XIX. A Harp to Practice On

Talhaearn was not best pleased. I could tell it from the tone of his voice, even before I opened the door and pushed aside the hanging flap of the leather curtain that helped to close off our thatched boothy from the cold, wet air outside. A carrying voice he had, Talhaearn, from a lifetime of bardic practice, and it was carrying clearly now—carrying a full weight of displeasure as well! I paused for a moment, but it was no place to linger, there in the wind and the rain, so I gathered my courage along with the tray I carried, and went it.

The two bards turned to face me, breaking off what they were saying. "It is Gwernin," I said for Talhaearn's benefit, though I think he had known my step already. "I have brought you the wine you wanted, masters, and cheese and cakes as well—the cook insisted!" I put the tray down on a small table beside the brazier and set about pouring the wine from its pottery flask into the cups—silver cups!—the steward had sent. The rich, fruity scent of the wine itself rose up as I poured, speaking louder than words of its quality. With two such famous bards at once in his *llys*, however briefly, Cyndrwyn clearly felt that no honor he could pay them would be too much: neither the cups nor the wine they held would have disgraced the table of a king.

I handed the first cup to my master Talhaearn, who took it silently, the displeasure that was still on him showing clearly in his compressed mouth and heavy frown. The second I gave to Taliesin, sitting across the brazier from him, who thanked me with a word and a slight, amused smile. "Leave us now for a while longer, Gwernin," he added, his blue eyes twinkling. "You shall come back soon enough, but just now you are better away, believe me!"

Talhaearn gave a sort of snort, and drank deeply from his cup. "Yes, leave us, lad," he said then. "Go away and practice." He drank again, and I paused, my hand hovering over the wine jug, but Taliesin shook his head at me, and under his amused and understanding gaze I went.

Go away and practice, I thought as I crossed the muddy yard toward Cyndrwyn's hall, ducking my head against the blowing rain. *What* shall I practice, and *how*? Harping would have been most appropriate, but the only harp to which I had any pretensions of use was Talhaearn's own, and that was safely back in the boothy beside him, nor likely to be released into my unsupervised hands, never mind the wind and the rain! Go away and practice, indeed!

The problem was hardly a new one; in a sense, it had been with me ever since I first offered myself to Talhaearn as apprentice and servant, back in that sun-lit courtyard at Deganwy. If Talhaearn's previous boy had owned or had use of a practice harp, he must have taken it with him when he left; certainly I had never seen one in the baggage that I packed and unpacked as we traveled. It was his own harp, intricately wrought and carved and gilded as she was, that Talhaearn had first placed in my hands; and it was on his own harp that he had begun my teaching. But lessons are one thing, and practice quite another. How could I come to make full use of the former, I wondered, without the latter?

Still musing on my problem, I made my way into Cyndrwyn's high-beamed hall, where many of the idle hands of the *llys*—and not a few of the busy ones as well!—had gathered on that wet day. Even as I dropped the door-curtain behind me and paused on the smoky threshold, waiting for my eyes to become accustomed to the change of light, I knew by the sound of harping that Taliesin's apprentice Neirin was here before of me, and at work. I could see him now as my sight cleared, a slender, red-haired young man of about my own age, seated beside the central hearth of the hall and surrounded by a small crowd of listeners. After a moment I made my way toward them.

If practice was Neirin's need, I thought, it was only in the sense that any learned skill must be maintained. His fingers danced freely and with mastery where mine stumbled but lamely. Even the small song he was playing now, a child's cradle tune, had a jewel-like clarity, and as I listened it changed under his hands to a dance tune, to a march, to a song of triumph, and then to one of mourning and remembrance. When at last the strings fell silent and the harper looked up, his audience burst into spontaneous applause.

"By Pryderi's Pigs!" I cried, coming forward. "If you are not a harper, Neirin, then may I never hope to hear one! However did you get such mastery, and you no older than you are?"

A slow, pleased smile spread over Neirin's thin face, and danced like firelight in his amber eyes. "I take that as praise from the heart, Gwernin," he said. "Still, I am thinking that you flatter me. Have you not heard your own master play?"

I nodded, sitting down beside him on an empty bench. "Yes, but that is a different sort of playing, and he has had a long life in which to learn it. *You* must have teethed on a harp, and composed songs in your cradle!"

"Na, na, not quite!" Neirin chuckled. He was putting his harp back into her case now, and seeing this, many of the listeners rose up and moved away, or at least drew back to give us space to talk. "Though true enough, I got my teaching first from my mother Dwywei, who was daughter to Lleenawg Elmet, and afterwards from her harper Cynan as well. I have been playing a harp, or trying to, since I could well hold one. Not so, I think, with you?"

"Na, na," I said shortly, frowning a little. "I had no such chance. Those who raised me were not kings, nor daughters

155

of kings. Such mastery as I have lies elsewhere, and comes at my own teaching."

"And yet you have now as good a master as any alive," said Neirin softly, but with something of my frown showing between his own dark brows. "The fame of Talhaearn Tad Awen is known throughout this land. He played before the Court of Arthur, surely, before ever you or I were born."

"That is true," I said, and sighed, and looked away toward the hearth, where the little blue flames were dancing over a bed of glowing logs and sending out grateful warmth. "And certainly I have no quarrel with his teaching—when he *will* teach me! But look you, Neirin," and I held out my empty hands, "how can I learn from his teaching when I have no way to practice? You did not come by your mastery from lessons alone, did you? Surely you have spent hours beyond counting by yourself with a harp!"

"Well," said Neirin, and again, "well," as if considering. He was frowning now as hard as I was. "Still," he said, "it is early days yet, and no doubt Talhaearn will be getting you a harp to practice on when you are ready, and have served him long enough. Or—might you be buying one for yourself?"

"With what?" I asked, more sharply than I had intended. "All that I own would not buy the bag *your* harp rides in, let alone an instrument." And that was true, for a very bonny case it was, the leather carved and tooled and gilded in the fantastic designs favored by the Picts of the Far North.

"I do not suppose your father–?" suggested Neirin delicately.

"Na, na," I shook my head again. "My parents are dead, and those that raised me—had other plans for me, which I would not follow. I would not ask them if I could." I sighed again in frustration. "Never you mind. I spoke only of what was gnawing at my heart. It is none of your trouble."

"That is no doubt true, and who am I to be taking another man's burden upon me?" said Neirin lightly, but the frown was still between his brows and in his amber eyes. Suddenly he snapped his fingers, and began to unfasten his harp case again. "Still, here we are, and *I* have a harp, and if you will submit to my watching, you may practice on it now as you will—is that not a fine offer?"

His manner was contagious, and I chuckled, but hesitated. "A fine offer it is indeed, and yet—"

At my tone Neirin paused, his harp in his hands—and a very fair harp she was, fairer even in her adornment that the case in which she rode! "And yet? And yet? *Hai mai*, you are very fine! Is she not good enough for you, then, this harp of mine?" And his mobile brows went up, half in humor and half in disdain.

"Ah, no," I said, before I could stop myself. "It is no such thing! It is only—" I stopped, and could have bitten my tongue.

"Well?" said Neirin, half-challengingly. "What, then, is it only?"

I felt a tide of red wash up from my tunic to the roots of my hair. "It is only," I said slowly, "that I am such a poor player as yet, I should be ashamed to play before you, never mind before all these who have heard *you* play," and I nodded at his erstwhile audience, disposed around the hall at their tasks.

Neirin met my eyes, and a flush dyed his own cheeks in their turn. "Well," he said after a moment, "I have no cure for your second objection, but as to the first—I have listened to a few bad players in my time, not all of whom would own it, and played good music myself before my betters. If you can master your shame at the playing, I think I can control my revulsion long enough to listen. *One* thing I know for sure, you will get no better by *not* playing! Shall we not try it?"

"Yes," I said after a moment, and held out my hand for his harp. "We shall, and I thank you!"

157

As a practice session it was less than a success, though it had other merits. Neirin meant well, but my ineptitude jarred on his sensitive ear, try though he might to hide it. He was also, I found, an instinctive teacher, and could not go for long watching me struggle, without wanting or trying to help. Indeed I got from him that afternoon as good a lesson as any I have had, and was properly grateful for it. But undisturbed practice it was not. I ended stimulated and glowing, but with my problem no nearer solution. Somehow, some way, I must get my own harp—my own harp to practice on!

That afternoon, though, was the start of our friendship. Even after Neirin had put his harp away, safe in her elaborate case, we sat on for a while beside the fire, talking each of our own backgrounds and desires. He had been four years already with Taliesin, traveling with him and learning, and was likely to continue so for some time to come: a bard's repertoire is not learnt in a season, nor even in a handful of years. Twenty years, I have heard, the Irishmen take for their teaching, though they are more formal about it than we could afford to be in those days, when our customs, our kingdoms, our very language was changing around us faster than we knew. Taliesin knew it, and knew the need to bend before the wind and the times. Talhaearn, too, bent in his own way, though being who he was, he also fought against the bending. But we were young, Neirin and I, with our lives before us, and had not yet felt the temper of that wind of change, or feeling, known it for what it was. We talked of what we had done, and, shyly, of what we meant to do: journeys to go, stories to tell, verses to make. There was a great contest held each summer in the North, in the lands of the Gododdin from which Neirin had come. He was yearning to enter it himself one of these years, when Taliesin's travels should take them again to the North. The subject set, it seemed, was usually heroism in battle, or deeds done by great warriors of old. I teased him gently about it, asking what either of us knew of battles, who had given up such practice for poetry.

"As to that," he said, "I am not altogether without experience, and have some verses already in my mind on the subject. Who knows, someday all the North may remember the Lay of the Son of Dwywei," and he laughed. But the fierceness of his eyes belied the laughter.

I watched him there, Neirin, as he talked, with the firelight bright on his bold cheek-bones, and leaping up now and then to stain his face red as blood. And just for a moment I thought that it *was* blood—his blood, and maybe mine as well. But the moment passed, and I forgot it; and the afternoon moved on toward its end. At last I rose up and went out into the darkening rain, to see if our masters needed ought from either of us before it was time for the evening's feast.

I had crossed the muddy courtyard, and was about to open the door to the boothy, which stood a little ajar, when something about the voices inside made me pause. In a momentary slackening of the wind, their words came clearly enough to me where I stood outside.

"He has not earned it," I heard Talhaearn say, fuming.

"No," agreed Taliesin's voice tranquilly, "but he needs it all the same."

There was a long pause, filled with the lashing rain, but I did not notice it. I waited, listening. Somehow I felt it was of me they were speaking.

"Have your own way, then!" said Talhaearn at last. "A stubborn boy were you ever, Gwion, and a stubborn man are you still!"

"As who should know better than yourself, who beat me often enough for it," agreed Taliesin with a smile in his voice. "Na, na, but you know I speak the truth, Father of Inspiration, or you would not be giving way! Stubborn I may have been and am, Iron Brow, but you are stubborner, if you will but own it!"

"Well, well," said Talhaearn, somewhat appeased, "there may be some truth in what you say. Have your own way, then, and give it to the boy now. He is waiting eagerly enough, I dare say."

"Or at least, in enough confusion," amended Taliesin. "Come in, Gwernin!"

Startled, I came back to life with a jerk, but there was nothing for it. I pushed the curtain aside and went in, dripping rain, and with my shame at having been caught listening flaming in my face like wine. I could tell from Taliesin's ironic smile that he saw my discomfiture, but he did not mention it. How I ever thought to conceal anything from that one, I will never know!

"Well, boy," Talhaearn was saying—and his voice was as stern as his face—"you come very aptly, just as we were discussing you."

"I—I came to see if you needed anything," I said. "I—did not mean to interrupt you."

Talhaearn gave a short, sharp bark of laugher. "I am sure you did not!"

"Gwernin," said Taliesin firmly, interrupting whatever else his former master had to say, "you have a certain gift of timing. Whether it is a good gift or an ill one, I hesitate to say, but certainly it *is* a gift. And indeed, it was of gifts that we were speaking, as you may well have heard. How much harp practice have you had in the last three days?"

"Why—very little," I said, astonished at the question. "In fact—" I paused, not wanting to further annoy my master, but unable to lie.

"In fact?" Taliesin's blue eyes were steady on mine, not questioning or compelling, but inexorable as fate.

"In fact," said Talhaearn, "he has had none at all, as you well know. And you know why."

160

"Peace, Father of Awen," said Taliesin quietly, his eyes still on me. "Gwernin?"

"As he says." I made it as neutral a statement as I could. "There's been no time for lessons while you were here, lord."

At that Taliesin smiled, a sudden blaze of amusement breaking up the gravity of his face like sunrise putting to flight darkness. "Aha! So now it is *my* fault, is it? You hear, Talhaearn?"

"I hear," and Talhaearn smiled too, if more grimly. "You are well answered."

"I am," said Taliesin, still gleaming. "I will amend my fault! Gwernin, bring me that sack—and bring it carefully!"

I brought the sack he indicated from beside his bed-place. Within it I could feel something light and hard, with a sort of singing feeling to it, even though it was silent. Taliesin untied the thong that bound the neck of the sack, and extracted from it with some care a scarred case of shaped leather, of a size to hold in one's two arms. Setting the sack aside, he settled the case on his lap, handling it gently. Well I knew that shape and that special kind of gentleness, and I caught my breath in anticipation. One by one he opened the bronze buckles that held the top of the case closed, and drew out a harp.

Not a large harp, she was, or a new one; not richly adorned with jewels or carvings, but only with the simple beauty of the wood, polished by much handling, and with her absolute fitness for the purpose for which she was made. My whole heart went out to her in yearning; I stood entirely still.

Taliesin looked long at me, and his look was stern, as though he weighed my worth with his eyes. Absently the strong fingers of his left hand caressed the wood of the harp, belly and fore-pillar and harmonic curve, as something well-known and well-loved. Full of unavailing words as I was, I could not speak, but simply returned his look. Things that I had overheard earlier came back to me, and they were true: I had not earned her, but I needed her all the same...

"Come on, then," said Taliesin at last, and held her out to me. "You had better take her, before Talhaearn changes his mind!" And the smile that lit his face this time was a reflection of my own.

That was how I got my harp, my harp to practice on, and practice on her I did—yes, and more than practice, over the flowing years. Many and strange are the places I have played her, and light she has brought to me often in darkness, and more than once has she saved my life...

But that, O my children, is a story for another day.

XX. A Winter-Tale

Before Samhain, Taliesin and Neirin had gone, on their way to Pengwern and the court of Cynan Garwyn where they would spend the winter, and from which they had turned aside to visit Talhaearn at Llys-tyn-wynnan. They seemed in their going to take with them much of the remaining sunlight, so that I felt the force of impending darkness more than I usually did at this time of year. There was little leisure, however, for missing them, what with the business of the autumn slaughter in hand, and the lessons that my master Talhaearn was now giving me daily, and the need—the passionate need!—to spend as much time as I could with my new harp. So the days passed, and the year turned, and it was the day before Samhain-eve.

Now, it may have been the time of year, that sends the buck and the boar alike battling in the woods; and it may have been that I was seeing nightly before me in hall the shining beauty of the Lady Angharad, Prince Cyndrwyn's new wife; and it may simply have been that I was young and lusty, and no longer wearing myself out with daily travel. But for whatever reason, the Woman Under the Hill whom I had met on Berwyn had been lately much in my thoughts—yes, and in my dreams as well. That was how I thought of her— the Woman Under the Hill—though even then I knew that she had other names and greater, some of which I may not mention here. Only the image of her fair skin and bright hair troubled my sleep, as that of Angharad troubled my waking. Knowing however that the one of these two noble Ladies was as far out of my reach as the other, I looked about me in *llys* and hall, to see what *might* come my way. And before long, my gaze and my fancy lighted upon Keinwen, daughter of Hueil Goch.

What can I say of Keinwen, after so long? Red-gold hair she had, I remember, flame-gold and flame-bright, and waist-long when she let it down from its plaits. Creamy-white skin she had, that begged to be touched; dark eyes; and a fine red mouth. Slender and graceful as a young birch-tree she was, and her voice like bird-song in its branches. Young she was—very young, as it seems to me now!—but not too young. And unwed!

Of course, I was by no means the first to have noticed her charms, and there were many before me in the contest. Chiefest of my rivals was Goronwy mab Gronw, one of Cyndrwyn's warriors. A young man perhaps two or three years older than myself, he was, but taller and broader by far, with a mane of red-gold hair nearly the equal of Keinwen's own, and a fine, full mustache which I envied him almost as much as his favor with Hueil's daughter.

For some days, as I saw her in the distance working, or down at the brook, washing off the blood and dirt of the day's labors—for we were all of us still hard about it with the autumn culling—or pouring mead in the hall at night, I had been mulling over in my mind how to make a proper impression on Keinwen. For though I was free-born man in my own kindred, and had some status as a storyteller, and would have much more when I became harper and bard, still I was as yet only an apprentice in these crafts, while Goronwy was already a blooded warrior, with prizes to show from his raiding. And there is no doubt but that glory—and prizes!—are impressive to girls. So I thought on my problem, rising up with it in the morning and lying down to sleep with it at night. But I was no nearer a solution when the thing happened which was to force my hand.

As part of my lessons, my master Talhaearn had been teaching me more stories—in private, for these were Winter-tales, not to be told in public in the bright half of the year. And wonderful stories they were—tales of Mabon son of Modron and his hunting of the king-boar Twrch Trywd in the Forest of Kelidon; of Llew Llaw Gyffes and his cousins Bleiddwn, Hyddwn, and Hwchdwn Hir, the three sons of Gilfaethwy the False; of the *Pair Keridwen*, the great Cauldron of Keridwen, and the three-and-twenty other Treasures of the Island of Britain, and their stealing and giving, winning and losing, hiding and finding again. Some of the stories I had heard before in different forms, and some of them were new to me, but all were wonderful, and I gathered them in hungrily. Talhaearn, in teaching them to me, had cautioned me not to tell any of them in hall until he was satisfied with my performance, or indeed to so speak any tale without his express permission. I thought his reminder needless, but I agreed. And I cannot truly say that I forgot my words.

It was, then, late afternoon of the day before Samhain, and a gray, cold, edge-of-winter day it was, with twilight coming on early. Some of us who had already finished our outdoor tasks were gathered about the central hearth in Cyndrwyn's hall, warming our cold hands and feet at the fire and looking forward with relish to our evening meal. Goronwy was there, boasting as usual of his warlike exploits, and Keinwen had brought him drink and stayed to listen, with her face bright and open as a flower drinking in sunlight—but turned, unfortunately, to him and not to me. And Goronwy grinned back at her like a hungry wolf, and took another swallow of ale from his horn, and wiped the foam away from that splendid mustache of his with the back of a broad brown hand.

I found myself yet again stoking my own upper lip with thumb and forefinger, as I had done so often before, and silently urging the few scant hairs on it to grow. And maybe it was the thought of the mustache that set my tongue wagging untimely, and maybe it was Goronwy's plodding blow-by-blow delivery of his battle-story which set my teeth on edge, but suddenly I heard myself saying into a moment's pause, "A fine warrior you may be in truth, Goronwy mab Gronw, but you should leave the telling of tales to those who understand that craft."

There was a little silence, and all eyes turned toward me, but not with quite the expression in them that I would have wished. "And you, I suppose," said Goronwy, looking me over as if I were something unpleasant he had discovered on the bottom of his boot, and meant to scrape off before long, "are such a one?"

"I am," I said firmly. "The length and breadth of this land I have traveled as *cyfarwyd*." And I cast a glance at Keinwen, to see if she was properly impressed. But she was looking at Goronwy.

"Traveled, I can believe," said Goronwy disdainfully. "The Bard travels, and you are his servant. And that is all that you are. Big talk for a horse-boy and bearer of burdens!"

I felt myself flush. "Before I came to study with my master," I said carefully, "I traveled my own circuit, and spoke myself in contest, and had silver laid in my palm as my prize. I am no up-country braggart, hero of a few cattle-raids; I have spoken before lords and princes—yes, before the King of Gwynedd himself—and been well rewarded for my tales." And if this was not full truth, still it was no lie, either.

Goronwy was growing red-faced in his turn. "Fine talk," he sneered, "but we have heard none of these tales here— unless this is a sample!"

"True," said one, and another, and "True!" cried a third, a dark girl named Rhiannedd whom I had hardly noticed in Keinwen's shadow. "But that can be amended here and now—for here we all are, and here is Gwernin, and time and to spare with all of us, is there not, for a tale before meat?"

They liked the idea; one and another took it up, and even Keinwen was watching me now rather than Goronwy.

Only I hesitated, remembering that I was bound. "Sorry I am to disappoint you," I said slowly, "but I may not speak my tales in hall without my master's leave. And that I have not got tonight."

The others' faces fell, but Goronwy laughed loudly. "Nor liable to get it, either, I should think! Shelter behind the bard's skirts, then, little cockerel! Only another time, do not crow so loud!"

I felt the heat rising again in my face, and saw Keinwen's eyes turning back from me to Goronwy, and I took a deep breath. "I do not promise," I said deliberately, "what I cannot perform. Listen, then, if you will, to the tale of Pwyll Prince of Dyfed, and his hunting of Glyn Cwch, and the task which was laid upon him there!" And as the hall stilled around me, I began to unfold for their hearing that ancient Winter-tale.

Not a long story, it is, but long enough, and dark enough for the darkness growing now outside the hall. It tells of Pwyll's meeting with Arawn, King of Annwn, and of the year that he spent in Arawn's own dark land as a result. My audience listened to me as silently as I could have wished; I held them in my hand. Only my voice, and the voice of the fire, and the voice of the wind outside, spoke in Cyndrwyn's hall until I was done. There is no other feeling like it in the world.

At the end I got my just measure of applause from all of them, even from Goronwy, and Keinwen's smile as my crown; and I was joying in it, when a slight motion at the back of the hall caught my eye; and looking over the intervening heads, I saw Talhaearn. What had brought him into the hall then I do not know, but there he was, standing quiet and listening near the door in the shadows that were not shadows to him, and his face dark and closed as the darkness outside. Quiet and patient as doom he stood, and let me have my moment in the light. I think I had enough control of myself, even then, not to show the shock that sight gave me, like a blow in the pit of the stomach that takes away the breath, but all desire for applause—or the sweet looks of a lass!—left me in that moment. When I could do so without loss of face, I left my audience and made my way to his side. "Master?" I said carefully. "You were wanting me?"

"Gwernin," he said, "come with me." And I came.

When we had reached the hut against the compound wall which Cyndrwyn the Prince had provided for our privacy, Talhaearn asked me mildly, "Do you know what you have done, Gwernin, and why you should not have done it?"

"Yes," I said, trying to match his tone, if not his detachment, for I knew what was coming, and I was not unafraid. "I do."

"That is good hearing," he said, and almost he smiled. "Now go down to the brook, and cut me a hazel rod as thick as your thumb, and bring it to me here." And I did so.

"Now bare your back," said Talhaearn when I had returned, "and kneel down, facing away from me." His aim was very good for a blind man, and his arm was not weakened by age; and that night I had other reasons to keep me wakeful than the red lips and fire-gold hair of Hueil's daughter.

This was not the end of the matter, of course, by any means.

But that, O my children, is a story for another day.

XXI. The Gifts at Arthur's Crowning

GOLD always gets one's attention. Once when I was I was young I went mining it with pick and shovel and washing-pan, and hard hot labor that was, for little return in the end. And once again in later life I went seeking it, in deeper darkness and by a light which I may not mention here. But the search for gold and treasure that I remember best was not my own—or at least, not mine in the flesh.

It was on a day in early winter when first I heard that tale. Samhain had long since passed, and the short, dark days were upon us. Wind and rain blew around Cyndrwyn's *llys* for days on end, and snow dappled the high hills above Nant Twrch, so that when a break in the weather finally came, everyone was only too glad to get outside and enjoy it. And on the afternoon of one such day of respite—a day of mixed sun and clouds it was, with hardly any showers, and those merely light and passing!—my master Talhaearn took it into his head for the two of us to climb the ridge above the Prince's court, and have our lessons in the out-of-doors, rather than in the smoky warmth of the hall to which we had been confined for so long.

We were still up there when the sun dropped behind the western hills, and began to paint the ragged clouds overhead with sunset colors, gold and rose and purple banners flung across the sky above us. And Talhaearn sat gazing up at the glowing light that came clear enough even to his age-dimmed vision with something very like a smile on his weathered face. "King's colors, Gwernin," he said then softly, "like unto the treasures at Arthur's crowning. Say for me again the list of the Three Crowns of the Island of Britain."

169

"The Three Golden Crowns of the Island of Britain," I said, reciting, "were the Crown of Maxen Wledig the Emperor, and the Crown of Bendigaidfran, and the Crown that Gofannon the Smith wrought for his sister's son Llew of the Skillful Hand. But greater than any of these three was the Crown of Arthur, which went with him into the West, and lies no more in this land."

"Fairly spoken. And who brought the gold to Arthur, to make the crown of Britain?"

"All the lords of the land brought it, that the crown which was forged for Arthur should represent the whole of Britain." I paused, and decided to venture, for Talhaearn was looking uncommonly mellow. "Were you there that day, Master, when the treasures were presented? Did you see them?"

Almost Talhaearn smiled. "I was, and I did indeed. Listen, then, for you should hear this story, and remember." And settling himself more comfortably on his rock, and still gazing into the colored West, he took up the tale in his storyteller's voice.

"After Arthur had won the last of his twelve great battles for the freedom of Britain, and crushed the Saxons at Badon Hill so that they came not west again for a generation, the Kings of the Britons met and agreed to have him as High King over them, who had until then been only *Dux Bellorum*, Duke of Battles, the War Leader of Britain. And they dispersed for a year and a day to prepare for the crowning feast, and each of them competed to gather treasure from his own lands or in his own way to give to Arthur at his crowning. For as you should know, overflowing generosity in peacetime is as praiseworthy in a Lord as is ferocity against his foes in battle; and as they had competed in war to be first on the foe, so now the Kings and Lords of Britain sought each to outdo his fellows in the richness of his tribute to the High King.

"Many are the stories that could be told of that search for treasure, and many the heroic deeds that were done. The Kings of the West, Custinnen of Dumnonia and Maelgwn Hir of Gwynedd, mined the riches of their own lands, setting slaves and free tribesmen alike to delve in the earth for gold, and some of that gold was as hard-won and blood-bought as any battle-plunder. And this they had wrought into twisted golden torques, bright-enameled brooches, and heavy two-handled cups set with rubies and other rich gems.

"The Kings of the North, of Strathclyde and Gododdin, set to work instead to mine their neighbors. They sent out raiding parties into the lands of the Picts and the Dalriads; and these brought back precious jeweled coffers, heavy silver chains and arm-rings, and stone-mounted, spell-carved swords with pommels of pale ivory.

"The Lords of the South and East, still Roman in name and nature, sent their agents out to lands overseas, to Gaul and beyond, to buy their treasures; and these brought back with them fine silks, colored like jewels or flowers; caskets of rare spice from the Middle Sea; huge amphorae of red Falernian wine; and high-couraged, battle-trained stallions whose harness was mounted with gold.

"The lesser lords and warriors, lacking the lands of the kings, competed each in his own way, and the treasure of many of these was bought twice over with blood. Fair Cai went wandering to Ireland and beyond, and many a giant or monster he killed on his travels, and gathered to him their hoard. Indeed I think he journeyed nigh to the Western Isles, reaving treasure as he went, though only seven of that party lived to bear it back. And these brought riches beyond mortal imagining… They are part of the Twenty-Four Treasures of the Island of Britain. Can you tell me some of their names?"

"The Caldron of Annwn," I said slowly, shutting my eyes the better to concentrate, "which can bring the dead to life again, but without speech; the Cloak of Manawydan Mab

Llyr, which confers invisibility on its wearer; the whetstone of Brân, which will sharpen the weapon of a brave man but blunt that of a coward; the gwyddbwyll-board of Math son of Mathonwy, on which the pieces play by themselves…" It is a long list, and I was sweating freely before I was done.

"Well said." Talhaearn was gazing still into the western sky, where the light was dying now. The cold of evening was beginning to bite, though I had hardly noticed it till then; it was time, I thought, to make an end. Drawing my cloak closer around me, I asked, "Was it Cai, then, who prevailed at the Crowning?"

"Not so," said Talhaearn, turning his face back to me, and still faintly smiling. "When the day itself came, all the Lords of the Island brought forth their treasures to present to Arthur, where he sat enthroned before them, until the whole room was full of the jewel-bright colors of silks and adornments, and the firelight gleamed and glittered on bright steel and silver and red-glowing gold. When at last the procession ended, Arthur stood up, tree-tall in his robes of purple and amber—robes as bright and glowing as those cloud-banners in the sky tonight!—and asked if any other wished to come forward before he chose and honored the one who had brought him the best gift of all. And out of the crowd there came a young boy, with a plain blue robe upon him, and his hair dark as the raven's wing, and a harp in his hands. 'Lord King,' he said in a firm clear voice, 'I have brought you a song, and ask your leave to sing it now before this company.'

"Arthur smiled and gave the boy permission to sing. And the song that he sang was a song of Arthur's twelve battles, and the great victories he won there over his enemies. And so vivid and cunning-wrought was that song, and so great the boy's *awen*, that every one of us there, well though we knew the story, was roused and caught and enchanted by his singing. And no one moved or spoke in that hall until the song was done.

"When the last words had died into silence, there was a sigh like a high wind in that place, as every man of us let out his hard-held breath. And Arthur, who had listened as intently and sighed as hard as any of us, asked the boy his name. And the boy replied that his name was Taliesin."

At this I sat up straighter, startled out of my stillness.

"Yes," said Talhaearn, as if I had spoken, "it was he. And Arthur thanked him for his singing. 'But why, Taliesin,' he asked, 'when others have brought me gold and weapons and treasure from the whole of Britain and beyond, did you think to come today bringing me merely words?'

"At that Taliesin smiled. 'Steel rusts, Lord King,' he said, 'silk crumbles, and gold is lost in the ground. But I bring you the gold of the Bards, which is their praise, and that shall last as long as the world stands and men remember our tongue.'

"Then Arthur smiled back at him and said, 'You have given me the best gift of all.' And he gave Taliesin a golden torque for his throat, and a golden ring for his finger, and a chair beside him at his own High Table for that night's feasting. And in after days he made him *pencerdd* to his Court, and Primary Chief Bard of the Island of Britain.

"And many and strange were the journeys that they went on together thereafter, and the many the wonders and marvels and dangers that they saw, until the Day of Camlann came at last, and Arthur went into the West."

With that Talhaearn rose stiffly to his feet and stretched himself to his full height. "But now the sun has followed him, and it is time for us go home. I will teach you more of their adventures tomorrow." And he put out his hand for my shoulder, to lead him down the hill. And we walked slowly down through the purple twilight, and into the smoky firelight of Cyndrwyn's hall, and I heard no more tales from him that night. But the pictures he had painted in my mind stay with me till this day, and I feel sometimes as if it had been I myself who had stood in that hall, and seen the treasures, and heard that first song of Taliesin: for such was the power of Talhaearn, who was truly called *Tad Awen*, Father of Inspiration.

As for the other tales he had mentioned, he did eventually tell them to me.

But that, O my children, is a story for another day.

XXII. Insult

A little blood goes a long way, especially when it is one's own. A spoonful appears as a serious wound, a cupful seems a mortal one, and a good nosebleed looks at first glance like a throat-slitting. But harder to wash out than blood itself is insult: *sarhaed*, as we are calling it now in the common tongue. For that stain, sometimes more blood is required—and sometimes another solvent.

Ever since my arrival at Llys-tyn-wynnan, I had had my eye on Keinwen, the fair daughter of Hueil Goch. Now as winter deepened, keeping us all enclosed together in Cyndrwyn's hall for days on end, I found my thoughts more and more returning to her beauty, and to my own desires. Busy though my master Talhaearn kept me now, and hard though he worked me through the days, often I lay awake at night dreaming of a fine red mouth, and creamy skin, and flame-gold hair. And I set myself to watch for my chance to do more than dream.

There was, of course, an obstacle in my way, and a large one at that. Goronwy son of Gronw was his name, and he had all the height and breadth and strength of arm I lacked—that, and a fine, full mustache that made the scanty growth on my upper lip seem even more pathetic than it was. Our initial confrontation had been in words, and there I had the victory, but words were all I got by it—words of praise, and maybe an admiring look from Keinwen, before she turned her gaze back to Goronwy again, and kept it there. Clearly more direct action was needed; but what it was to be, as yet I did not know.

That was how the situation stood one cold day not long before midwinter, when I came out of the stables after seeing to Talhaearn's pony and heard the sound of cheering. Curious, I traced it to the practice ground outside the court, where a group of the young warriors were entertaining themselves. It was a day of broken clouds and shadows after several days of heavy rain, and the tracks were deep in mud, so much so that even the better weather had not tempted Cyndrwyn out to hunt. Instead, someone had set up a wooden post as a mark, and the young men were taking it in turn to throw spears at it. As I came up, Goronwy made a mighty cast and hit the post dead center, and another cheer went up. Looking around, he saw me and smiled, but it was not a friendly smile—more the smile of a wolf who sees dinner approaching. "Ah," he said, "here is our Bard's horse-boy. Come and join us, horse-boy, and show us how well you would fight if you rode with the war-band as *bardd teulu*."

"Better would I fight, I think, than you would sing our success afterwards," I said, as the crowd parted for me. "What would you have me do?"

"Why, show us the strength of your arm, and the straightness of your eye. It is simple enough even for a horse-boy—there is the post, and here is a spear." And he held one out to me.

"The ash spear of a bard is his *awen*," I said, temporizing. The crowd looked expectant, and the Prince was watching me with interest.

"This one is of holly, then," laughed Goronwy. "Can you not throw it, little bardling?"

As I reached out to take it, he suddenly thrust it hard at me. I stepped back, slipped on the muddy ground, and fell, as Goronwy released the spear shaft. There was a burst of laughter, which quietened as I stood up. The spear shaft had struck me in the face, and my nose was bleeding. I wiped it with the back of my hand, and looked hard at Goronwy, and he stared back at me. If we had been dogs we would have been growling.

Then I turned away, facing the post, and stood for a moment hefting the spear in my hand, gauging its weight and balance. I was out of practice, but still... I wiped my nose again, tasting the blood in the back of my mouth, and thought. Blood shed is insult, but blood from the nose carries no payment. But there might be a way... I turned to the Prince, trying to sound calm. "Let us make this a contest, Lord, for the better entertainment of the household. I will throw against Goronwy now, if he will match me in storytelling tonight in the hall. And you shall judge the victor."

Cyndrwyn smiled. "Ah, now that should be a good contest. Let us have it so. Goronwy, fetch back your first spear, and you shall both cast. Then tonight, you shall both entertain us."

Goronwy looked uncertain, but after a moment he nodded and went to retrieve his spear. He was now, I thought, not so happy with his stratagem, but could see no way out of the situation he had created. "What shall we compete for, Lord?" he asked, coming back.

Cyndrwyn looked at me, still smiling. "Gwernin? What would you think a fair prize?"

"Oh," I said, "I would compete for something of little cost but great value." And I looked at Keinwen, standing near Goronwy. "A kiss from a fair lady would content me."

"Would you do this, lass?" the Prince asked her. And when she nodded, blushing, "What say you, Goronwy? Would this content you?"

"Yes, Lord," said Goronwy. His face, too, was red, but not from modesty. "I will play this game gladly."

"Then Gwernin shall cast the first spear," said Cyndrwyn, "and tonight you shall tell the first tale." And he stepped back, giving us room to throw.

I took a deep breath, settled myself, and drew back the spear, remembering all the things I had learned in my boyhood training. I had not been bad then... I sniffed, and tasted blood again in the back of my mouth, and threw. The spear sailed through the air with all the strength I could muster. It struck the post fairly and stayed there, quivering. But it was at least three finger-breadths from the center.

Now it was Goronwy's turn. As everyone watched in silence, he stepped to the line, drew back his arm, and threw, all in one movement. It was almost casual; it spoke of great practice and great confidence. Straight to the post his spear flew, and struck, and stayed. It was not dead center this time, but it was undoubtedly closer to the center than mine. I sighed.

Goronwy threw me a glance of triumph, and turned to Keinwen, who came happily into his arms. The kiss he claimed lasted long and long, and I did not enjoy the sight, but I made myself wait until it was over, and even to smile. Tonight in hall I foresaw my revenge, and hoped that it would be complete indeed. My ash spear, I thought, would take him as Llew Llaw Gyffes' took Gronw Pebr, and no defense he could put between us would stop it. And then we would see who Keinwen would prefer.

In the meantime, I now had another problem: I needed Talhaearn's permission to perform in hall, and I had not yet got it. Chewing my lip thoughtfully, I headed for the fire-hall, where I knew he was usually to be found at this hour. Manipulation was unlikely to work in his case: it would better, and certainly safer, to be straightforward with the thing. I had never yet tried to deceive Talhaearn, but I had a fair idea what his response might be if I did so and he found me out, and the prospect was not inviting.

I found the old Bard in a corner of the hall, tuning his harp in the dim firelight. Three or four of the women-folk were nearby, working at their sewing and obviously hoping for music by and by. This was something I had not bargained for, and I came to a halt uncertainly, but Talhaearn had already heard and recognized my step, and looked up from his tuning. "Gwernin?"

"Yes, master," I said. "Is there anything you are needing?"

"Na, na," said Talhaearn. But he continued to look at me.

I took a deep breath. "I have a thing to ask of you."
"Yes?"

"I have—the Prince has asked me –" I paused and tried again. "Goronwy mab Gronw challenged me just now to a throwing competition, and I suggested to Cyndrwyn that I would throw against Goronwy if he would compete against me tonight in telling stories, and they both agreed. And I threw and lost, and now—and now I have remembered that I need your permission to speak in hall."

"And have not yet got it," said Talhaearn, and turned back to his tuning, leaving me to stand silent before him. I was beginning to know, however, that this was one of his ways to test me, or to punish my presumption, and so I stood quietly, trying to ignore the curious glances of the women. One of them, I realized, was Rhiannedd, the little dark girl who I had noticed sometimes with Keinwen. She was smiling a little, looking at me as if I amused her, and I felt the hot blood rising into my face at her glance. I turned back to Talhaearn, but I was aware of her still, as I had not been before.

After what seemed a very long time, Talhaearn looked up at me again. "You are still here," he said quietly, making it half-question, half-statement. "Is there yet something you are wanting?"

"Yes, master. I wait for your permission, if you will give it."

"You have not asked for it," said Talhaearn. "You have only told me that you have done a foolish thing, and I have taken note of it. Is there more?"

Behind me I heard a giggle, and my face turned hotter still. "I—yes, yes there is. I am asking your permission to speak in hall tonight."

"Ah." Talhaearn nodded. "And do you expect to get it?"

Another of the women giggled; I wished I could sink into the floor and disappear. "I—I am not knowing. But—but if I do not speak, with the Prince expecting it, I will look very foolish."

"Indeed. And you are implying that this will make me look foolish by association?" Talhaearn's voice was still calm and even, but I cringed. I remembered my friend Edern saying of the old Bard's reputation: *folk here call him a proud, cold man, with a tongue that can flay you alive while you stand.* I thought I knew now what they meant.

"Yes," I said. And waited. At least there were no more giggles behind me.

"Ah," said Talhaearn again, and struck a few experimental notes from his harp. "Then I think I had better command you to speak. But you have *not* got my permission, and presently there will be a price for that." And he turned back to his harp, and began to play.

After a moment I mastered myself enough to turn away and leave the hall. If I was going to compete against Goronwy, at I knew not what cost, I had better prepare myself, and be good at it. Keinwen's kiss was likely to be dearly bought indeed.

As I left I felt Rhiannedd's eyes following me, but I could not meet her glance. I already felt as if I had been stripped naked before her, and I was afraid to see amusement in her face—or worse, pity. If I had looked at her then, what came after might have been different—or it might not have.

But that, O my children, is a story for another day.

XXIII. King Arthur's Raid on Hell

The performer who says that he is never nervous lies. We have all known it—the quiver along the nerves, the flutter in the stomach, the shortness of breath, the accelerating beat of the blood. Even Taliesin felt it sometimes beforehand, when the stakes were high enough. (I remember—oh, yes, I remember!) Some feel it to extremes, so that it cripples their performance, either in the errors they make, or in the cost afterwards to body and mind. For others it merely lends spice to the occasion. So I have generally found it myself—a heightening of the senses, an increased aliveness as the moment of challenge approaches. But I have seldom been as nervous as I was that evening in Cyndrwyn's court, knowing that even if I won the cost would be high, and if I lost—but I would not let myself think of that. I could not afford the distraction.

The evening meal was over, and the trestle tables cleared away. Cyndrwyn sat at the upper end of the hall in his great chair, with Angharad his wife beside him and his favorite hounds sprawled in the rushes at his feet. With night the rain had come on again, and I could hear it now and then, in moments of quiet, hushing on the thatch and splashing steadily into the puddles under the eves. The central fire had been built up, and the blue wood-smoke hung thick under the roof-tree and twisted now and again in the icy draft from the door-place when someone pushed the hanging curtain aside. The hall was full, benches and floor and all, with the people of the *llys* who had crowded in to hear the competition between myself and Goronwy. As I stood waiting, not far from the Prince, my glance traveled over their faces—old

181

and young, men, women and children, all the faces that had
become familiar to me in the handful of months since I had
come here with Talhaearn. Faces curious, eager, expectant,
and not unfriendly—but none of them that of a friend who
would stand by me however well or ill I did, my master
Talhaearn least of all. For just a moment, in that crowded
hall, I felt very much alone.

Then the Prince, who had been speaking to his lady wife,
looked up and caught my eye, and beckoned for me and
Goronwy to come forward. "Are you ready?" he asked us. "I
am," I said, and Goronwy beside me made some affirmative
noise that might have been "yes." Glancing up at him, I saw
his tongue come out unconsciously to moisten his lips, and
he swallowed; and I realized he was as nervous as I was, if
not more so. With that my confidence came flooding back.
This time we would meet on my ground, not his.

"Goronwy, then, will go first," said Cyndrwyn, still regarding us friendly-wise. We nodded solemnly, and I went a
little aside, to stand by my master where he sat on his bard's
stool with his harp silent between his knees, while Goronwy
took his stance facing the hall and began.

He told the tale of a cattle-raid he had been on last
summer. At first his words came haltingly, and with pauses,
but with the encouraging murmurs of his friends, and the
obvious admiration of Keinwen (sitting near the front and
smiling at him), he began to get into his stride and even to
enjoy himself. He told of the journey; the stealthy approach
in the night; the surprising of the cattle-guard and the blow-
by-blow combat he had exchanged with one of them; and the
running off of the cattle. He even remembered to mention—
briefly!—the achievements of the other men in the party. By
the time he finished, to the cheers of the crowd—some of
whom had been along on the raid—he was grinning broadly,
and I was frowning. This would not be so easy as I had
supposed. Goronwy was popular with his fellows, and now I

saw why, for all men love to hear themselves praised, and he had not been ungenerous. I should have to go carefully.

"That was well told," said Cyndrwyn, and he beckoned his cup-bearer, who came forward with a horn of mead for Goronwy. And when Goronwy had gone to join his friends on the benches, the Prince turned to me, still smiling. "So, Gwernin," he said, as I stepped forward, "what do you have for us now?"

"With your permission, Lord," I said, "the tale of another raid, but not for cattle." Outside I could hear the wind rising; the hall had fallen silent to listen. I smiled. "This is the story of King Arthur's journey to Annwn, and his raid on Hell itself."

"This tale I would hear gladly," said Cyndrwyn, his eyes sparkling. "Let you begin." And so I did.

"In winter's darkness, even as now we are," I said, "this tale begins, at the place called Caer Camel, one of Arthur's chief courts, where the King had come to keep the Midwinter feast with his lady wife Gwenhwyfar, and his Companions, and all their folk besides. And one evening as they sat at their meat, into the hall came the gatekeeper, Glewlwyd Mighty-grasp. 'Lord King,' he cried, 'come out and see! It is a great wonder, and I do not know what it means!'

"Arthur and all his people came out of the hall; and behold, in the eastern sky there shone a great star, as bright and as red as a firedrake. They looked up at it and exclaimed, some in awe and some in fear and some in both together. Arthur himself looked at it and marveled, and he asked if anyone there could explain this sight, for he could not. And Emrys son of Myrddin, who was in those days Arthur's Chief Bard, spoke up.

" 'Lord King,' he said, 'last night I dreamed, and in that dream I stood beside a fortress whose name I did not know. And as I stood there, I heard a voice of one within the fortress, crying out and lamenting his imprisonment. Then I

183

awoke, and I knew the voice for that of Mabon son of Modron, who was stolen from his mother's side before he was three days old, and none now knows where he lies. It is he who must read you this riddle, and no other.'

" 'If none knows where he lies, then who shall find him?' asked Arthur. 'Can you do so, O my Bard?'

" 'Far have I traveled in my long life, and much do I know of this world,' said the old Bard, 'and yet there are those who have lived longer than I, and know more. I will seek them out and ask if any knows where Mabon is confined.'

" 'Go, then, and ask,' said Arthur, 'and when you bring me word of his prison, we shall go there and free him.'

"Far to the north Emrys traveled, to the distant marshland where the Blackbird of Kilgwri lived. 'O Bird,' he said to her, 'so old are you, that you know the names of all men, living or dead. Can you tell me where Mabon lies imprisoned?'

" 'Alas,' said the bright-eyed Blackbird, 'although I have lived so long that I have worn a smith's anvil down to the size of an nut, only through sharpening my beak on it once a year, yet I do not know where in this world Mabon lies. But if you come with me, I will take you to one older than I who may know.'

"They journeyed until they came to a mossy glade in the deep forest where the Stag of Rhedynfre lived. 'O Stag,' said Emrys, 'your life is long and your ears are keen—have you heard where Mabon lies imprisoned?'

" 'Alas,' said the brown-coated Stag, 'although I have lived so long that I have watched an acorn grow into a mighty oak, age, and fall, and turn to dust, yet I do not know where in this world Mabon lies. But if you come with me, I will take you to one older than I who may know.'

"They journeyed until they came to a trackless glen in the shadow of the mountains, where the light beneath the trees was only a green twilight even at midday, and there they found the ancient Owl of Cwm Caw Llwyd. 'O Bard,' hooted the gray-feathered owl, 'I know who you are, your birth and kindred and fame, and I have forgotten more than you will ever know. But although I have lived so long that I have seen two forests grow up in this glen and be cut down, before this present forest grew, yet I do not know where in this world Mabon lies. But if you come with me, I will take you to one older than I who may know.'

"Far and far they journeyed, until at last they came to a high mountain where the Eagle of Gwernabwy lived. 'O Bard,' said the sharp-clawed Eagle, 'Eldest of all the birds am I, and in my lifetime I have seen the very mountains themselves wear away to pebbles, yet even I do not know where in this world Mabon lies. But if you come with me, I will take you to one older than I who may know.'

"Long and long they journeyed, until they came at last to a deep lake and saw before them the oldest creature of all, the Salmon of Llyn Llyw. 'O Salmon,' said Emrys then—and he was weary, for despite all his powers he was only a man!— 'far have you journeyed in your lifetime, and all the lakes and rivers and oceans of this world do you know. Can you tell me where Mabon lies imprisoned?'

" 'I can,' said the silver-scaled Salmon. 'His prison lies on the shores of the Dark Land itself, in the castle of Arawn Lord of Annwn, and I alone of all the creatures on this earth can lead you there; but you must bring an army with you when you come, for none but the bravest can pass those gates and come out again as living man.'

" 'Salmon,' said Emrys, smiling, 'my thanks to you. In a year and a day, we will meet you at Severn-mouth, and follow where you lead, though it be to Hell itself.' "

(I paused for a moment. In all that crowded hall there was no sound but those of wind, and rain, and hearth-fire. I smiled and went on.)

"When he had heard the news, Arthur gathered his men and his three ships, and brought them to Aber Hafren as his Bard had promised. Prydwen and Gwennen and Bronwen were the names of the ships, each of them more beautiful than the last, and five-score men in each of them. And there on the appointed day they met the ancient Salmon, himself tree-long and mighty, and followed him away from the land and into the trackless sea. Nine days and nights they sailed without sight of land, over green waves like mountains, and all the time the Dragon-Star burned above them. At last black clouds came up from the west and covered sun and star and sky and all, and they sailed on through storm and darkness, following the Salmon as their only hope. Then far in the west through the bitter rain they saw a tiny spark of light, which grew as they came nearer until it was a beacon-fire burning on a high black tower, and that rising in the midst of a mighty fortress on a dark shore. 'Here is the place you seek, Arthur,' cried the Salmon then. 'I have done as I promised—the next deed is yours to do!' And with a flash of his tail he was gone.

"The ships came to land, and the warriors gathered on the beach, and they climbed a winding path to the gates of the *caer* above them. As they went up the black walls towered higher and higher over them, and the three-score-hundred men who stood on them called down mockingly to the three hundred who came. But Arthur cried, 'Open now the gate for Arthur King of the Britons,' and the gate swung open, and the gate-keeper who stood within led them through the fortress to a lofty gold-roofed hall.

"And when they came into the hall, they saw that it was hung with tapestries of many-colored silks, and lit with fifty-score silver lanterns, and each lantern had within it ten candles of the finest beeswax, which burned with a steady flame. In the midst of that hall they saw a man sitting upon a charven chair of gold; and his hair and beard were as black as jet, and his skin as white as the fresh snow of one night, and his eyes as green as the grass below the walls of Caer Camel in the first week of May; and the robe on him was of blood-red silk embroidered with thread of gold. 'Be welcome, strangers,' he said in deep voice which rang throughout the hall like a bronze bell. 'Tell me your names, and from what country you come, and why you are here.' And that asking without first offering hospitality was grave discourtesy, as you all know well.

" 'I am Arthur King of the Britons,' said Arthur, 'and my mission to you, Lord, is easily told. I seek Mabon son of Modron to set him free, and I have heard that you hold him prisoner here.'

" 'Not for gold or silver,' said the green-eyed Lord of Annwn, 'shall Mabon ever be set free, but only for the doing of a task.'

" 'Let you but name that task,' said Arthur, 'and if I can do it, it shall be done.'

" 'Long years ago,' said Arawn, 'I alone ruled over all this land. Then one day came a stranger, and warred on me, and I could not defeat him; for however many blows I struck him, always he rose up stronger than before. At last I made truce with him, and gave over half of my land and three of my greatest treasures to seal the peace: and these were the Speckled Ox, whose collar is of gold and who alone can draw any cart, however heavy it might be; and the Cauldron of Pen Annwn, which can hold enough meat to feed every man in this castle, and still be full when they all have eaten their fill; and the Sword of Llemnawg the Strong, which opens every door. If you can meet my enemy in combat and slay him, and bring back these three treasures to my hall, then Mabon is yours.'

" 'How shall we travel to meet this enemy,' asked Arthur, 'and where in this land shall we find him?'

" 'Mabon himself shall be your guide,' said Arawn, 'and three and three hundred silver-white stallions shall bear you; but I will have a surety for your return. I see one here in your company whose *awen* burns within him like a white flame: your Bard Emrys shall bide here in my hall and sing for me until you come back.'

" 'A short time that will be,' said Arthur. 'And when we return, Lord, be very sure that I will keep you to our bargain.'"

(I paused again. The hall was if possible quieter than before; even the rain had stopped. I drew a deep breath and went on.)

"For three days the Company rode across Arawn's gray land, which neither snow nor rain can wet, and where neither winter nor summer ever comes. Arthur and Kai and Bedwyr led, and Mabon rode beside them as their guide: a beardless, slender, golden boy he was, glad beyond words to be out of his prison. 'Lad,' said Arthur to him as they rode, 'tell me where we are going, if you can, and against whom we shall fight.'

" 'His name is Hafgan,' said Mabon, 'and we shall meet him and fight before his *caer*. He has many warriors, and strong indeed are the walls that guard his treasures. Only by his death can you come at them and buy my freedom.' And he smiled.

"At last they saw before them a gray fortress upon a high hill, and in front of it a vast army standing ready for battle. Arthur saw that they were greatly outnumbered, but it was not in him to retreat, so he stopped his men and set them in good order. Then he rode forward slowly with Mabon beside him, and from the other group a man came spurring out to meet them, a tall man in shining black armor with a golden crown on his helm. 'Who are you, Lord,' he cried out to Arthur, 'and why do you come here in my land with your war-band? For I have not done you wrong.'

" 'I am called Arthur, King of the Britons,' said Arthur, 'and if your name be Hafgan, I have come here to take your head, in satisfaction of a vow.'

" 'Have I no choice but to fight you?' asked Hafgan.

" 'None, by my God,' said Arthur.

" 'Then draw your sword,' said Hafgan, 'and let us straightway begin.'

"With that Mabon lifted a hunting horn and blew it, and Arthur's men charged forward with a great cry. Arthur drew his sword, and it met Hafgan's, and they spoke no more that day but with steel.

"In the first hour of that fight, Kai slew a hundred men, and Bedwyr slew two hundred. Menw mab Teirgwaed slew three score and one before he fell, and Gwarthgydd mab Caw slew twice that number. Four score men and two was Rheiddwn's count, and Ysgawd son of Glew clove five-score men before his own blood flowed. Six score and three men Isgofan Hael killed with his great sword before he himself felt death's chill, and Isgawn son of Ban died on a hill of bodies; Gwydre Llaw Goch cut down two hundred, and splintered shields he scattered all around. No man before or since has seen such valor as Arthur's war-band showed that day; with their red blood they bought Mabon, and great was the slaughter that they made there.

"Arthur was laughing as he fought, though his own blood ran thick upon him; and his sword Caledfwlch sang as she repaid blow with blow. Hafgan had long since cast away the broken remnants of his shield, and only his fierce pride kept him afoot with wounds past counting. At last his sword-stoke missed, and Caledfwlch came down upon him like lightning, cutting through armor and bone and flesh and all, to cleave his heart. Even as he fell mortally wounded, Arthur swung again and struck off his head; and this he tied to his own saddle by its long black hair, and slung Hafgan's sword in its scabbard beside it. Then he stood still at last and looked around him. Of all who had fought on that field, only five men besides himself remained alive: Bedwyr the Gentle and Kai the Fair, Manawydan Long-Sight and Gwrgi Golden-Hair, and lastly Mabon the Young. Hafgan's army they had slaughtered to a man, but the gates of his fortress stood closed against them still.

" 'Back from here we cannot go,' said Arthur to his friends, 'without the treasures we were sent to find.'

" 'Lord, can you name them for me again?' asked Manawydan. 'For I am unsure of my memory.'

" 'An ox, and a cauldron, and a sword,' said Arthur. 'But how shall we come at them now? For the door we needs must open is still closed.'

" 'By God's Word,' swore Manawydan, '*that* is the key: Llemnawg's—no, Hafgan's—sword, which opens every door!'

" 'Then we shall try it,' said Arthur, 'and God send that you are right.' And with that he drew the sword from the scabbard where he had hung it, and stood before the oaken door of the fortress, and swung at it. The shining blade sliced through wood and iron and stone as if through water, and the gate lay open before them.

"They bound up their wounds then, and set the people in the fortress to work to dig a great pit, and there with many tears they buried their friends. Then, when they had taken rest and food, they harnessed the Speckled Ox to a wagon, and Arthur alone lifted the mighty Caldron onto its bed—a feat beyond the strength of most men!—and they set off.

"The way was long, but at last they reached Caer Annwn again, and the porter led them once more to the gold-roofed hall. And there Arawn awaited them, sitting in his great carven chair, and beside him Emrys the Bard sat playing on his harp.

" 'My Lord,' said Arthur then, 'I have done as I promised, and brought back to you your Ox, and your Cauldron, and your Sword.'

" 'And is Hafgan dead?' asked Arawn, frowning.

" 'He is.' And Arthur pulled the bloody head out of the sack where he had carried it, and flung it down before Arawn, and drew Caledfwlch from his scabbard. 'Now give us leave to go, and to take Mabon with us, as you did promise.'

"Arawn smiled, and he spoke a word of Power. The sword fell from Arthur's hands and rang on the floor of the hall, and Arthur himself and all those with him stood like stone, unable to move or speak. 'If I wished, man,' said Arawn then, 'I could chain you now with Mabon in my black dungeons, never again to see the light of the sun, or taste clean water, or breathe the free air. Give thanks to your God that I do not do so. Take with you him for whom you came, and leave while you still can: your Bard Emrys shall stay here with me, for I am grown accustomed to his song, and would not be without it.'

"Then the old Bard put a hand on his strings to still them. 'Lord,' he said, 'grant me that I may sing one song for Arthur before he goes.'

" 'It shall be as you wish, O my Bard,' said Arawn. 'For indeed, it is only for your pleasure that I leave him man alive, and free.'

"Then Emrys smiled, and he began to sing and to play. And such was the power of his *awen*, that everyone in the hall felt themselves overwhelmed with grief, and Arawn himself began to weep. Then the music changed, and suddenly all their hearts were light within them, and Arawn himself was laughing. And for a third time the music changed, and upon his throne Arawn closed his eyes, and slumber took him, and all of his men as well.

"Then the power of the enchantment was broken, and Arthur and his men were freed, and could move and speak as before. And Emrys stood up with a smile, and placed his harp—still playing by itself—carefully on the chair where he had been sitting. And so they came away.

"They took the Sword, and the Ox, and the Cauldron—all bought by blood—and left the fortress, and none sought to hinder them. They took ship in Prydwen, and sailed, and left the Dark Land behind them. And seven alone they came at last to Severn-side on one clear spring night, with the Dragon-Star still burning low in the east before them. 'Tell me,' said Arthur then to Mabon, 'what is the meaning of that star? For it was to read that riddle that we came to free you from your prison.'

" 'Not hard, Lord,' said Mabon. 'That Fire-Drake is your Red Dragon, and so long as it burns in the sky, so shall your memory burn in the hearts of men.' And under the light of the Star they came ashore."

For a moment after I finished the hall was quiet, so quiet that the dripping of the rain from the roof sounded loud, and far away in the forest I heard the cry of an owl. Then the room exploded in noise, in the drumming of feet and clapping of hands and crying of applause, so that it seemed to shake me as I stood: for I was far spent with the effort of telling so great a tale, and one that I had never told before, having learned it only recently from Talhaearn. Then the Prince himself was putting his own mead-horn into my hands and bidding me drink. I took a mouthful of the golden liquid, and swallowed, and the world came back into focus, which before had seemed a little fuzzy around the edges, a little unreal. But then, it is not often that one travels to the halls of Arawn, and comes back as living man.

I raised my eyes from the mead-horn and looked up at the Prince, who was smiling and thanking me for my performance. And beyond him I saw Talhaearn, still seated on his bard's stool, and watching me with the unreadable expression which I had seen once or twice before on his worn face; and the warm glow which the mead had been starting in my stomach turned to ice. I still had a price to pay, and it was likely to be a heavy one: for not only had I now spoken without permission, but I had also told a tale which I had been expressly forbidden to tell. That I had told it, as it seemed, very well indeed was not likely to prove an adequate excuse.

Then the Prince was leading Keinwen forward, and she was in my arms. And in the process of claiming my prize— which I did with enthusiasm—I missed seeing several things I should have seen, and was the poorer for it thereafter.

But that, O my children, is a story for another day.

XXIV. Midwinter Night

There are two points of balance in the turning year: midsummer and midwinter, when the sun reaches its highest and lowest points. As in the brightest, longest days we can foresee the decline into darkness, so in the pit of darkness we can look upwards and foresee the light. In hope and in despair are each the seeds of the other: in the year, and in the life of a man. But on the morning before this particular midwinter night, the world looked dark to me indeed.

It is true that my storytelling in Cyndrwyn's hall had succeeded beyond my wildest hopes, and moreover had won me Keinwen's kiss, which I had longed for. But one kiss, and that in public, is hardly a satisfaction of desire, however long it lasts; and my storytelling success looked likely to cost me dear, for I had doubly defied my master Talhaearn in winning it, and he was not one lightly to forgive such defiance. It is true that when I put him to bed that night, combing out and plaiting his long iron-gray hair, he had said nothing of punishment, but that had not relieved my mind: rather it gave my fear and uncertainty time to grow. And the following morning he had only reminded me to come prompt and prepared to my harp lesson later in the day. All in all, by the time I sought him out in our lodging that afternoon, I was worried indeed, and the greeting I got did not abate my nervousness. He seemed absent-minded, a rare thing for him, and listened to my playing, or rather my succession of errors, with an unvarying frown and no comment.

At last, when I had paused, uncertain which tune to play—or rather mis-play!—next, he held up a hand, saying,

194

"That will do for today, Gwernin. Put your harp away now, for we must talk."

"Yes, master," I said, almost thankfully, and stowed her in her leather case as carefully as I could, for my nervousness was making me clumsy. And I waited, and waited, until at last Talhaearn sighed.

"Gwernin," he said then, "I do not know what to do with you. You flout my commands, and offer neither explanation nor apology. Who are you trying to impress? For it cannot be me."

"I—there was –" I stopped, confused. I had not expected this.

"Yes?" His voice was still mild and even. I took a deep breath.

"A girl. Keinwen. I wanted –"

"Oh, yes," said Talhaearn. "I know what you wanted. And have you got it?"

"I—no. I thought –"

"Did you? Did you indeed? I have not seen signs of it," said Talhaearn scathingly.

I closed my eyes for a moment; it did not help. "No, master."

" 'No' to your thinking, or to my seeing? Although indeed it could apply to both. Gwernin, I think you are either too old or too young to be my student, for your mind is not on your business. Are you sure that you wish to continue?"

The shock of this suggestion took my breath away. I had been prepared for pain and humiliation, but not for the snatching away of all my hopes. "Master," I gasped, "I—I do indeed wish your teaching!" I raised my hands in an involuntary gesture of supplication, then let them fall. "I—I beg of you, do not turn me away!"

"Ha!" Talhaearn gave a bark of laughter. "And why should I believe your words? Your actions speak very loudly to the contrary."

"I—I know. I—please, do not send me away."

"Hmm." Talhaearn stroked his beard. "And if I do not, will you promise to amend? Follow all my instructions, without failure or question? Never look at a girl again, unless I bid it? Well?"

"I –" I could not speak; my mouth was too dry. I tried again. "I will try. I will do my best. I—I cannot promise more." I felt hot tears on my face; I knew it was not enough. "I am sorry."

To my surprise Talhaearn laughed again, really laughed. "Well, well," he said after a moment. "I suppose I must be content with that. At least you are honest. And even Gwion did not always obey me, though he did not complain when I beat him for it afterwards. You do not think yourself better than Gwion, I hope?"

"No!" The idea was incredible: Gwion was Taliesin, his boyhood name. "No, master, never!"

Talhaearn chuckled. "Are you willing, then, to accept the price?"

"Yes, master," I said, and stood up. "Very willing."

"Then you know what to do." Talhaearn was serious now. "I believe the same hazel rod will serve—it is in the corner." And he stood up as well and took the rod from my hand, and I pulled off my tunic and knelt down before him.

The beating went on for what seemed a very long time, and it was not pleasant. Talhaearn had a way of pausing for a moment between his strokes, so that the anticipation was almost worse than the pain, and that was bad enough. Clenching my teeth, I managed not to cry out—I was of man's years, after all, and should bear it like one!—but before he was through my face was wet again with tears, and there was more than one trickle of blood making its way down my back to tickle my bare ribs. I understand now that it was his intention not merely to punish me, but to lodge this moment deeply in my memory, so that he would not have to repeat his efforts. In that he certainly succeeded, but at the time all I knew was that it hurt.

At last, however, it was over. As I struggled painfully back into my woolen tunic, Talhaearn surprised me yet again. "Go you now and see Gwawr the herbalist," he said. "I think she will be expecting you. And Gwernin –"

"Yes?"

"It was a very well told story indeed. But *next time*"—and I winced at that—"you might first inquire if I plan to tell the same tale soon myself." And when I turned back in horror at this new and previously unrecognized offence, he shook his head at me. "Na, na, away with you now. Enough!" And I went.

Gwawr the herbalist was indeed expecting me in her hut at the back of the compound. She was one of the women who had been in the hall the day before and witnessed my dressing-down by Talhaearn. Moreover, as I soon discovered, she was also the mother of little dark-haired Rhiannedd, who was there helping grind some aromatic mess in a mortar, and who showed no signs of leaving when I arrived. I would have turned and gone away again, however sore my back, but Gwawr stopped me. "Come in, boy, and sit down. I thought we would be seeing you presently." She put a firm hand on my shoulder and I gasped, and she shifted her grip quickly. "Fool that I am! But here, let me help you off with that. Rhiannedd, the green jar with the white thread on it. Now, Gwernin, sit down."

I sat on the bench with hanging head while she talked on behind me. Taking off the tunic again had hurt even more than putting it back on, but presently cool fingers began to spread something soothing over the burning weals on my back. It was a while before I realized that the fingers in question were not Gwawr's, but by that time it seemed too late to object.

197

When she had finished, Rhiannedd bound a piece of linen over her work, and watched critically while I worked my way back once more into the clinging brown folds of my tunic. "He has a heavy hand," she said then.

"He does, but I deserved it." We stood looking at each other for a moment, while her mother worked on in the background, then we both smiled. "Would I be seeing you, maybe, tonight at the dancing?" I asked.

"It may be that you would." I saw that her eyes were blue, the deep dark blue that surrounds the stars in summer, and her softly curling hair was the dark glossy brown of ripe chestnuts. And she was still smiling. My heart felt suddenly light within me, and my back hurt hardly at all.

That was how I came to stand beside Rhiannedd at the midwinter bonfires that night, as the year turned again toward spring. Dancing there was, and music, and much food and drink; for the harvest that year had been good, and the Prince was generous. And if the priest from down-valley was there to lead us in the prayers for the birth of the Christ, we also had Talhaearn to sing the old songs to us, and the Prince Cyndrwyn himself to lead us in the dance round the fire. And although Rhiannedd was not by my side all the evening, yet always she came back again, and from time to time our hands touched as we stood together watching the leaping gold of the flames. And later in the night we withdrew for a while to a sheltered corner of the *llys*, and stood for a long time locked in each others' arms, and I kissed her, as the great stars of winter sailed silent overhead.

Just for a moment as we stood there, the two of us folded warm within my cloak, I had a sort of vision or waking dream. I saw a different midwinter bonfire, in a different place, and a man standing near it as I had stood earlier, with a woman beside him; and that man was Taliesin. Only for a moment the vision lasted; and then Rhiannedd turned up her face again to me to be kissed, and I forgot it.

And above us the sky in the east paled slowly towards morning.

It was a long time before I knew the meaning of that snatch of vision, and to this day I am still not sure whether it came from Taliesin himself, standing alone that night by the fires in Pengwern, or from some other source.

But that, O my children, is a story for another day.

XXV. Wolves

Wolves are always gray. Gray shadows in the dusk, stealing closer and closer to the sheep, their eyes full of hunger. Gray ships upon the gray sea, bringing their Saxon crews to land, ready to burn and kill. Gray steel of swords and spear-points, weapons of the war-band, carried with them as they set off to raid. But whether the wolves in question are our ancient enemies or our ever-new ones, or even we our own selves, the end is the same:

> ...like the pack on the track of the sheep that they rack,
> in the mud like a flood they will spill the bright blood...

And always, always, there will be wolves.

Some little while after Midwinter, the cold began to bite. It came with an icy wind cruel and sharp as wolf's teeth, and a chilling rain that changed first to sleet and then to snow. All night it howled round Cyndrwyn's halls, and morning brought little light and no improvement. Indeed, as the day wore on, the storm seemed to grow worse, and the cold even more bitter. All who could slept that night in the hall itself, rather than in the various hutments built around the *llys*, and I thought myself fortunate to command a scant strip of rush-strewn floor fairly close to the central fire, while my master Talhaearn spent the night on a pallet in the Prince's own brazier-warmed chamber, with a feather-stuffed pillow and a coverlet of martin skins to add to his comfort. I was glad to have him so well provided, for even in the hall it was not warm. The wind shook the shutters ceaselessly, and icy drafts prowled along the floor, so that sleep was hard to come by. I had my harp with me, and made myself popular for a while with some quiet practice, for I had found that even my poor playing was acceptable if the harp was in reasonable tune and there was no better musician by. And indeed, of the three musics, it is with the music of sleep that most harpers begin their mastery.

After a while a horn of beer appeared at my elbow, and I paused to make use of it and look around. Here and there in the hall there were quiet conversations going on, and other activities as well. At the far end of the room a baby was fretting; somewhat closer, a dog was searching for fleas. A higher than usual tongue of flame in the hearth showed me Goronwy and Keinwen lying against the east wall, face to face and intent on each other. This I no longer minded, for Rhiannedd herself was sitting close beside me, watching me play with the slightly amused smile which no longer troubled me, since I had discovered it was her habitual approach to the world, and as likely to be turned on her mother or the Prince Cyndrwyn himself as on me.

When the beer was gone I picked up my harp again. As I was checking the tuning, I heard it—a far-off, mournful howl, almost lost in the voice of the storm. I paused to listen, but there was only the one cry. Even a wolf, I thought, as I returned to my playing, would not be out on such a night by choice.

Towards morning the storm blew itself out. Dawn showed a world wrapped in crystal and silver, and glittering in the light of the early sun. As I picked my way across the courtyard towards the stable, I thought of Arawn's hall in Annwn—the same exquisite and unhuman beauty, indifferent to life or change, not so much unreal as belonging to a different reality altogether. Nothing seemed to move in that frozen world but myself; there was no sound but the crunch of snow under my boots and my own breathing. My breath itself smoked white in the bitter air, and the cold found out every gap in my defenses. Even the sunlight had little heat in it, and I was glad, when I had finished my business, to return to the smoky darkness of the hall, warm by contrast with the silver world outside, and human.

As the day went on, the clouds grew again in the west, and by evening snow was once more falling, but without the punishing wind of the night before. That night the hall was quiet except for the sort of snores or grunts that people make in deep sleep, but sometime towards morning I awoke, and heard once again that far-off distant howling. And this time it was answered by others, in a call and response sequence that went on for some while. I lay and listened until at last they quietened, and I drifted back to sleep. But my sleep was troubled. I dreamed of the forest, and eyes in the dark, yellow eyes that followed me however fast I fled, until at last shadowy figures leapt upon me, grasping and catching me to pull me down. Then I awoke to find it was dawn, and Rhiannedd was shaking my shoulder. "That was an ill dreaming," she said when she saw I was awake.

"It was." My heart was still pounding with the fear of it, but I reached out and caught her hand, smiling up at her, and she smiled back. "But it is over now." And indeed I thought it was.

It seemed I was not the only one to have heard the wolves in the night; there was some discussion of it over breakfast in the hall, and when a messenger came in presently to tell Cyndrwyn that the sheep folds had been attacked, everyone's interest redoubled. Some of the warriors decided to ride out and see if they could trail the pack, but they soon came back discouraged, for the snow, which was still falling, had covered the tracks. Goronwy offered to go and reinforce the sheep-guard, and asked for volunteers to join him. I was standing beside Talhaearn at that time, and whether because I was simply restless, or because the memory of the dream was still on me, and I wanted to face down my fear, I asked him suddenly, "Master, may I go with them?"

"Hmm," he said, cocking his head for a moment as if he listened to a voice I could not hear. "Yes, do you go. Take Llwyd if you need a mount. You have a good cloak?"

"I do," I said, and I hurried to join the group that was forming by the door.

If Goronwy was surprised to see me—his eyes widened as I came up, and his eyebrows rose into his shaggy hair—he took me with him all the same. And soon, mounted on Talhaearn's gray pony, I was making my way through the early twilight up the muddy track that led to the sheep folds, in company with a dozen other young men.

The shepherds were pleased to see us. They brought us into their hut and showed us several injured sheep being doctored there, and a couple of dead lambs. The flock was gathered in a pen, but the wolves, hidden by the falling snow and the darkness, had broken in before the shepherds were aware. Tonight they had built up fires around the pen, and we would take it in turn to man them. With luck, they said, the fires themselves would keep the wolves away, but one could never be sure.

Unlike most of the young men there, I owned no spear, but Goronwy had brought several extras and casually handed me one. It was the same holly-shafted spear I had thrown in our competition, not so very long ago. I hefted it in my hand, checking the shaft for marks of my own blood, but it was clean. Glancing up, I saw Goronwy grinning at me, his teeth very white under his red mustache. "Do you not worry, horse-boy," he said lightly, "I wiped it carefully afterwards." And he turned away before I could think of an adequate response.

He had split us up into pairs, two young men and a shepherd at each fire, with half of us in reserve in the hut getting warm, and he rotated us at regular intervals. After the first excitement had died down, we found the time dragged slowly. Staring into the fire, as we tended to do while warming ourselves, destroyed our night vision, but facing away from it, we faced the snow and the cold. Fortunately there was not much wind, but even so the chill crept into the bone. Like my mates, I was soon stamping my feet to keep the feeling in them, and blinking at the snowflakes which tickled my face and tried to settle on my cheeks and lashes. My cloak, too, was not so warm as I had thought. The shepherds, short dark men with weathered faces and big sheepskin hats, regarded us tolerantly, and the sheep, huddled in their pen like shaggy, snow-covered boulders, watched us all with their yellow eyes and narrow suspicious faces. Now and then one bleated or stirred restlessly. After a while I started to watch the sheep as much as the darkness, and the shepherds' dogs more than either. Their senses were sharper than mine; they would give the first alert.

When our turn came for the hut, I was full glad. We crowded around the fire, stuffing our mouths with stale barley-bannock and cold bacon—for we had left Cyndrwyn's hall before the evening meal—and sharing round a jug of beer. There was a little talk at first, mostly about the wolves, but after a while the warmth and food made us drowsy, and we sat blinking into the fire, half-dozing.

Goronwy, who was taking a break with us, looked around the circle. "Na, na," he said, "this will not do. How will we respond to an alarm, and most of us half-asleep? Horse-boy, do you tell us a story to keep the life in us."

I shook myself awake, frowning. Did this come under Talhaearn's performance ban? Well, I would deal with that later, and take my beating if need be. "What sort of tale would you have, then?" I asked.

"Something with blood in it," said Goronwy, and grinned, and "Yes!" said some of the others. "Something to stir the heart!"

"Hmm," I said, thinking briefly. "Would you hear the tale of Cuchulainn's weapon-taking, then? Here it is…"

This is an Irish tale, one that I had learned somewhere along the way during my summer wanderings. The young boy Cuchulainn, having heard from a Druid that whosoever took honor that day would have everlasting fame, but also a short life, went to the King his father and demanded weapons. Every weapon they brought him he broke, until at last the King gave him his own; and the same with chariots. Then Cuchulainn mounted his new chariot and rode out, and slew his first men, and came back bloody and victorious, with their heads hanging from his chariot-rail and their arms and armor beside him. It was just the story to appeal to Goronwy and his friends, who had never heard it before, and they listened open-mouthed, cheering at all the right spots, their sleepiness forgotten.

At the end Goronwy passed me the beer jug, now much depleted. "That was better than hot wine, horse-boy," he said. "We shall have to find you a new name."

" 'Storyteller' will do well enough," I grinned; and so they called me thereafter.

"Time we were stirring, and relieving the others," said Goronwy then, standing up and stretching. And we rose and went reluctantly back into the winter darkness.

The snow was coming down harder than ever, but I thought the clouds seemed to be thinning; and as I watched, the Bright One herself showed suddenly in the heavens, with a mottled silver skein of clouds sailing fast around her, and making it seem as if were she who was in rapid motion, and not they themselves. Then they thickened, and the dark closed in again; and quick on its heels, as if summoned, came the cry of the first wolf. It was answered almost immediately by a second, and then a third, and none of them was far away. All of us, new watchers and those who were half-way into the hut, turned toward the sound, heads up and spears ready, peering into the mealy flakes of snow that seemed to dance in the firelight, as if our own determination could somehow sweep aside that veil and show us our enemies.

The silence stretched out and out, and still we waited. At last Goronwy nodded to the men by the hut. "Get you in and warm you while you can, but be alert." And they went thankfully, while we others settled down to wait in their place. And gradually, as the time went by and nothing happened, we began to relax, and think more of our other enemy, the cold, which gnawed at us like wolves' teeth. But even as I stood there, stamping my feet from time to time like the rest, and shifting my cold hand on the spear-shaft, something within me was coming alert. Maybe it was the dream last night, and maybe it was the bard's other sense waking in me, as it had once or twice before, but I could feel motion somewhere out in the dark beyond the range of my eyes. When I concentrated, it went away, but always it came back again. The dogs felt it too; they were prick-eared and whining, but the wind was too light and uncertain to bring them the scent they were seeking.

For a moment I saw a flicker of light; I blinked, and it was gone. Then it came again, a pulsing light like flames. It was not before me; there was nothing there but snow and darkness. I closed my eyes, and understood: it was not with my own eyes I was seeing; the warning came from behind me. The hairs stood up on my neck, and I whirled, in time to see, across the sheep-pen, the flickering gray shadows come breaking out of the dark, running for the wall and the sheep inside. I gave a yell that roused my friends from their cold-induced stupor; then everything was confusion, men and dogs and wolves and sheep running and dodging and leaping and shouting in the wild firelight and the snow, and I somehow in the midst of it, trying to put my spear in the path of a wolf while avoiding the spears of my fellows. Fortunately they were more experienced at the hunt than I, and no one was killed, except for one wolf, slower or more unlucky than his fellows, who took Goronwy's spear in his side and snarled out his life in the snow, leaving a great puddle of blood, black on white in the firelight.

Presently the surviving wolves were gone, and everyone was picking themselves up and checking the damage. The sheep were mostly frightened but unhurt, although one ewe had a bleeding slash on her rump which the shepherds fussed over. Goronwy's following were almost as lucky, although one had slipped in the snow and taken a bad fall, and had to be helped indoors, limping on a wrenched knee. "I think," said Goronwy, "that they will not be back tonight, but I and Selyf will stay and watch a while to be sure. The rest of you, go and get what sleep you can. Oh, and Storyteller..." I turned, surprised, and he motioned to me with a jerk of his head. I went back, while the rest sorted themselves out and went indoors.

"You must have hearing like Cuchulainn himself," said Goronwy after a moment. "I would like to have you with me on the war-trail. How did you know they were coming, and from that side?"

I was looking down at the dead wolf. The yellow eyes were clouding, and the gray fur looked soft, soft, but the white teeth exposed in his death-grimace were sharp. I looked up at Goronwy then, and saw the kinship. He had blood on his sleeve, too, and I think it was not the wolf's. "I do not know," I said simply, and that was true enough. "I was watching the dogs... I think the dogs knew, and I turned, and saw them." And that was true, too, so far as it went.

Goronwy gazed at me a moment, out of those pale eyes so like the wolf's, and then nodded. "That is as good an answer as any. Go you in and get your rest, then, Storyteller. I think you have earned it tonight."

We rode back down to the *llys* in the morning, a bright sunny morning without snow or clouds. We laughed and boasted as we rode, and our breath and that of the ponies made a cloud around us in the cold, and their feet threw up the melting snow in clods behind us. Goronwy had skinned out his wolf, and carried the gray pelt flung over his pony's withers before him—not much to the pony's pleasure. He offered me the pelt later, and I took it, though not for any reason he could guess.

Talhaearn as usual had the last word. I had poured out all the tale of that night to him, and he sat for a while mulling it over. "Na," he said at last, "no beating is due to you this time. And do you know why?"

"I think so," I said. "But I hope you will tell me."

At that Talhaearn smiled thinly. "*Sa, sa,* I begin to have hopes of you. Well, then, because you did not speak this time for your own glory, but for the good of the war-band. You may make a *bardd-teulu* yet. But on this other matter..."

"Yes?" I said after a moment. "The warning I—saw? Master, I do not know what to think of it."

"And that is as it should be," said Talhaearn. And he smiled, and no more did I get from him then on that subject. So instead I went away and told the tale of my adventures to Rhiannedd, and it was properly appreciated.

But that, O my children, is a story for another day.

XXVI. The Making of Arthur's Crown

The learning that it takes to make a bard—or a master storyteller, for that matter—is not got in a few days, or even in a few seasons. The Irish, indeed, are said to take twenty years for its teaching—but then the Irish have not the Saxons on their eastern border, and coming closer to them every summer, as we had in those days. Quite apart from *cerdd tafod*, the craft of poetry itself—which comes in its own time, through aptitude and practice, and sometimes not at all—there are lists upon lists of names to be learned by heart, names of people and places, battles and weapons and treasures, and the songs and stories that go with them. Some of these are grouped in triads—the Three Loyal War-bands, the Three Noble Prisoners, the Three Futile Battles—and some are longer lists, such as the Twenty-Four Treasures of the Island of Britain, of which I spoke earlier. Talhaearn had been gradually teaching me many of these lists over the winter—yes, and testing me on them from time to time as well!—and his tongue could be sharp indeed if I stumbled or made mistakes. Sometimes, however, I found that I could interrupt his questions and get a breathing-space by asking for more details—and sometimes I got more than I bargained for.

Even so it happened, on one dark winter day not long after Imbolc. The two of us were sitting in one corner of Cyndrwyn's hall, as far out of the drafts from the door as might be; for though the bitter cold we had suffered earlier in that winter had somewhat relaxed its grasp, it was still a long while until spring. Talhaearn had been drilling me on triads again, and for some reason I was making hard going of it that day. "Na, na," said Talhaearn. "Three *golden* crowns, boy. Elmet's is silver. Start again."

" 'The Three Golden Crowns of the Island of Britain,' " I said carefully, " 'were the Crown of Maxen Wledig the Emperor, and the Crown of Bendigaidfran, and the Crown that Gofannon the Smith wrought for his sister's son Lieu of the Skillful Hand. But greater than any of these three was the Crown of Arthur, which went with him into the West, and lies no more in this land.' Master," I added hurriedly, "tell me more of Arthur's crown. Who made it, and how, and when? For you should know better than any man now alive what passed in those days."

Talhaearn, who had been about to speak, paused with his mouth half open, then closed it. "Hmm," he said after a moment. "Well, it is a long story, but we have the time. And you should hear this." And having said so much, he sat for a while in frowning thought, while I congratulated myself on the success of my stratagem and composed myself to listen.

"It was in the days of Arthur's later victories," said Talhaearn slowly, "when some of us began to have hope that such a crown might be needed. Indeed, we hoped at one point that he could push the Saxons back entirely from our shores, and rule again in the White Tower, in Londinium, like Maxen Wledig before him... But it was not to be. However, those of us who hoped, and who had the skills, began to make preparations. It was my Master himself who gathered the gold for the making of that crown, and I with him—I who was man-grown and many years a chief bard in those days, but followed him in this like an ignorant boy, for in the Druids' arts, the arts of magic and enchantment, I was not and never shall be his equal. In truth, in the history of the world, there have been few who were... But I was speaking of the Crown.

"The gold of seven kings went into it, and the gold of three emperors—and one of those was Maxen Wledig himself—and last and greatest in magic was the gold which was part of the treasure of Caer Sidhe, part of the spoils we brought back from that adventure…"

As he spoke his voice was changing, and his language. The words twisted, shifted, drifted backwards in time, half-way back to the Old Tongue itself. I had been struggling, that winter, to understand some of the older songs he had taught me in that language, but now it seemed as clear as if I had learnt it in my cradle. Talhaearn's voice went on, sweeping me with him, sweeping us both away, while such other people as were in the hall crept softly closer to listen.

"But before that journey could be gone or thought of, we first needed gold from seven British Kings. Now the crowned Kings of Britain in those days were Tudwal Tudclyd of Strathclyde, and Cynwyd of Eidyn, and Cynfarch Oer of Rheged, and Lleenawg of Elmet, and Maelgwn Hir of Gwynedd, and Brochfael Ysgithog of Powys, and Geraint mab Erbin of Dumnonia. And this gathering of gold from them was no easy task; for many considered Arthur to be an upstart, with no good claim to Uther Pendragon's chair, while others had ambitions themselves to be High King. And in order for our magic to be true and right and potent, we might not get the gold other than by free gift.

"So my Master devised a plan, and it was this: no King could risk the dispraise of a *pencerdd*, a master bard, however strong he felt himself, whether the dispraise was only by silence, the mere omission of his name from a list of Generous Ones, or by the sharper attack of satire. If each King were to believe that all the others in our list had given generous gifts to our endeavor, than each in his turn would give as well, not to be outdone. The difficulty lay in starting the process.

"We went, therefore, first to the court of Rheged, which was ruled in those days by Cynfarch Oer, Cynfarch the Cold, who could as well have been called Cynfarch Caled, Cynfarch the Miser. For as my Master said truly, if we could win gold freely given from that skinflint, than no one else would dare to hold back, for fear of dishonor. And we arrived on the eve of Samhain, then as now one of the great festivals of the year, when even Cynfarch would be forced to hold a feast.

"Now my Master's name was known in those days the length and breadth of Britain, and not for lack of resource. So in order not to put Cynfarch on his guard, we agreed that I would appear in my own proper person, but that he would dress himself in our oldest clothes and pretend to be my servant. And thus we arrived at Cynfarch's hall, where a feast—of sorts—was in progress.

"Cold, did I say was Cynfarch's calling? Cold was the hospitality of his hall as well. Few indeed were the torches that lit that hall, and small and feeble the hearth-fire, so it was little enough that could be seen through the drifting haze of smoke. The benches were thronged by such as had no hope of better entertainment elsewhere, but little good did they get by it, for the bowls of broken meats came half-empty to the table, and the drink was small sour beer. It is true that Cynfarch's retinue was served somewhat better—a war-band which is not feasted will soon find another lord—and better yet was the food on Cynfarch's own table, but I swear to you that Arthur's war-band in the field after a three-day's battle ate better than he. Nevertheless, we came into the hall, and I followed close after the porter to be announced, while my Master joined the servants near the door.

"Now Cynfarch, though a miser, was no fool; and my own name was not unknown in the land of Britain. Yet like all those who value gear and goods above honor, he could not resist the prospect of getting something for nothing, or nearly nothing: in this case, my songs in exchange for his poor entertainment. It would be a bold bard who satirized him there in his own hall; and if my praise was less than fulsome, why, he could live with that. Indeed, he had been doing so for a long time. So he waved me to a seat at his own table, and presently he bade me sing.

"I sang, first, a song in praise of Arthur, calling him Bull of Battle and Bulwark of Britain, Red-Ravager and Gold-Giver. This produced a little applause from Cynfarch, but rather more from his war-band, who like everyone else had heard tales of Arthur's success. Clearly they were now wondering if he might be a more generous provider than Cynfarch. Next I told the tale of Pwyll's winning of Rhiannon, when he comes to her wedding feast dressed as a beggar but carrying a magic bag which cannot be filled, however much is put into it. At this I heard one of the retinue say to another, 'Well for him that he came not here!' and laugh, and Cynfarch shifted uneasily in his chair. 'Have you no better tales than this?' he asked me. 'Give me something new.'

" 'Alas, Lord,' I said, 'I am weary from traveling and need food and time to rest. Perhaps you would hear a tale from my servant while I eat? He is not without experience.'

" 'Gladly,' said Cynfarch. 'Let him come up.'

"My Master came to the front of the hall, still in his disguise. 'Good evening to you, Lord,' he said. 'Would you hear a tale suited to the night, which I learned long ago in Ireland?'

" 'Gladly,' said Cynfarch. 'Tell your tale.'

"My Master then began to tell the most terrifying story I have ever heard, of unquiet spirits and monsters which could not be killed, and murdered men returning from the grave for vengeance, their empty eyes burning with the fires of hell. And as he spoke the hall grew darker, and the torches burned faint and blue, and outside the wind rose and moaned about the hall, and there were voices in it. Even the retinue grew quiet and huddled closer together on their benches; and their faces were pale, and their hands moved uneasily now and then to their knife-hilts. Cynfarch's eyes went round and round the hall, as if he saw movement in the shadows, and sweat stood upon his brow; and I myself felt the skin creep on my shoulders, and the hairs on my neck stand up. And still my Master spoke, and the wind rose, and one or two of the torches flickered and went out.

"At last Cynfarch could stand no more. 'Enough!' he cried. 'End your tale now, old man!'

" 'But how shall I do that,' my Master asked, 'and the tale not half finished?'

" 'I will pay you to end it,' said Cynfarch. 'In silver, if need be.'

" 'Nay,' said my Master, 'that would be ill doing. For it would be bad luck to me to end the tale untimely, and silver is not enough to pay for that misfortune.'

" 'Let it be gold, then,' said Cynfarch, and he hauled off from his arm the great twisted bracelet of red gold which he wore there, and which no one had ever seen him without, and threw it into my Master's hands. 'Take it, and be silent.' And my Master bowed, and turned away; and as he did so, the torches burned up again, and the wind died away to nothing.

"We did not linger long at the hall of Cynfarch Rheged, but went on with our journey. At all the other Kings' courts we showed the arm-ring, and praised Cynfarch's generosity, and we had no trouble in getting their gold. And so the first of our tasks was accomplished."

Talhaearn paused and took a swallow from the wine-cup which had somehow appeared at his elbow. Everyone else in his audience—by now a substantial one—sat entirely still and waited. After a moment he smiled in his beard, and went on.

"Our second task now was to find the gold of three Emperors, and this was harder. For several men of Rome had become Emperor while in Britain, but only two had ruled here for long, and those two were Maxen Wledig, of whom many tales are told, and Carawn Wledig of the Blue Ships, who kept the Saxons from our coasts, and was slain by false Allectus. But who should count as the third? One possibility was Custennin mab Custenwy of the North, who built the great churches at Eboricum and other cities; another, Carcolen mab Septwm, of whom little is now known and less remembered. After some discussion, we decided to start with the first two emperors, and let the gods guide us to the third in due course.

"We searched in many places, and in many ways, some of which I may not mention here, though I think, Gwernin, you will come to them in your time. And at last our journeying brought us to Londinium, which was then still in the hands of the British. There in a ruined temple near the river, once sacred to the Bull-slayer, we found what we sought." Talhaearn paused, and a look almost of pain crossed his face; then he shook his head and continued.

"I have never understood why the followers of the Christ must destroy the worship of all other gods in order to exalt their own. We walked in silence through that empty place of broken stone, and hollow hopes, and unquiet memories. Nettles and willow herb grew thick in the corners where the wind had whirled the leaves of a hundred autumns; white bindweed covered the stones of the floor, and ivy hid the roofless walls. No one came there but the beasts. And yet my Master went straight to a spot in one corner, no different, you would have said, from anywhere else in that place, and parted the ivy, and put his hand on one of the stones of the wall; and that stone moved. We lifted it out of its socket—it took both of us to do so—and found behind it a hollow space, and in it an iron box or casket, corroded but whole, and heavy. It needed all my strength to lift it out and place it gently on the ground. Then my Master knelt down beside it

215

and touched the lid, and spoke a Word. And the lid lifted lightly in his hand.

"There were many things of great value in that box, and many things of great beauty as well, but we took only those for which we had come: a gold coin of Custennin mab Custenwy, and a golden military badge with the name of Carawn Wledig on it, and a heavy gold ring: and this last came from the hand of Maxen Wledig himself. I remember still the feel of it on my palm, the warmth and power and resolve that still clung to it..." For a moment Talhaearn seemed to be looking at something very distant which only he could see. Then he sighed and went on.

"We closed the box, and put it back in the wall, and sealed it with the stone; and we made sacrifice to such gods or spirits as still dwelt in that ruined place. Then we came away, and traveled to my Master's home on Ynys Môn, to rest and make ready for our third trial, beside which the first two were as games for little children. And when autumn had come again, we took the boat which we had built that summer, and on Samhain Eve we sailed."

Talhaearn paused again, and drank from his cup, and Cyndrwyn's steward appeared at his elbow to refill it. The afternoon was drawing to an end, and the light outside was fading. Most of the folk of the *llys* had come into the hall now, including its Lord himself, and sat quietly listening. There was no talk; only a few people moved softly here and there, building up the central hearth-fire. As its flames reached up to finger the fresh wood, they drew leaping patterns on the walls, and painted with gold and shadow the faces of those who listened. The crackle of the fire was all the sound in the hall. And in that silence Talhaearn began again to speak.

"We sailed on a dark wind, a wind from the north and the east, a winter wind with no kindness in it. Three days and nights we sailed, and always to westward. Three days and nights, until we reached the Glass Isle. None but my Master could have steered us there, by mind and music; none but the boat the two of us had built could have endured that voyage…"

I could see it as he spoke, the great gray waters, the waves mountain-high in storm, foam-capped and angry, or glassy and green in the calm. As he spoke, I could have been myself on that endeavor, crewing the ship, swinging on the oars as she brought us into that bay. Bitter salt air, seaweed-reek from the rocks, and birds all around us. Bright wave-glint on the waters, black sands before us as we ran our ship ashore. In a mist, in a haze, in a sparkle of cloud, in a light that faded toward darkness, we climbed the hill…

"We climbed the hill," Talhaearn said, "and with every step we went up, the darkness and the cold increased, until it was hard to remember the light of the sun, or the look of a living land. The air around us was streaming wet, like fog or cloud, but not so clean. Bitter as poison it was on my lips, burning my eyes and my lungs. Each step I took was harder and won with savage pain, and all the while my heart was near to bursting in my chest with the labor of it. I am an old man now; I have ridden to war sword in hand, and seen my own blood flow, and walked the field of Camlann after the battle, but never before or since have I suffered as I did that day.

"At last, when it seemed that mortal flesh could endure no more, we reached the top, and saw before us through the moving murk the lights of the gatehouse. No honest firelight that was, no gold or red flame that burns on oil or wood, no second-hand sunlight—oh, no! This was the greenish-white glow of corpse-candles, the little flame that burns on the marsh at night to lead the traveler astray. In its light the walls rose up, glassy and black. I could not see their tops, nor did I wish to. The gate-guards I *could* see, and that was enough to freeze my blood where I stood. But my Master walked on confidently, as if entering his own hall, and what could I do but follow?

"Some say that the world one enters after death is conditioned by what one has experienced in life and can imagine. It may be that Tir Gwastraff also takes its shape from the fears that dwell in our own innermost hearts. I do not know; I only know I was afraid almost beyond bearing while I was there, and yet I followed my Master, and spoke, and acted, and played my part at need. Each of us, at the end of his days, in the bitter need of death, will find his own answer: I pray that none of you will ever see the sights that were before my eyes that day.

"We went into the fortress, passing the gate-guards—I will not describe them—as if they were not there. Through court after court my Master walked, as serene as if in his own chamber, and at last we came to the hall. In it, the light was brighter, but cold, cold. My breath steamed before me like cloud, and the bitter fog from outside froze on my clothing and hair. There was no one in the hall that I could see, and yet my Master stopped before what seemed to be an empty chair, and spoke long in a tongue I did not know. The blue flames of the hall-fire rose and fell, and the time went by, and went by, and still he spoke; and gradually I began to hear the voice that answered, though I could not understand it. It spoke as a ringing in the air; it spoke as a beating in my blood; it spoke in tones as sharp as glass and as subtle as silver; and it spoke like the falling of the leaden lid of a coffin, in a crypt, in a cave, in darkness…

"And at last it stopped, and I saw my Master bow, and hold out his hands; and something was dropped into them, something small and heavy. I saw the tension in his shoulders as they took up the weight; I saw the stiffening in his back, as he turned, still holding whatever it was away from his body; and I saw the pain in his face. His eyes were wide and dark; his mouth was set hard, and as he passed me he managed only a jerk of his head, and a whispered 'Come!' And I went after him, all that long way, through court after court, with the fear of the place clutching at my breath, and tearing at my heart; and when I would have touched him, to help brace his steps or lift his burden, he only shook his head at me; and we walked on.

"At last we passed the gate-house, and started down the slope. Then I did get an arm around him, for I think he would have fallen else, and so we descended the mountain; yet still he kept his hands before him, clasped now tightly together, although as the light increased I could see his own blood running from them and dripping onto the dead ground. Not until we reached the strand, and stepped aboard our ship, and she bore us out into the bay, did he open his hands and show me, smiling, the single precious sharp-edged disk of gold that lay in them, cutting his flesh and bathed in his own blood."

Talhaearn sighed, and was a long while silent. Then he looked up at the folk of the hall, who still sat all about him watching. "We bore it back to Ynys Môn," he said simply, "and put it there in safekeeping with the rest. And when the time was right we took all that treasure to the foremost goldsmith of Britain, and he made from it Arthur's Crown. And after Camlann it went with him into the West, and lies no more in this land.

"But that, O my children, is a story for another day."

XXVII. The Wild Geese

The sound of spring in Wales is the sound of running water. Not the voice of the cuckoo calling from the woods; not the *baah*-ing of the lambs from their green pasture; but the drip and splash of the rain from the thatch, and the chuckling of full-running streams, and the distant roar of the river, loud in the stillness of the night. That, and the high, far-off barking of the wild geese in their flight, like the hounds of Gwyn mab Nudd, somewhere in the vaults of the dark sky.

Rain, of course, leads to mud, and that day the *llys* was full of it. In the courtyards it was churned to a porridge-like consistency by the comings and goings of men and beasts, and even to cross the main courtyard was to be mired to the knee. The women picked their way around the edges, their skirts kilted high; the men strode through the middle, affecting a lordly indifference. The wooden floor of the great hall was set above the ground on stone footings, and even the fire-pits were paved, but the wet found its way in regardless, and there was more smoke than fire in the hall that night. The hutments around the *llys* wall, ours included, were flooded, and the stables so wet underfoot that we turned the horses into the paddocks, where at least they could come at fresh grass and fare no worse otherwise than indoors. Those who could not fit into the hall slept in the haylofts, thin though they were of hay at this time of year. My master Talhaearn was snug enough in the Prince's own chambers, and I myself, to my surprise, found a refuge in the *penteulu's* room at Goronwy's invitation, along with himself and a few of his friends. He was well in with the chief of the retinue, was Goronwy; I could see him in that post himself in a few years.

The current *penteulu*, Tudfwlch by name, was a broad brown-faced man in his middle years, with a fiery mane of hair that showed well the relationship between them, for they were close cousins. He asked me some questions about my background and warrior training, and seemed satisfied with the answers. I had my harp along, for crowded as this lodging was, it was at least dry; and I played her for a while at their urging; and the rattle of the rain against the house made a quiet counterpoint to the music of her strings. After a while we shared around a jug of ale, and the talk grew a little louder, mostly of last summer's raiding, and of what might happen this year. I sat fingering my strings and listening to it, wondering what my part might be in all of this; wondering, too, what Talhaearn's plans were for the summer, for he had not yet told me. It was one thing to winter in the Prince's court, and quite another to strike root there permanently—though at Talhaearn's age permanence might have its attractions. Whichever way he chose, I was bound to follow, for I had learned just enough that winter to know how little bardic lore I possessed, and I hungered and thirsted for more. At last everyone stretched out where they could find a spot, and we drifted off to sleep, lulled by the monotonous sound of the rain.

The next day was drier, and I was glad, for it meant there were less people in the hall, listening to my lessons. Talhaearn had started me on the different forms of poetry, reciting examples of each for me to memorize, and then requiring me to compose on the spot: an exciting challenge, but tiring after a while. Eventually he released me to practice on my own, and I was glad to go. Outside I met actual sunlight, the first in days. I also met Rhiannedd, on her way to the wood-shore to look for herbs, and naturally I went with her.

Some time later, the herbs forgotten, we were sitting together on my cloak on a rock on top of the ridge, looking over the country as an eagle might. To the west the hills climbed higher and higher, leading to the water-break between Banwy and Dyfi; to the east the country dropped off in waves of green and silver toward the distant blue valley of the Severn. "Somewhere over there," I said, "around the curve of the Breidden, is Pengwern." And I fell silent, thinking of the past.

Rhiannedd leaned back a little against my encircling arm to look up at my face. "You have a family there still, have you not?"

"Yes," I said. "Aunt and Uncle and cousins." And I frowned. "It is a year that I have been gone now; they must be thinking me dead."

"Could you not send them a message?" asked Rhiannedd sympathetically. "There will be travelers now and then, with the roads opening."

"Well—yes, I suppose I might. Or Talhaearn and I might be going that way soon enough, when we take up our travels again," I said without thinking.

"Yes," said Rhiannedd after a long moment. "I suppose you might." There was something odd about her voice, and I looked at her in surprise, but she was staring at the ground, her face turned away from me, showing me only her dark hair. Then she jumped up suddenly, picking up her basket. "I must go and look for the herbs Mother was wanting; she will be waiting for me. I will see you by and by." And before I knew it she was gone, leaving me feeling confused and rather foolish, with my mouth half open to call her back. Then I sighed and sat down again, and tried conscientiously to work on my poetry lessons. But it was no use; my thoughts kept wandering off to Rhiannedd and her strange behavior. At last I gave it up and followed her back down the hill to the *llys*.

That night I spent again in the *penteulu's* room with Tudfwlch and Goronwy and their friends, for one day's sunshine was not enough to undo the damage of a week's rain. This time the talk ran on women, with more than a little boasting. Tudfwlch of course was long married, with sons almost old enough for the war-band, and I, as the youngest there and the stranger, kept my peace and pretended to be tuning my harp. I was still wondering what was wrong between me and Rhiannedd; she had not come near me since the afternoon. Goronwy's voice broke into my thoughts.

"Yes," he was saying, "I will be giving the bride-price to Hueil Goch before Beltane. I am ready for it, I can tell you, and so is she." And there was laughter all around. Goronwy flushed a little redder, and not entirely from the beer, but he was still grinning. "We will not be the only ones jumping the fire, I am thinking: it was a cold winter." And they laughed again.

"Cyndrwyn did not find it so," said Dynfel slyly. He was a thin dark fellow, very proud of his young beard. "They say the Lady Angharad is breeding."

"Well, well," said Tudfwlch indulgently. "Even a keen hunter must sometimes bide at home, and keep his spear sharp while he does so." And he laughed at his own humor.

"Ho, Storyteller," said Goronwy. "How are you coming with your little dark filly? Is she ready for bridle yet?"

"Oh—oh, I think so," I said at random, startled. "Soon enough, soon enough." And I blushed even redder than Goronwy, and they laughed. Then the talk drifted off to raiding again, while I sat chewing my lip and thinking. I did not much like my thoughts.

The next day I found occasion to ask Talhaearn if we would be spending the summer at Llys-tyn-wynnan. "Hmm," he said. "I do not know. Why do you ask?"

"Oh—oh, no reason," I said. "I was only wondering." And then, inspired, "I have kin at Pengwern who were expecting me back last autumn. I was thinking I should send them a message."

"Ah," said Talhaearn, and he looked a little amused. "That is most dutiful of you, of course. Yet you did not seem to think of them these many months past, I wonder what has changed?"

"I—I do not know," I said. "Only I was talking with someone yesterday, and it—it came into my mind. That is all."

"I see. Well, then, to answer the question you did *not* ask: the Prince Cyndrwyn has asked me to bide with him as his *pencerdd*, and I have accepted. But that does not mean we will always be staying in this court: he will go a circuit presently around his lands, and he may also visit his cousins in Deva and Pengwern. But this is his favorite *llys*, and I expect we will winter here again. Is that what you wanted to know?"

"Yes," I said. "Yes, it is. Thank you, master."

Talhaearn gave a sort of snort. "I am relieved to hear it. Now, if I may direct your attention again to the *awdl* we were discussing yesterday, regarding Cunedda and his sons: recite for me the first twenty lines, and explain the meter." And he kept me fully occupied for the rest of the afternoon. It was only when I had been dismissed at last, and was standing up to go, that he called me back. "Gwernin… a word of advice."

I sat down again, startled. "Master?"

"Just this: remember that bards travel. We are like the wild geese, always wandering, always in flight." Talhaearn sighed. "Stability will be the exception in your life. Do you understand?"

"N–no." I frowned.

Talhaearn snorted again in exasperation. "You will in time. Think about it, boy. Now go away and practice: I want to hear a better recitation tomorrow." And he turned away and picked up his harp, and paid me no more heed. After a moment I stood up and left, intending to follow his instructions.

At the doorway of the hall I paused. Again the day was almost sunny; the mud was retreating in the courtyard. Almost against my will I headed for Gwawr's hut at the back of the *llys*. If I could find Rhiannedd anywhere, I thought, it would be there: but I was wrong. Only Gwawr herself was inside, bending over something she was mixing in a bowl. When I pushed aside the curtain she looked up; then seeing who came, she smiled. "Gwernin," she said. "I thought I would be seeing you before long."

"Did you?" I asked. "It is your daughter I was seeking."

"I know." She made a tutting noise. "Gwernin, have you been deceiving her?"

"No more than myself," I said heavily. "Lady, do you know what is wrong between us? For I do not."

At that she laughed. "Oh, child, you make me feel old. Sit down and tell me, then, what has happened, for my daughter will not."

Instead I stood, looking restlessly around the room. I had been there often enough before, but my attention had always been elsewhere. A small room, it was, and looked smaller because it was so full, with shelves of jars and bottles on the walls, crocks on the floor, and hanging bunches of herbs in the corners. A bench, a work-table, and a brazier took up most of the remaining space, and a hanging curtain in the back wall sectioned off the area where the two women presumably slept. I remembered that Gwawr was a widow of some years.

She had gone back to peering at her bowl, which was full of something dark green and viscous. "What are you mixing?" I asked, and she looked up again, smiling. Her smile was very like her daughter's, and I could not help smiling back.

"A salve for cuts and grazes." She held the bowl up to me. "You should know the scent."

I did: it was the salve Rhiannedd had used on my back, after Talhaearn beat me at Midwinter. My face changed; I controlled myself with an effort. Gwawr watched me for a moment, then asked again, "Gwernin, what happened? What did you do or say?"

"I—do not rightly know," I said. "We were talking about Pengwern, where I yet have family. She said I should send them a message to let them know where I was, and that I was well, and I said Talhaearn and I might be going that way ourselves soon, when we took up our travels again. And that is all—but she has not spoken to me since. Lady, what have I done wrong?"

Gwawr shook her head, frowning. "I told her this might happen," she said, more to herself than to me. "Gwernin, it is not your fault, or not all of it: but this is not something I can mend. You will have to talk with Rhiannedd yourself."

"But how can I do so, if she will not come near me?" I asked, bewildered.

"I will tell her she has to talk to you," said Gwawr. "When are you likely to be leaving us?"

"Why—I do not know. Whenever the Prince decides to go a circuit, I suppose. I asked Talhaearn, and he says he will be staying with Cyndrwyn as *pencerdd*." At that Gwawr laughed. I stared at her. "Where is the humor in that?"

"Oh, my dear," said Gwawr, still chuckling. "Do you not see? No, I suppose you do not. Rhiannedd is upset because you are about to leave, and did not tell her so, but only mentioned it in passing, as a thing of no importance. And now you tell me you are not leaving at all, but merely traveling with the Prince, and will likely be back come autumn." And she laughed again. "Go and find her, boy, and give her the news: I think you will both be glad of it. She will be down by the stream, looking for the comfrey roots I sent her for."

"Thank you, Lady!" I said, my face clearing. "I will do so!" And I turned and went out on my errand.

I did find Rhiannedd, and we talked for a long while, and the outcome was happy—or so I thought then. And when later I was kissing her, and we heard the distant clamor high up in the sunset sky, I did not take it for an omen, as I should have done. For Talhaearn was right: we bards and the wild geese are close kin. We may settle for a time, for summer or winter, to rest or to breed; but when the wheel turns, we must once again be on the wing. I knew it then with my mind, but I know it now with blood and bone and heart, as the turning years have taught me: and that lesson was not lightly learned.

But that, O my children, is a story for another day.

XXVIII. Beltane Fires

Time goes by quickly in spring-time, and a month will show great changes. By the time the moon that was new when Rhiannedd and I had our falling-out was new again, what had been only yesterday a haze of green on the wood-shore was now full leaf; and it was almost time for the Beltane fires, before the cattle were driven up the mountain to their summer pasture. Of late I had often been providing the evening entertainment in hall, as Talhaearn ran me through my repertoire of winter-tales: for as I have said before, some tales belong to the dark half of the year, and some to the light, and it is not well to mix them. And Beltane is *Calan Yr Haf*, the beginning of summer, when the plowing is over, and the first crops in, and the increase of the land begins to be felt. It is also the time for wedding.

Goronwy had paid the bride-price to Hueil Goch the Smith, and taken Keinwen to his *tref*—and his bed—with all the blessings of the Church. Now, with the Beltane fires, it was time for blessings of another sort. When the fires were sinking, we would drive the cattle between them, for protection and increase in the coming year. It was the custom, too, for men and women, those who desired this sort of blessing, to leap between the fires themselves. Goronwy and Keinwen, I thought, would be first in line.

Rhiannedd and I would not be leaping the fires this year. We had talked long and long about it, for I had come to know that I loved her, and she loved me. But I had no way to support a wife: no land, no livelihood, no way to raise a bride-price. By my own action in choosing the bard's path, I had cut myself off from my kindred and my possible inheritance there. I was free-born, yes, and had some status in the *llys* as my master's apprentice, and lately also from my own talents: but that was all. Some day, perhaps, when Talhaearn was satisfied with my training, I might become *bardd teulu*, the bard of the retinue: so I was becoming unofficially already. Some day, perhaps, I might be a *pencerdd*, a master bard, myself. But these possibilities were long years in the future: not enough to build a life on now. All this Rhiannedd and I knew and had discussed: but knowing in the head is not knowing in the blood. What might have happened next I do not know: I only know that fate intervened.

It was on a bright spring evening two days before Beltane Eve that it happened. I was sitting on a bench with Rhiannedd, close to Cyndrwyn's fire-hall, waiting for the time to go inside, when we heard the sound of approaching horses. Into the court there rode three men, and two of them, to my astonishment, were familiar to me. Taliesin Ben Beirdd I would know, I think, at the world's end—providing only that he himself wished it!—and Neirin mab Dwywei's dark red hair and lean build were hard to disguise by any light. The third, a fair-haired youth who rode behind them and led their pack-horses, was a stranger to me.

With a startled word to Rhiannedd, I leapt up and ran to meet them. "Taliesin! Neirin! By all the gods, what brings you here?" Then there was confusion and shouting in the court-yard as others ran to greet them or to hold their horses, to carry word to the Prince and make ready hospitality, or merely to participate in the excitement. In the midst of it all, I found myself face to face with Taliesin himself. "Gwernin!" he said, and reaching out, he took me by the shoulders, and looked me up and down, his blue eyes sparkling. "Yes, I was right. Being with Talhaearn suits you, I think. And you have grown."

It was true: I had grown a finger's breadth over the winter, and was now as tall as he. It seemed very strange, but I

had no time to ponder it then, for Taliesin had released me
to Neirin, who stood beside me grinning, and had turned to
greet the Prince and Talhaearn. I did not see what passed
between them, for Neirin had flung an arm around my
shoulders, and was introducing his companion. "Gwernin,
this is Pedr mab Rhys, from Dyfed. He wants to learn the
harp, and Taliesin has brought him along to take your place
while you are gone."

"Gone?" I cried. "Where am I going?"

Neirin laughed. "To the North with me, I hope! But only
for the summer! Na, na, but I should have let him tell you the
story himself! No doubt but that I have spoiled it!"

"Now that you have started, go on!" I said. "But first let
us take your horses to the stables, and you can tell me as we
go. Besides, there will be less of a crowd there, while they are
all gathered around our masters, and we shall have more of a
chance to speak!"

"How was your winter?" Neirin asked as we walked.

"Good," I said, and thinking back I smiled. "Most of it,
at any rate! And yours?"

"Good indeed. Your Pengwern is a most fair place, and
her Prince very generous. He loaded Taliesin with treasures,
and could hardly be persuaded to spare him for a few days to
make this trip. Indeed, I thought at one point I would have
to come alone to make my request, and glad I am that I did
not! Talhaearn would have made short work of me! How do
you get on with him now?"

"Very well nowadays," I said with a laugh. "He is no
easy master, I can tell you, but he has taught me much—if
only to know how little I really knew!"

"That is the first lesson," said Neirin seriously, "and the
hardest. I mind me well when I first came to Taliesin… *Hai
mai*, I was full of myself! But he soon showed me the error of
my thinking!" And he chuckled reminiscently.

Cyndrwyn's chief groom was waiting at the stables with boys to take the horses, so Neirin and I loaded ourselves with harps and saddle-bags and went out again, leaving Pedr behind to deal with the packhorses. "I do not know where they will be putting you," I said, "but come to our boothy first and leave your gear. Then we can talk properly, and I can introduce you to Rhiannedd."

"Oho!" said Neirin. "This has the sound of news! Should I remember her?"

"I do not know," I said, shouldering aside the door-curtain and beginning to set down my load. "You will have seen her, I know, but there are others more memorable at first glance. I will let you decide."

Neirin grinned. "A good winter indeed, I think you must have had! Though I was not lonely in Pengwern myself. Where now?"

"The hall: I want to see what is passing between our masters. And you still have not told me about this trip we may be making, or about Pedr. He had little enough to say for himself."

"I doubt we gave him a proper chance," said Neirin, falling into step beside me. "He is here because Taliesin wants to borrow you from Talhaearn to be my companion on a mission, and feels that he should provide the old man with a substitute while you are gone. Their discussion, I think, should be well worth the hearing!"

"I hope we are in time," I said, and laughed.

We found Taliesin still talking to the Prince, while Talhaearn stood by with an expression that spoke to me of gathering storm. "Ah, Gwernin!" said Cyndrwyn as we came up. "I have been offering Taliesin the guest lodgings across the courtyard from yours for himself and his party. Would you take them there?"

"Gladly," I said, keeping a weather eye on Talhaearn. "Neirin and I have just been stowing some of their baggage in our own hut, so…"

"Let us all go and get it, then," said Taliesin, "and you can be our guide, Gwernin. Prince, we will talk more at meat, if it please you. Talhaearn, give me your company now, please." And he swept us off with a hand on Talhaearn's arm, gesturing to myself and Neirin to go ahead as he did so. "So, here you are again, and unexpectedly as ever," I heard Talhaearn say behind us. "What are you playing at this time, Gwion?"

"A diplomatic mission, as I said: can you doubt it?" I could hear the laughter in Taliesin's voice, and Talhaearn's snort in response. "Na, na, Father of Awen, we will talk of it soon enough, and I hope you will not be displeased. Wait you only until we are indoors and private."

"As you please, as you please," said Talhaearn, and was silent until we reached our lodging. As Neirin and I were leaving with the baggage I heard him say, "What news from Rheged?" But the curtain closed and I lost Taliesin's answer.

"Phew!" said Neirin as we crossed the court again. "We are well out of that, I am thinking! Ho! Pedr! This way!" waving to his companion, who was standing irresolute and burdened at the entrance to the stable-yard. As he came up I saw that he was Neirin's age or a little older, a well-grown handsome young man, with the golden hair and blue eyes you often see on the Saxons, and sometimes on the Irish as well. His voice when he spoke sounded pleasantly of the southwest. "I thought I would never find you," he said. "This place is like a maze!"

Neirin chuckled. "You would not say that when you had seen Deva, or any of the old Roman towns."

"I have seen Caerwent," said Pedr, "but that is mostly straight lines. This is different."

"Did you pass through Caerllion on your way?" I asked.

"Let me think: no, we went by Severn-mouth, and up through Glevum: another Roman town, and bigger than Caerwent, but fewer people in it. A place of the dead: I did not like it."

"Well, well," said Neirin peacefully, as we entered the guest lodging. "That is as it may be. Put the packs down over there, and let us sort things out."

At this point a servant boy arrived with a flask of wine and three cups on a tray, saying, "Cyndrwyn sends it for the bards."

"I will take it to them," I said, and the boy grinned and left. Pedr made to reach for one of the cups, but I pulled the tray back in surprise. "Pedr, I meant what I said."

Pedr frowned briefly. "My apologies," he said then. I looked at him for a moment longer, my brows raised, and he continued unwillingly, "I thought you meant for us to share it ourselves: we are bards, too."

"Speak for yourself," I said reprovingly. "I am Gwernin Storyteller, and I serve Talhaearn." And turning, I went out of the room with the tray. Behind me I heard Neirin's voice speaking to Pedr: the words were muffled, but the tone was not kind.

At the door of my own lodging I paused, hearing the rumble of Talhaearn's voice within. But I had been here before; balancing the tray one-handed, I tapped on the doorpost and went in. "Wine from the Prince, masters," I said, and setting the tray down on a low table, I poured a cupful and took it to Talhaearn. His color was high, and he was frowning, his bushy white brows almost meeting in the middle, but he took the cup readily from my hand and drank. I turned back to do as much for Taliesin, but he was already helping himself. Before drinking he poured a few drops, neatly and deliberately, onto the floor in libation. Looking up he caught my eye and smiled. "No, Gwernin, not about you this time," he said. "Though that will come soon enough, no doubt. Has Neirin told you my plan?"

"Part of it, lord," I said, and looked at Talhaearn. "Master? Do you know?"

"Not yet," said Talhaearn. "He has only told me that the North is a tinderbox, about to burst into flame, and the Saxons are stirring again in the east, and Cynan Garwyn is doing his best to foment war in the south and west: nothing of great moment, you perceive. Why, what is it that he has yet reserved? Something to do with you, Gwernin, I feel." He did not add, "as usual," but I felt it in the air.

I turned back to Taliesin. "Will you tell him, lord? It will come more completely from you."

"Gwernin," said Taliesin lightly, "are you trying to force my hand? Well, then," and he turned to Talhaearn, "it is true I have come to ask you a favor, Iron Brow, though I would have preferred to choose my own time for the asking. The North being, as I have said, a tinderbox, I am sending Neirin up there this summer to gauge the accuracy of my news and do what he can to soothe things down in his own home country, while I do my best to restrain Cynan. And as he is still young, and only one man, I thought to give him company on this trip by borrowing Gwernin from you for a few months. I have brought a young man with me to serve you while he is gone, Pedr mab Rhys by name, who says he wishes to learn the harp and the other arts of the bard. I think," and here he grinned unexpectedly, "that you will soon get his measure. Treat him as you will, Father of Awen: perhaps he will last out the summer!"

Talhaearn smiled grimly in his beard at that. "Well, we will see," he said, and then to me: "Gwernin? What do you think of this? Are you ready so soon to leave me?"

At that I went down on my knees beside his chair. "Master," I said, "you know I am not. I admit that the adventure tempts me, but it is for you to decide, yea or nay. I will do as you desire."

Talhaearn's expression softened a little. "Well, well," he said, "you are very docile. Is it only my company you would be missing, I wonder? Never mind: but do you come back to me in the fall, and strive not to forget all my teaching in the meantime." And he laid his hand on my head for a moment as if in blessing. "Now go along with you: Gwion will see me to the hall when it is time." And I went.

The next two days were busy ones. Taliesin and Neirin were staying to keep the Beltane feast with Cyndrwyn before they left, the one for Pengwern again and the other with me for the North. Talhaearn was continually thinking of last-minute instructions or bits of advice for me, some of which I managed to remember. And for myself, I had an urgent desire to spend as much time as I could with Rhiannedd before I left.

She had taken the news philosophically, though whether she believed my promises to return I am not sure. "It will be as the gods allow," she said once when she saw I was troubled, and she smiled up at me so sweetly, her blue eyes so full of understanding, that I could not but kiss her. I had introduced her to Neirin, not without qualms; but he took the measure of our relationship at once, and although he teased me, he treated her like a sister. For her part she soon lost her awe of him, and dealt with him much the same. Pedr, on the other hand, she took in dislike at once, and I cannot say that I was sorry, for there was no denying he was a very handsome man.

On Beltane eve we stood near the fires hand in hand, as we had stood at midwinter: but this was a calm, mild night, not one of icy cold. We watched as the black and brown cattle were driven bawling between the fires, the cows with their calves at their heels, and the sparks flying wild about them; and after the cattle, the sheep, with the sheepdogs barking behind. Then, as the fires were dying down, the men and women went through, the young ones running and laughing, some of them holding hands; the older ones more deliberately. At last, when it was very late, and few folk were left, I looked at Rhiannedd, and she looked back at me, and something passed between us. Then we, too, ran between the sinking fires, holding hands; and that night we did not go back to the court at all, but spent the time together on the green hillside, with one cloak beneath us, and another above, and the pale stars of summer overhead. And when we went home in the dawn, still holding hands, we knew that we were bound as sure as any, though no priest had blessed our union—no mortal priest—and no bride price had changed hands. And the next day I took horse with Neirin and we rode north.

But that, O my children, is truly a story for another day.

POSTSCRIPT

The 6th century in Britain is in some ways the darkest part of the European Dark Ages. As direct evidence of people and events in this period, we have a handful of poems, a few historical references in accounts written 200 years or more later, and a set of genealogies of doubtful value. In addition, there is a growing body of archeological material, some of which contradicts (or at least fails to support) the above sources. In attempting to write a series of somewhat historical stories based in this period, the prospective author must leap from rock to rock, occasionally walking on water in between. Inevitably there will be some splashes.

For those who care about such details, then, the following summary is provided. Actual physical locations (i.e., towns, forts, roads, etc.) are based on archeological reports where available, but details (buildings, general appearance) of these places at the time of the story are speculative or wholly invented. Territorial units such as kingdoms fall in this category as well; there are no maps of Wales or of the lands of the Men of the North from the 6th century. Most of the kings or princes are at best names in a poem, history, or genealogy, and their characters (to say nothing of their appearances) are largely inferred from their reported actions. Five of the more important bards are listed (as names only) in *Historia Britannica*; from two of them—Taliesin and Neirin (later called Aneirin)—we have poetry as well, although the degree to which these poems may have mutated during oral transmission is debatable. This poetry, incidentally, provides a large amount of the detail for material and social culture in the courts of the time.

Finally, a word on the magical or supernatural element in some of these stories. Many of the "supernatural" characters encountered by Gwernin, especially in the first part of this book, derive from the collection of Welsh medieval tales called the Mabinogion, and especially the section called the Four Branches. In a time and place where there was no clearly perceived distinction between spirit world and "real" world, I submit that these characters would have seemed, to a person in touch with their stories, to have as much "reality" as many of the "historical" ones. Indeed, so I have found it myself on some of my own journeys through Britain, over 1400 years later.

Appendices

A Note on Welsh Pronunciation

The spelling used for Welsh words and names in these stories is mostly that of Modern Welsh. The most important differences between the English and Welsh alphabets are these:

Welsh	English
c	k
dd	th (as in "bathe")
f	v
th	th (as in "bath")

The Welsh "ll" has no English equivalent; an approximation can be reached by putting the tip of the tongue against the roof of the mouth behind the teeth and hissing—good luck!

Names of Some People and Places

key: **historical** invented *legendary/mythical*

(**accent** usually falls on the next-to-last syllable)

Angharad ferch Rhun (ang-**hă**-rad verch hrēn)–Cyndrwyn's wife

Anwen (**ăn**-wen)–little dark girl on Ynys Môn who fell in love with Gwernin's friend Ieuan

Caradog (ka-**ră**-dog)–miner and trickster

Cynan Garwyn (**kĭn**-an **găr**-win)–prince of eastern Powys whose court was at Pengwern

Cyndrwyn (kin-**drū**-in)–prince of western Powys whose court was at Llystyn-wynnan

Dyfed (**dŭ**-ved)–kingdom in southwest Wales

Edern mab Rhys (**ē**-dern mab hrēs)–a storyteller from Aberdaron in western Wales

Emrys (**ĕm**-res)–Arthur's bard; an old man on the road

Eryri (e-**rŭ**-re)–Snowdon and the mountains around it, "land of the eagles"

239

Goronwy mab Gronw (go-**rōn**-we mab **grō**-noo)–young warrior in Cyndrwyn's teulu

Gwawr (gwaur)–herbalist and mother of Rhiannedd

Gwernin Kyuarwyd (**gwĕr**-nin ke-**văr**-wid)–Gwernin the Storyteller, the narrator of the story

Gwion (**gwē**-on)–Taliesin's boyhood personal name

Gwydion mab Dôn (**gwĭd**-yon mab dōn)–Gwydion son of Dôn, the magician (Mabinogion)

Gwynedd (**gwĭ**-neth)–kingdom in northwest Wales

Ieuan mab Meurig mab Pedr (**Yē**-an mab **mīr**-ig mab **pĕd**-ur)–Gwernin's friend Ieuan

Keinwen (**kāĕn**-wen)–daughter of Hueil Goch at Llys-tyn-wynnan

Llys-tyn-wynnan (llēs tēn **wĭn**-nan)–Cyndrwyn's court, near Caereinion in mid-Wales

Maelgwn Hir (**măĕl**-gun hēr)–"Maelgwn the Tall", King of Gwynedd (deceased)

Modron ferch Afallach (**mōd**-ron verch a-**vă**-llach)–wife of Urien Rheged; possibly legendary.

Neirin (**nāĕr**-in)–Taliesin's bardic apprentice

Pengwern (pen-**gwĕrn**)–Court of Cynan Garwyn, possibly located on the site of modern Shrewsbury

Powys (**pō**-wes)–kingdom in east-central Wales, including part of today's Shropshire

Rheged (**hrĕ**-ged)–kingdom in the north of Britain

Rhiannedd (**hrĕăn**-neth)–friend of Keinwen at Llys-tyn-wynnan

Rhun Hir (hrēn hēr)–Rhun the Tall, Rhun son of Maelgwn Gwynedd

Talhaearn Tad Awen (**tăl**-**hāĕărn** tad **ă**-wen)–Talhaearn "Father of the Muse", Taliesin's and Gwernin's bardic teacher

Taliesin Ben Beirdd (**tă**-lē-**ā**-sin ben bāĕrth)–Taliesin "Chief of Bards", most famous bard in 6th century Britain

Tristfardd (**trēst**-varth)–sometime bard to Urien Rheged, and killed by him; the name means "Sad Bard"; probably legendary.

Ugnach mab Mydno (**ēg**-nach mab **mēd**-no)–bard of Caer Sëon who competed against Taliesin at Caer Seint; possibly legendary.

Urien Rheged (**ēr**-eun **hrĕg**-ed)–King of Rheged in the North of Britain

Ynys Môn (**ĭn**-is mōn)–the Island of Môn (Anglesey) off the northwest coast of Wales

Yr Wyddfa (ur **wēth**-va)–Snowdon, the highest peak in Wales

Other Welsh words

afon (ă-von)–river

bardd (bărth) pl. beirdd (bēīrth)–bard

caer (kăĕr)–fortress, castle

cerdd tafod (kĕrth tă-vod)–poetry; literally, "craft (of) tongue"

coch (kōch)–red

ferch (vĕrch)–daughter (of)

glas (glăs)–blue, gray, green

hafod (hă-vod)–summer hut

llwyd (llŏēd)–gray

llys (llēs)–court, fortified complex

mab (măb)–son (of)

pencerdd (**pĕn**-kerth)–"head of song", master bard, bard of the court

penteulu (**pĕn-tăĕ**-lē)–chief of retinue, leader of the body-guard

teulu (**tăĕ**-lē)–retinue, war-band

uchelwr (**ĕch**-ul-ur), pl. uchelwyr (**ĕch**-ul-ēr)–nobleman, literally "high man"

Selected References

A full listing of the sources I consulted for this book would run to many pages. For those wanting to read on, however, two places to start:

Ford, Patrick K., 1977, The Mabinogi and Other Medieval Welsh Tales: University of California Press, Berkley, California; ISBN 0-520-03414-7.

Evans, Stephen S., 1997, Lords of Battle: Image and Reality of the *Comitatus* in Dark-Age Britain: The Boyell Press; ISBN 0-85115-662-2.

Made in the USA
Lexington, KY
22 February 2010